She couldn't believe it—everything was going so well and then this...

"What do you want?" she asked sharply.

Something about Adam immediately put Mia on her guard. She remembered how he had invaded her personal space when she had only just met him, the way he stood just a little too close, the way his lips had been centimetres from hers, and the way his breath had touched her skin. She shuddered at the thought.

Despite the opinion of millions of female fans, Mia couldn't see the appeal in Adam Morgan. She could practically hear the hysterical shrieks of millions of Glasshearts fans as she thought those thoughts. She could hear the catcalls, the hisses, and the insults hurling her way. But all Mia wanted to do was scratch her skin or take a running leap into the nearest shower.

"You," was all he said.

His voice was low and quiet, his tone deep and seductive, but it paled in comparison to Joel's. His voice lacked that same empathy, his tone was deep but meaningless, the seduction in his voice failed to match the leer in his eyes.

"No, you don't," Mia said firmly, shuffling back in her seat. "Get out of here, Adam."

"Do you know how many girls would kill for this opportunity?" he scoffed, flaying his hands up and down himself in appraisal.

Mia pulled a face. "I'm not one of them, sorry."

Her voice was low and steady. On the outside, she appeared calm and controlled, but inside, she could hear her heartbeat pounding loudly in her chest. Her nerves crashed and toiled and her blood was pumping so fast she could hear it in her ears.

Adam scared her.

That was the simplest way she could put it.

He cocked his head to one side and took a step toward her. "But you will be."

Mia Ryan used to think things like this didn't happen to girls like her. Barmaids from small Irish towns didn't get song-writing jobs with LA record labels. Girls like Mia also didn't land rock-star boyfriends like Joel Coben.

But one night changed everything.

The last thing Mia remembers of that night is the sickening crunch of metal as their car was hit, bounced over the edge of a bridge, and plunged into a dark abyss. As she begins to regain consciousness, she has no idea where she is, who survived the crash…and who didn't. But most of all, she has absolutely no idea who the dark-haired figure is that continues to fade in and out of sight.

KUDOS for *Chasing the Dream*

In *Chasing the Dream* by Melissa Speight, Mia Ryan is recovering from the car accident she suffered in the first book *Chasing Shadows*. She wakes up in the hospital, and the first thing she notices is the dark figure lurking in the background. He's familiar, but she can't place him. Is he a threat? Should she be afraid? And how will the studio react to her being off work for so long after the crash? Add to that the fact that her three-month contract with Sixth String Studios is now up, and Mia doesn't know if they will keep her or say, "It's been fun, but no thanks." And what will happen to her relationship with rock star Joel Coben if the studio lets her go? Without a job, she'll be forced to return to Ireland, and long-distance relationships rarely work out. With her life in turmoil, Mia's frightened about what her future might hold. But even her wildest imagination can't prepare her for what's to come. Like the first book in the series, this one is a touching story of an ordinary girl with an extraordinary talent who is thrust into an overwhelming world of fame and fortune for which she is totally unprepared. ~ *Taylor Jones, The Review Team of Taylor Jones & Regan Murphy*

Chasing the Dream by Melissa Speight is the story of what happens when dreams unexpectedly come true. We all have dreams—some big, some small. While we often realize the small dreams, most of us go through life, hoping and praying our big dreams will also come true, without really understanding the consequences that might have. Mia Ryan—a small-time singer and performer in a pub in Dublin, Ireland—has two big dreams. One is to find her long-lost brother, whom she hasn't seen since she was a small child when her parents died and she and her brother were put into separate foster homes. And the other is to break into the big time and take her singing career to the next level—a contract with a record studio, world tours, fame, fortune, the works. However, when she's scouted by a record studio, flown to California, and offered a three-month contract as a singer/song-writer, she's totally unprepared for the fame, the hounding by paparazzi, and the need for full-time security that follows. Nor is she prepared to gain a rock-star boyfriend, Joel Coben, and be suddenly hated by millions of Joel's female fans. But Mia's life is still changing, and she needs to adapt fast if she is going to survive in the unfamiliar world she finds herself in. *Chasing the Dream* gives us a glimpse into the world of stardom that few of us will ever see, as well as exploring the negative side of realizing dreams that most of us rarely consider while praying for our own dreams to come true. All in all, a thoroughly entertaining and thought-provoking read. *~ Regan Murphy, The Review Team of Taylor Jones & Regan Murphy*

Chasing the Dream

Melissa Speight

A Black Opal Books Publication

Black Opal Books

BECAUSE SOME STORIES JUST HAVE TO BE TOLD

GENRE: STEAMY ROMANCE/ROMANTIC SUSPENSE

DEDICATION

For my mum

Chapter 1

*B*eep.
    Beep.
    Beep.
That noise played on a never ending loop in her mind. She was sure this was how supermarket checkout assistants felt when they tried to sleep at night.

Beep.

Beep.

Beep.

A light overhead flickered irritatingly as she tried to open her eyes. Why was everything in this room so irritating? There was a sharp pain in her left hand, as if a splinter had been jammed there for days.

Beep.

Beep.

Beep.

What on earth was that infernal noise?

Someone really needed to change that light bulb, she thought as she squinted her eyes. All she was trying to do was get some sleep.

There were parts of her body that ached, some more than others. Some parts she couldn't feel, which was disturbing.

She tried to twitch her fingers, to wriggle her toes. But nothing.

Days and nights had no significance in this place. Time was a never ending entity. There was no concept of hours elapsing, minutes passing or seconds ticking. She thought back to another time in her life recently where she wished time could have stood still. She remembered being alone in a room, feeling very comfortable on a leather sofa and also feeling very content. But that was all she remembered. She was getting sleepy again and the flickering light blurred out of focus as her eyelids flickered closed.

Beep.
Beep.
Beep.

She tried to open her eyes but they felt heavier than lead. She tried to move a hand to rub against her eyelids but that felt worse. A searing pain in her ribcage had forced her from her blissful slumber. Why was she feeling that sharp pang in her side? She wanted to cry out in agony but nothing would come from her throat. The pain forced her eyes open a fraction.

A face hovered over her. She couldn't tell who it was. They blurred in and out of focus. They turned and said something to someone else nearby, but she couldn't hear what they said. Their words were muffled as if someone were holding their hands over her ears.

Sleep reclaimed her soon enough and the mumbling disappeared.

Beep.
Beep.
Beep.

She awoke sharply with the pain in her side. Her head felt dizzy and confused. She wanted to sit bolt upright and cry out but her body failed her. Still the light flickered on overhead. Didn't anyone ever turn that thing off? A face appeared over her own again. No features came into view. They spoke but their words were still muffled. Something told her there was feeling in her hand. Someone was holding hers. Maybe it was the face she could see. Exhausted, she closed her eyes again.

Mumbling. Why was everyone always mumbling in this place? Why couldn't she hear them properly? Their hushed voices, saying words she couldn't understand, kept rousing her from her sleep. It was happening more and more often. She knew soon enough the fog would wear off and she would have to face the world.

Beep.

Beep.

Beep.

Faces. Another one was peering over her as she opened her eyes. She recognized this one. But she didn't know how. She knew it from somewhere but her confused memory failed her. She wanted to reach up and touch the features that were so close, but her body failed her again.

Who was that?

Again. The face was there again.

There was something so familiar about it, but she just couldn't put her finger on it. Darkness.

That's what was recalling in her memory.

Darkness of the person's hair and features.

The hair was so very dark. And the eyes too.

Who was that?

She was hearing things better. Finally, words were turning into sentences. She could hear them without having to open her eyes and struggle to make sense of what was happening.

"He's here?" a voice asked. Female, she decided.

"Yes," answered a male.

"Does she know?" asked the woman.

A sigh came from the man. "I don't think so."

The face was there again. Why wouldn't it leave her alone? Every time she opened her eyes, it was there, peering over her.

Words were no problem to her now, but faces were still an issue. This one still wouldn't come.

So dark.

But so familiar?

She smiled as she opened her eyes. Things were finally beginning to make sense now. She could hear clearly and the blurry outlines that were once only shadows of people were beginning to become clearer.

"Mia?" a voice asked, "can you hear me?"

She smiled as she recognized the voice. She opened her eyes and the outline steadily focussed into a familiar female face. The quiff of hair that was usually so quirkily styled looked ruffled. She smiled and the woman laughed.

"She knows!" she cried out.

Mia closed her eyes again to the sound of a low, male voice in the corner of the room.

"Hey, sweetie," a soft, familiar accent cooed in her ear.

The accent sounded different from all the others.

The sound of this voice made her think of green fields and gentle music.

Ireland. That's what the voice reminded her of.

"Niamh," she croaked out. Her voice sounded horse and alien, as if unused for a long time.

"I'm right here, sweetie." Niamh's soft accent sounded close in her ear and a familiar hand curled around her own. "There's people waiting to see you," she whispered. "You can't sleep forever, you know?"

Mia's face creased into an unfamiliar smile. That was a sensation that felt alien too.

"There's my girl," Niamh's voice sang, "come on, sweetie, wake up. We all want to see you."

"I'm trying," Mia croaked out.

Niamh sat with her for a long time, patiently talking to her as Mia tried to open her eyes. They closed again and she would try to open them again. Eventually, she could hold them open and focus on the room around her. She was propped slightly upright in a hospital bed. The beeping noise was coming from the numerous machines that whirred beside her. The damned fluorescent bulb overhead was still flickering. There was a long needle inserted deep into her left hand with a tube that ran to an IV drip beside her. So *that* was why her mind was foggy. Medication.

"How are you feeling?" Niamh asked as she handed her the paper cup of water from the nightstand.

"Like death," Mia croaked.

At those words, Niamh's eyes misted over and a tear quickly ran down her pale face. She managed to squeeze her hand.

What had happened? It must have been bad.

The door to the tiny hospital room cracked open and a figure stepped through it.

"No, no, no," Niamh called out, "not yet!"

Darkness.

He was here.

The darkness she had been seeing. He was there, standing before her.

His dark hair, his dark eyes.

Everything about him seemed dark. And strange.

Who is that?

Chapter 2

The realisation then immediately came crashing down upon Mia. She hadn't needed to ask herself. She already knew.

So many images, so many memories. They were all so faded now. So many times she had pictured this moment, so many times she had dreamt of it, and now it was finally here.

But in her medication fuddled state, it had taken her a moment to realise who he was.

The shock and the realisation had suddenly hit her like an oncoming truck. So many memories of tidal waves of emotions that had often threatened to crash down upon her and break her during her darkest hours were immediately awakened when she realised who was standing before her.

The machine beside her bed began beeping at twice its usual speed as Mia's memory cranked up a gear.

The faded photograph that was stashed away inside a notebook in her hotel room came flooding into her brain. So many times she had opened the top drawer of the cabinet back in her flat in Dublin and seen his little face staring proudly back at her, and now he was standing before her.

Only that proud little face looked so different now. But

still, she knew straight away who he was. Luke Ryan was standing in her hospital room.

Her brother was alive.

He was here.

So many years of helplessly searching, wondering, hoping and praying and now he was finally here. So many memories, so many years spent not knowing, and now the answer was finally standing before her. So many songs she had written, so many tears she had cried over this man and suddenly he was with her.

She wondered for a moment if she were dreaming, if her all the medication still floating around in her system was causing her to hallucinate. She then heard the machine beside her bed began to beep a little faster as she began to wonder if this was it, if this was the end. Had she finally crossed over to the other side and this is where they would at last be reunited? But where were her parents?

It couldn't be the end. This couldn't be the other side. Mia had seen him so many times, she was sure it was him she had been seeing in her hospital room.

No, she thought, she was definitely still in the hospital. The searing pain in her side was a sharp reminder that she was still among the living.

And the cause of that searing pain was what had brought Luke before her now. It had taken Mia's near death experience to bring him out of wherever he had been hiding all these years to surface, but he was there. He was finally here.

He looked up at her from under the brim of his dark, hooded eyes.

"Hello, Mia," he whispered nervously.

Mia opened her mouth to speak but no words would come out.

Niamh began to get up from her seat. "I don't think this is a good idea, she's only just woken up."

"I want to see her," he whispered again, not taking his eyes away from Mia.

"She might not recognize..." Niamh's voice faltered and

her sentence trailed away. She glanced back to Mia and saw her eyes were riveted on the man standing before her.

"I know who he is," Mia managed to croak out.

"You do?" Niamh asked. She whipped around to stare at Mia, her face full of surprise.

Mia nodded.

It was true, time could change so much about a person, but Mia would recognize those eyes of his anywhere. The eyes were the window into the soul, and those same dark brown eyes, that had stared back at her for eighteen years from a faded old photograph, were now standing before her.

Those were the only thing about Luke that hadn't changed.

Everything else about him seemed strange.

Different.

Alien.

Mia had spent those eighteen years wondering where Luke was, what had become of him, and eventually wondering if he still walked the earth at all, and now he was here.

All that time she had wondered, hoped, despaired, longed, and he had been alive all along. All the hours she had cried, all the songs she had written and the lyrics she had sung about him and here he was.

Her muse had finally come home.

She had often wondered if they would ever meet again. How many times she had envisioned this moment, and in not one of those visions did she picture herself strapped to a hospital bed, unable to get up and greet her brother.

After eighteen years of silence, eighteen years of not knowing if he was alive, and Mia couldn't even get up to greet her brother with a hug.

When she was still a little girl, she would picture them meeting one another across the park, or that her brother would be waiting beyond the school gates for her, and every time they would both run as fast as their little legs would carry them until they collided into one another with open arms.

As she grew older, she envisioned them meeting awkwardly at a café or restaurant, they would get up and greet one another, ask a few questions before one of them—usually Mia—would burst into tears at the relief of finally being reunited.

Mia often imagined Luke would appear in the crowd at one of her shows. She would look up from her guitar or the microphone and there he would be. Just standing, watching and listening to the lyrics that she had penned about her heartache over their separation.

But every time she looked up from her guitar, there would only be the usual sea of glassy-eyed spectators, each one unrecognisable and unnameable.

But that moment had finally arrived, and it was nothing like Mia had imagined it to be.

"Do you want me to stay?" Niamh asked, still caught in mid-motion of leaving her seat.

Mia shook her head. "No."

Niamh nodded, understanding, and left the room. She paused on her way out, "I'll be right outside," she said with her hand on the door.

Mia nodded.

With a soft click, the door to Mia's hospital room closed, and they were alone together after eighteen years.

An eerie silence fell on the room.

Eighteen years' worth of silence descended upon the room. Eighteen years' worth of unspoken words fell down between them and suddenly the hospital room became unbearably claustrophobic.

Luke made no motion toward Mia, and she was unable to make one toward him.

He continued to stare at her, looking both awkward and lost in the middle of the hospital room.

"Do you want to sit down?" Mia asked, pointing to Niamh's recently vacated chair.

Luke nodded and crossed the room to sit beside her in the uncomfortable plastic seat. He untangled his hands from his pockets as he sat and clasped them in his lap. He looked up at Mia from under tired, hooded eyes. His mop of dark brown hair was a long, unruly mess of curls on top of his head. Some strands of hair fell loosely around his face as he looked down at his lap. Mia noticed the edges of those curls appeared lightened by the sun. Now that he was closer, she noticed his skin appeared dark and weather beaten, too. His arms were deeply tanned and had freckles running up their lengths and a pattering of freckles ran across his cheeks too.

A person didn't acquire a look like that from eighteen years spent hiding in the streets of Galway. Mia wondered where Luke had been all these years. She had assumed he was still in Ireland. Stupidly and naively, she hadn't contemplated he could have been anywhere in the world.

By the looks of the man now sitting before her, Luke had long ago left Ireland and Mia behind him.

Where did she begin to start this conversation? Eighteen years of waiting and searching and her long awaited moment was finally here. What did she ask someone who had been missing for the most part of that time? *How have you been? What have you been doing?*

Her mouth was already beginning to form sentences though.

"I thought…" She swallowed, that sentence was too difficult to finish. Instead she tried another. "Where have you been?"

Chapter 3

Malaysia?

Of all the places in the world: Malaysia.

That's where her brother had been hiding?

"As soon as I was released from the system—" His faded Irish accent croaked into the room. "—I took off traveling with my inheritance."

Mia's parents had left a modest sized estate upon their deaths, all of which was bequeathed equally to their two children upon their eighteenth birthdays. Mia had only bought her small flat in Dublin with her money. The rest was still stashed away in the bank. Luke had obviously taken off with his at the first chance he got. He was three years older than Mia, so by the time she had finished her stint in the care system, he had been long gone on his travels. It was no wonder he had been untraceable.

"I got as far as Malaysia before someone offered me a job." He shrugged and stared down at his feet. "I had no reason to come back. It seemed like an easy way of life."

His words stung Mia. So many years she had searched for him, and he had given up so easily. In the blink of an eye, he had left both Ireland and her behind and not looked back.

"I met a few guys in a bar who were fishermen and they needed some help. I said yes, I had nothing to lose. I spent months out on the ocean just staring out to sea as we worked. No one asked any questions, no one cared who I was or where I came from. I was invisible out there, which was what I wanted. I had no idea what had happened to you," he continued, "my time in care was very different from yours, I suspect. I left as soon as I could, I never wanted to set foot in that country again."

"In Ireland?" Mia asked, disbelieving.

Luke nodded. "I left the care system when I was sixteen. Up until that point, I'd spent the last eight years being passed from pillar to post. I was originally sent to Galway, which I'm sure you heard."

Mia nodded. She was sent to Kinsale, Luke was sent to Galway, which was as far as her search had ever got.

Luke was eight years old when he was placed in the system, which meant he was old enough to remember more than she did, Mia realized.

"The family I lived with in Galway were nice enough, I suppose. I think I just rebelled against them after everything that had happened to us." He paused and Mia could feel her tears beginning to form. "I gave them a hard time and, eventually, they moved me on, they couldn't cope. I was placed into the foster system from then, and I think, at the last count, I'd been in twelve different homes." He attempted a wry smile. "Almost two a year."

Mia could feel her eyes glass over. *Two per year?* She had remained with Mike and Sharon from day one. Luke had been passed on like an unwanted Christmas gift.

"It could be more, I stopped counting after a while." He shrugged. "Some homes were better than others. Some I don't think the foster mothers even noticed I was there. A lot of them were just in it for the money. Anyway, I took off the first chance I got, I turned sixteen and I was out on my own. I don't remember a great deal about the next two years after that. I tried working various different jobs, I then ended up homeless for a while, mixed with the wrong crowd, and drank my way through life until I reached that magic number eighteen."

How very different their lives had been, Mia was beginning to realize. Today truly was a wakeup call, in more ways than one.

"Then bam! I turned eighteen and all this money was mine."

His eyes sparkled as he obviously reminisced over the day he received his inheritance. Mia remembered that feeling too. Thankfully, she had two special people in her life to guide her through that time, and she hadn't frittered away her money.

"As soon as the money cleared, I packed a bag and headed to the airport. I caught the first plane out of there. Morocco was the first flight out of Dublin with a spare seat on the flight, so that's where I went. It was liberating, just packing up and not looking back."

Mia looked away. She had spent years searching for Luke, and he had left without a second glance.

"Mia." He placed his hand on her arm. "You have to understand. I was a very different person back then. I hadn't had the same rosy upbringing you had, mine was dark and miserable. I wanted to get away, to leave it all behind."

She nodded, trying to understand. "How did the police not realize your passport had been used?" she found herself asking. If a missing person's report had been filed and investigated, surely a passport record would be one of the first places to check?

Luke pulled a strange face, it was almost smug, yet almost regretful. "It wasn't my passport." He shrugged. "I've never even had one. It's amazing what money can buy you."

Mia simply stared back, uncomprehending. Their lives really had been worlds apart.

"So I took off from there. I traveled across Africa, Europe, and the Far East until I landed in Malaysia. I spent years traveling, just wandering, searching, exploring. I'd planned to travel the world, to cover as much ground as I could. I had no idea what I'd do when I reached the end of that plan, but it was all I had to go with. But I got as far as Malaysia. I'd been in the country a few months when I met these guys. They were on the mainland for a few days. They were leaving to go back to this island and asked if I needed a job. I said yes. I've been there for three years now."

He made it sound so simple, just packing up your life on an illegal passport and traveling the world, casually agreeing to work with strangers on a remote island. But then again, Mia realized her life would have sounded so surreal when compared to the life Luke had been leading.

"Three years?" she repeated.

Luke was twenty six now. Mia quickly did the math and realized he had spent five years traveling across the world until he had landed in Malaysia. Then for three years he had lived anonymously, invisibly, in some remote corner of the globe, while she had stayed in their home country, fruitlessly searching and hoping.

"Three years living in paradise." Luke smiled, his smile finally meeting his tired eyes and creasing his weather-worn skin. "I'll take you there one day."

Realizing he may have overstepped their fragile, new boundaries, he quickly added, "If you would like to."

"I'd love to, one day."

Chapter 4

Technically the island of Koh Li Pe belongs to Thailand, but I met the fishermen on mainland Malaysia," Luke explained. "It's paradise. Truly, it is."

Mia now knew her brother had spent the last three years living on a remote island off the coast of Malaysia and Thailand.

His story sounded like the ultimate cliché—a wandering European traveler with nothing to lose, drifting across the Far East before settling on a Thai island. How many others like him were out there? Mia wondered. She also wondered if those others had family back home, like her, who still wondered what had become of them.

Luke had spent the last hour explaining to Mia what had become of him since their separation. He had described to her the island of Koh Li Pe, with its turquoise blue oceans and white sand beaches and its lush, dense jungles that climbed its rising hills. The place sounded like the setting of an episode of Survivor or Castaway.

"It was heaven for me," Luke continued. "I could leave everything behind and got to live in paradise. There was virtually no communication with the outside world. I had no TV, no phone, no radio, no internet, nothing. I was living as simply and as invisibly as I wanted to. The police had stopped looking for me a long time ago."

"I didn't," Mia said quietly.

"I always thought about you, Mia. I knew you would be out there somewhere, living the perfect life. You got the better deal out of the two of us, you got the perfect family." Luke's face became overcast. "I didn't think you would want me back in your life. I turned out to be the complete opposite of you. I didn't think you would want someone like me in your life. You would have been better as you were, thinking I didn't exist anymore."

Mia could feel her eyes brimming with tears. She had waited so long for this day, but it was nothing like she had expected. She never imagined Luke's life would turn out like this. They were both each other's only living relative. They had to hold onto one another.

"How did you find me?" was all she could manage to say.

"We sailed into Phuket one morning. The one guy out there who could speak English told me they needed to meet with some people they knew there for business. I had no reason to ask anything more." He shrugged again. "While they carried out whatever business they needed to in the port, a few of us took a walk into the city. The village I was living in was so small and so remote, it was like living in another universe. I was keen to see the hustle and bustle of a city again, if only for a few hours. We walked past a news-stand on our way back to the harbor and, low and behold, there was a pretty face staring back at me from the cover of one of the magazines there," he said, nodding at Mia.

Mia's faced creased into a deep frown. "Me?" she asked. Incredible that news of her and Joel's relationship had be-gun traveling across the globe.

"Uh huh." He nodded again. "Even though I hadn't seen you since you were tiny, I knew straight away it was you. I grabbed the magazine, and there you were, strolling hand in hand down a street in LA somewhere with some rock star."

Mia smiled wryly to herself. How strange that must have seemed to someone who had spent years of his life isolated from the world in a remote fishing village off the coast of Thailand.

"He seems like a good guy." Luke's lips curled into a soft smile. "We've had plenty of time to talk while you've been out of it."

Mia made a mental note to ask how long she had been "out of it." She smiled. "He is."

"Anyway, there you were, happy, beautiful and on your way to becoming a superstar," he continued. "I never in a million years expected to see you again, let alone to see you on the cover of a gossip magazine with a rock star. So I bought this rag of a publication and got one of the guys to read it to me. My Thai is still a bit rusty even after all these years." He grinned. "I couldn't believe my ears when they read it out loud. You were working for some huge recording label and dating one of the biggest stars in the world." He shook his head. "How different our lives have turned out."

He was right, Mia realized. Their worlds were poles apart.

"We ended up staying in Phuket for a couple of days so, while we were there, I went to an internet café and stared doing some research. I wanted to find out more about you and this life you had for yourself in LA. There's not much out there," he quickly added, seeing Mia's worried expression. "They don't really know that much about you, yet."

"They will do now." Mia gestured down at her body lying in the hospital bed.

Luke nodded grimly. "Anyway, on the third day I was heading back into the city when I passed the newsstand again and there were pictures of this awful car crash plastered all over the press."

He paused and Mia could no longer hold his gaze. Her memories of the crash were still painfully vivid, up until the point where the car rolled over the edge of the bridge. From there all she could recall were flashes of consciousness as she lay in the wreckage, the flashes of light and loud bangs as the metal of the car was cut around her, the ambulance sirens wailing overhead as she was hauled on a stretcher into the back of the vehicle and then blurs of hospital lights as she was rushed through the emergency doors.

Luke exhaled deeply. "I just acted on instinct. I don't know why. I guess I just needed to get to you. I grabbed a passing taxi and went straight to the airport. I caught the first flight out of Phuket to Los Angeles and tried to find you."

Mia stared, baffled at how, after so many years, her brother had so drastically appeared at her side. He'd just upped and left his life in a heartbeat to come rushing to her side.

"And here I am." He shrugged again.

"You make it sound so simple." Mia stared, baffled. "After all these years, you just appear."

Luke cast his eyes away from her. "It was never easy, Mia. You seem to think I chose to leave, that I didn't want anything to do with you, that I never gave you another thought."

She didn't answer.

"I was young, stupid, uneducated. I wouldn't have had a clue how to find you, all I cared about was getting away from the place that had made me what I was. Living in Koh Li Pe has changed me for the better. You have to understand that. It's made me a better person, the person I should have been years ago. If I had come to find you back then, you wouldn't have liked what you saw. I doubt we would have even stayed in touch. Everything happens for a reason. That I'm sure of. I know there's a reason we haven't met again until now."

His wise words hung in the air, lingering in the room with their deep meaning.

Living in paradise had made this young man much wiser than his years, Mia thought. It had given him many hours of serenity to contemplate his mistakes and his choices.

"You're long past visiting hours." A female nurse came bustling into the room. She strode over to the side of the bed and began ushering Luke away.

"No, please," Mia began.

"Nuh uh." She shook her head and waggled her finger at Mia. "You can see him tomorrow. You need your rest."

"It's okay, Mia, I'm not going anywhere." Luke smiled a sad, knowing smile and his eyes crinkled at the corners. "I'll be back in the morning."

He silently crossed the room and opened the door. He paused with his hand on the door handle and took one last look at Mia and waved softly. And then he was gone.

Mia found herself repeatedly blinking at the spot where he had stood moments ago. Had her brother really just reappeared in her life? After so many years he had shown up, just like that. Or had she imagined the whole thing? Perhaps the drugs really were causing her to hallucinate.

"You're stats are good, you're doing better each day." The nurse's voice brought Mia's attention back to the present. She checked the ever-beeping machines beside Mia's bed and began ticking off things on her clipboard. "The doctor will be in to see you in the morning," she added as she hung the clipboard back on the end of Mia's bed. "We're glad to see you finally awake. You gave us all quite the scare."

Mia stared after her. So many questions she had were still unanswered. She assumed she had to now wait until the arrival of the doctor in the morning to get those answers. She watched the nurse quietly shuffle back across to the door. As did Luke, the nurse paused at the door.

"There's quite a gathering of people waiting for you out here." She gestured to the hall beyond Mia's hospital room. "They've been here the whole time. They'll be so glad you're finally awake."

Chapter 5

A gentle knock sounded on the door to her hospital room, before it was slowly cracked open. "Mia?" A deep Californian accent whispered her name into the room as Joel poked his head around the door.

Even though night had fallen and her hospital room was enveloped in darkness, Mia would recognize that silhouette anywhere.

"Hey," she said softly as he shut the door behind him and strode quickly across the room to the side of her bed.

Wordless, he came to her side, knelt one knee on her bed, and leaned over her body, pulling her tightly to him and wrapping his arms around her.

Pain immediately shot through her right side and she winced loudly.

Joel immediately released her. "What's wrong?" he asked, grabbing her shoulders and scanning her over for the cause of the pain.

"My side." She winced again and gently placed a hand on her rib cage.

"Shit, I totally forgot, I'm so sorry." Panic crossed his face and his hand covered hers on her ribs. "I'm not even supposed to be in here." He shook his head and briefly closed his eyes. "I'm just so relieved to see you awake."

"You forgot what?" Mia asked.

Joel cocked an eyebrow at her. "Hasn't anyone told you yet?"

"Told me what?" she asked, frowning at both the pain and her confusion.

"About your injuries? About what happened?" he asked carefully.

"No." Mia sighed. "I met Luke today."

Joel stared wide eyed at her admission.

"He kind of appeared without warning as soon as I woke up and, naturally, we started talking. I haven't had chance to ask about anything like that yet. The nurse came in and checked me over before I went to sleep. No one's told me anything yet."

She looked away from Joel and began pulling at a loose thread on her bed sheet at the thought.

Joel sighed heavily. Clasping Mia's shoulders, he leaned forward and softly kissed her forehead before pulling up the plastic chair beside her hospital bed. He took her hand—the one that wasn't hooked to an IV drip—away from the sheet and protectively wrapped both his hands around hers. "You've had a lot to take in today, huh?" he asked with a sad smile.

"Yeah." Mia half-heartedly laughed. "It's not quite what I was expecting. I'd been seeing blurring images of faces these last few days. I knew there was someone there who I did, but didn't, know." She tried to explain to Joel how she'd been seeing and hearing the people in her hospital room before she woke up. "Niamh was with me when I woke up," she continued. "I hadn't been awake more than a few seconds before he appeared at the door."

Joel exhaled, shaking his head. "Wow."

"Yeah, I know. But somehow I just knew. He didn't say anything, Niamh didn't say his name. Somehow I just knew who he was."

Joel stared up at her in the darkness, patiently listening.

His face was illuminated by the soft glow of the machines beside her bed.

"Everything else was forgotten about. Right then I didn't care where I was, what had happened to me or if I was going to be okay. I was awake and Luke was there and that was all I knew." She took a deep breath. Joel squeezed her hand in reassurance. "I had eighteen years' worth of questions to ask him," she said. "Right then I didn't care that I'd woken up in hospital. I'd no idea what had happened to me, but I didn't care. I needed other answers first."

Joel nodded, understanding. "You've had chance to talk?" he asked. "Did you get some of the answers you needed?"

"Yes and no." Mia shrugged. "I know where he's been all this time. He's told me why he left and why he lived his life the way he has. I guess the only answers I don't have are the ones to my own questions. The not-so-straight-forward ones."

"That's understandable," Joel agreed.

He had adopted his listening, understanding and allowing Mia to let it all out until she was done mode.

"It's just…" She trailed off, her eyes scanning the darkness. "…a lot to deal with in one day. And I still have no idea what happened."

She didn't know whether she meant the accident, Luke, or her injuries.

"I wish I'd been here for you when you woke up." Joel winced, hating himself. "Niamh and Charlie insisted I go home to shower and rest. I've barely left you while you've been here."

"How long have I been here?" Mia asked.

He clasped her hand tightly and his eyes roved up and down the hospital bed before settling on her face.

"Joel?" she asked.

He cast his eyes downward. The glowing machines with their green lights beside Mia bathed his face in an eerie light. He sighed again. "I—I don't really know where to start. I don't think I should be the one to tell you."

"Why?" Mia's voice began to quiver. "What happened? Is everyone okay?"

She immediately began to think of Charlie, Josh, Chad, TJ, and Ruben and even the driver who had all been in the car with her that night.

"No, it's not that. They're all okay—" He looked up to her face, his eyes darker than usual. "—for the most part anyway."

Mia began to ask why but Joel cut her off. She realized that his eyes were darker than usual because they had huge dark circles around them. The shadows in the room only amplified their darkness. Joel looked as though he hadn't slept for days.

He probably hadn't.

"The doctors should be the ones to explain all of this to you," he said without looking at her. "Not me. Now that you're awake, I think they were waiting until the morning, when you've rested."

"What do you mean?" Mia's head swam with confusion. "Why can't you tell me?"

He loosened one hand from hers and gestured to her body lying in the hospital bed. "Because I'm the reason this has happened to you."

"How is any of this your fault?" Mia asked.

Joel looked away from her face and began talking to the hospital floor. "I'm the reason everyone was injured. I'm the reason the car was pushed over that bridge. I'm the reason you all ended up in hospital. That accident happened because of me."

"Joel, you weren't even in the car," Mia tried, her head pounding with confusion.

"My dad—" was all Joel managed to say before his voice cracked, and he swallowed hard before continuing. "—my dad was the one who followed you all. He saw you and Josh getting into the car. He was watching from across the parking lot. It was dark and the paparazzi were in the way. He thought Josh was me."

It was an easy mistake to make, but Mia wriggled her fingers in between Joel's and gripped his hand tightly.

"He followed the car away from the studios, as you probably saw." Joel looked up briefly and Mia nodded. "He ran the red light at the junction before the bridge and caught up with your car," he continued. "He slammed into the car, causing it to flip onto its roof. I'm told he then reversed and did it again, sending the car straight over the bridge."

"He…" Mia's voice trailed away. She couldn't believe what she was hearing.

They were both silent for a moment as Mia let the words sink in.

"He planned it. The whole thing was deliberate," Joel finished her sentence.

"Why?" was all Mia could ask.

Joel shook his head. "Because he thought I was in the car. He wanted to take me out. He thought getting rid of me would leave everything I had to him. He risked everyone in that car's lives because he thought if he got rid of me, he would land everything."

Mia stared open mouthed at the darkness at the end of her hospital bed, her eyes and mouth unmoving. She was frozen. It was one of those rare, surreal moments where shock froze the world as you knew it.

She felt a ringing in her ears as her eyes misted over. All she could see was the blinding flashes of memory, the re-plays of the accident. She could see the glass of the window shattering beside her on impact, she saw limbs flailing wild-ly in the air as the car twisted and flipped. She heard metal either side of her crunching as the car landed on the ground. She could hear screaming, banging of metal as it bounced again and more crashing of glass. She remembered covering her face as the glass exploded beside her. Subconsciously her hand went up to the side of her face and she could feel faint scratches, she knew she hadn't been fast enough.

She remembered her body slamming into Josh sitting beside her and they both collided with Charlie on the other side of the car. She remembered the shouts from those sitting in the front of the car, unable to see or hear what was happening when they were hit.

She remembered the deafening bang as the car was shunted once again and the panic that flooded her body as they realized the car was going over onto its roof once again.

But nothing compared to the feeling she remembered when realizing the car was careering over the side of the bridge.

A cold chill ran across her body and she could feel the tingling sensation in the back of her throat that told her bile was rising. She swallowed it away, the action causing tears to fall down her cheeks.

She reached her IV drip laden hand up to wipe away her tears and saw that her hand was shaking. Joel squeezed her other hand tightly.

"You can't blame yourself," she croaked out.

"I have to, Mia. None of this would have happened if it wasn't for me. You all almost died because that bastard thought I was in the car."

"No, Joel." Mia's voice hardened, and she felt anger replacing the fear inside her chest. "You can't keep blaming yourself for him, for his mistakes, his actions. He was the reason this has happened to me, to all of us. Not you."

Joel stared at her for a moment, his face completely unreadable, before staring down at the floor again.

Mia took several deep breaths. This was a hell of a lot of information to deal with in one day.

Despite her fatigued, injured body crying out for sleep, she focussed on her midnight visitor and urged Joel to continue, by tugging on his hand. "What happened to everyone?"

Joel glanced back up at her. Seeing the look on her face he continued. "The car went over the bridge and fell around

thirty, forty feet before hitting the ground. The police were
there within minutes, ambulances, fire crews—the works.
The car was a complete mess. They had to cut most of you
out of it. Thankfully, no one was killed, I've no idea how
they weren't. The police said it's a miracle you're all alive."

"Everyone's okay?" Mia's voice breathed out in relief.

"Not quite." Joel gritted his teeth. "The driver came off
the worst. He's got two broken legs and a fractured skull.
Ruben is pretty cut up and bruised, but, for the most part,
he's okay. TJ and Chad are pretty cut up too. TJ broke a
couple of ribs, and Chad took a nasty hit to his head."

"And Josh? Charlie?"

"Josh came out of it the best. He's got a few cuts and
bruises, but he's fine. Charlie's got a broken arm. She was
thrown around a bit, so she's cut up, like everyone else, but
they'll be okay."

"And me?" Mia dared to ask. After Luke had left, the
nurse had been in to check on Mia, she had told Mia her
stats were good and she was improving, but that was all.
Mia had no idea what injuries she had sustained. Thankfully, she could feel and move everything, other than her ribs,
she seemed to be functioning okay.

Joel's eyes welled up as he looked up at her face. He
scanned up and down her body again in disbelief. "You
broke three of your ribs in your right side. You've got a few
nasty cuts and bruises from the glass."

"That's it?" Mia asked, relieved.

Joel shook his head. "You were on the side of the car
that hit the ground first. They had to cut you out of the car,
it was so messed up. You had one hell of a head injury. You
fractured your skull, there was bleeding internally. You've
been out of it for five days, Mia."

"Five days?" she repeated.

Joel nodded. "You've been in a drug-induced coma to allow your body to recover. You were touch and go for the
first couple of days. The doctors weren't sure if you were

going to come around at first." He paused. "I thought I was going to lose you."

His words hung in the room, allowing the realization to sink in with Mia.

After a moment's pause, she gingerly shuffled to one side of her bed and pulled Joel by the hand.

"What are you—" he began.

Mia pulled him toward her, and he took a seat by her on the edge of her hospital bed.

Ignoring the firing pain that was searing through her side, she wriggled closer to Joel and nestled in the crook of his arm, wrapping her arm across his chest.

Joel let out a long, relieved exhale as he gently placed his arms as carefully as he could around Mia's body and rested his head on hers.

Mia felt a sharp pang of pain as he did. She now knew why her head hurt so much. It wasn't from the confusing, information-overload day she was having, after all.

"It'll take more than that to get rid of me," she whispered against his chest.

She felt the low rumble of a chuckle come from beneath her cheek as Joel laughed faintly. "I hope I don't have to find that out," he murmured against her hair.

Surrounded by darkness and shadows cast by the green lighting of the machines, Mia closed her eyes and drifted away. Ignoring the never-ending beeping, she laid her cheek against Joel's chest and imagined they were back in the safety of his house, and all was right with the world.

☾☽☾☽

Niamh looked down at Mia from her perch on the edge of Mia's bed. "He's been here for the best part of five days, you know?"

"He got to the crash soon after the police. He was with us the whole time they were cutting us out of there," Charlie added from Mia's other side. "News traveled fast. As soon as he heard, he came rushing to you."

"He came with you in the ambulance, Mia," Niamh said.

Mia smiled softly to herself. Despite the other images that were flooding her mind of that night, she marvelled at Joel's loyalty to come rushing to the scene of the crash and straight to her side. Apparently, he had rarely left her since.

"I practically had to drag him out of here to go and get a shower." Charlie laughed. "I didn't want him looking like that when you woke up."

Mia let out a laugh and had to wince at the pain in her side. She was still forgetting all the things she couldn't do while her ribs were in bandages. Some things were involuntary, though. Mia giggled, wincing again. "You should have seen the nurse's face when she came in this morning and found him in here."

Both Niamh and Charlie lunged forward as Mia winced. "Are you okay?" they asked simultaneously.

Mia looked up at them both mirroring one another, and managed not to laugh again. "Yeah."

"What is it?" Charlie asked, looking puzzled.

Mia grinned from ear to ear. "I knew you two would get along just fine."

"Well, we've had a lot of time on our hands these last few days," Charlie said with a glint in her eye.

Niamh winked. "Yeah, not having you around has its perks."

Mia tried not to laugh. She knew her friends were making a positive out of a bad situation. She mentally thanked them. She needed some humor right now, despite the pain it caused her ribs. After hours of listening to Luke and Joel's painful tales of recounting recent events, Mia needed some time like this with her friends.

Charlie and Niamh knew just how to cheer her up. Mia was over the moon to see her two best friends from opposite sides of the globe getting along so well together. She had always known these two were cut from the same cloth. "So I've been out of it for five days?" she asked.

Charlie nodded. "You and the driver came off the worst."

"Great," Mia mumbled. "How is everyone else doing?"

Joel had told Mia about her injuries and how close she had come to not making it, but he'd only briefly touched on the subject of everyone else. She was still desperate to hear how her friends were doing after the accident.

Charlie gestured at her bandaged arm. "They'll be fine. The driver's still in here, but the rest of us were discharged earlier this week."

Mia noticed Charlie's cast was wrapped in bright blue bandages. *Of course*, she thought, *Charlie wouldn't make do with any plain old cast.* "How did you get here so fast? The flight must have cost you a fortune?" she asked Niamh.

Niamh quickly looked at Charlie before glancing away. "Erm—" she stumbled, her expression looking almost guilty.

"What is it?" Mia asked.

Charlie shrugged from the other side of the bed. "Just tell her."

"Tell me what?" Mia exclaimed. She couldn't deal with any more surprises.

"Joel paid for my flight out here." Niamh's voice, for once, was barely a whisper.

"He did what?" Mia exclaimed, her ribs painfully resisting against her lungs at the rise in her voice. She winced and clutched her side, sitting back down in the covers.

"Relax, Mia," Charlie soothed, placing her hand on Mia's leg. "He just wanted you to have a familiar face here for you. He thought someone from home might bring you round faster."

Niamh giggled. "He was right."

Mia smiled, remembering it was Niamh whose voice she had woken up to. "Okay, okay," she said, holding up her hands in surrender.

"I stopped him bringing Mike and Sharon out here, though," Niamh added. "You need to call them as soon as you can, I've let them know you're okay."

"I will," Mia said.

"They've been beside themselves," Niamh added, "Sharon calls me almost every hour."

Mia smiled ruefully. "I'll call them today."

The anguish it caused her to imagine what Mike and Sharon were going through on the other side of the world was more painful than any of her injuries. She knew they wouldn't have the money to fly out to Los Angeles at short notice and the agony at being so far away from Mia at a time like this must have been unbearable for them both.

The hospital room door opened and, for a moment, Mia thought Joel had come back. "What the—"

"Glad to see you're finally awake, beautiful," Dylan's familiar accent sang from across the room.

She looked from Niamh and Charlie back to Dylan again, shaking her head in disbelief. "This medication really is going to my head."

Everyone in the room laughed, and Dylan made his way over, hugging Mia as carefully as he could before taking a step back.

"I guess Joel flew you out here too?" she asked.

Dylan grinned as he looped his arm around Niamh's shoulders. "Sure did."

"Is there anyone else out there I should know about?" Mia asked, grinning from ear to ear. She didn't have the heart to be mad at Joel. Why should she? Her friends were her family, and they cared about her as much as she did for them. Having them with her at a time like this meant the world to Mia.

"No." Charlie giggled. "Josh took Joel and Luke home to shower and get some sleep. They should be here later."

"Good." Mia exhaled. "I don't think my heart rate can cope with any more surprises."

Chapter 6

"Have you got everything?" Joel asked for the third time before they left the room.

"Yes, come on." She laughed. It was almost like having Sharon with her.

Joel's arm was protectively around Mia's shoulders as she clasped onto him for support.

Outside her room, in the corridor, stood Charlie, Niamh, and Dylan, all waiting to escort her back to her hotel.

"You be careful now." Mia's nurse appeared in front of them. "There's an awful lot of press outside, waiting for you two."

Mia looked from Joel to Niamh, Dylan, and Charlie. All four nodded in response.

"Oh, god," she answered.

She dreaded to think how many paparazzi were about to bombard them as soon as they stepped foot outside the hospital doors. How long had they been waiting? Mia wondered. Surely they hadn't been there all this time?

They said their thanks and goodbyes to the staff, and of course, Joel had paid the extortionate hospital fees. He wouldn't even let Mia see the pieces of paper that were stuffed inside his pocket.

"It's been taken care of," was all he had said when she asked.

The perks of having a multi-millionaire rock star boyfriend, Mia thought. She hadn't even begun to think about the hospital fees while she was lying in the hospital bed. She had medical insurance for her stay in the States, but Joel had ignored all of that, paying for her fees outright.

The elevator pinged loudly, signaling their arrival onto the ground floor.

Wordlessly, they made their way across the foyer, their group naturally taking shape surrounding Mia, protecting her from the media scrum they were about to face. Joel's arm tightened around her shoulders as the hospital doors slid open and they stepped outside.

That all-too-familiar noise was once again clicking in her ears like dozens of birds taking flight all at once. Flashbulbs blinded her as dozens went off simultaneously.

"Mia!"

"Joel!"

"Over here!"

"How are you feeling?"

"Can you tell us about the crash?"

"Joel, have you spoken to your dad?"

Dozens of questions were fired at them from every angle as they made their way across the car park.

Mia squinted in the bright glare of the camera flashes and clung to Joel as he followed Dylan pushing his way through the crowd. Their noise was overwhelming. Mia's ears were flooded with the clicking of shutters and an endless stream of questions. Joel pushed another camera out of the way as a journalist shoved it dangerously close to Mia's face.

Another microphone was thrust under their noses, and Charlie swatted it out of the way, closing in tighter around Mia.

Thankfully, Joel wasn't parked too far away and, with the help of the others, they were soon at his car. The paparazzi followed them every step of the way and surrounded Joel's car as they tried to get in.

Niamh, Dylan, and Charlie stood protectively around Mia as Joel helped her climb into the huge Escalade, preventing her recently healed body from being barraged by the surrounding press.

Joel slammed the door shut and, after ensuring Niamh, Dylan, and Charlie were safely stowed in the back of the car, he dashed around to the driver's side and started the engine.

Mia leaned her head back against the seat, exhausted, realizing she wasn't as well rested as she thought she was.

"Are you okay?" Joel asked, his hand hovering over the gearshift.

"I'm fine, let's get out of here," she said, looking through the window at the media still surrounding their car.

Joel knocked the car into reverse and eased his way out of the cluster of paparazzi. One by one they began to scatter as they realized their photo opportunity was gone and the car was leaving.

Mia couldn't help but glance in the wing mirror to check they weren't being followed.

"Relax," Joel said, placing his hand on her knee, as he watched her eyeing the mirror.

Mia curled her fingers into Joel's and clasped his hand tightly for support. She exhaled heavily once they were clear of the hospital and she was sure they weren't being followed.

"Where are we going?" she asked, realizing Joel wasn't driving in the direction of her hotel.

Joel kept his eyes on the road. "My house."

Mia stared out of the window, her mouth half open in unspoken words.

"Charlie picked up your things yesterday and brought them over. We thought it was best if you stayed with me. It'll be safer," he added.

Mia hesitated for a moment. She watched Joel's face. He

was still concentrating on the road before him but stifling a smile all the while. She grinned. "Sure you did."

Joel shrugged, feigning innocence. "What?"

Mia heard muffled laughter coming from the back of the car.

"Subtle, dude," Dylan quipped.

Joel laughed, the tension draining from his face as he relaxed. "All right." He shook his head. "Keeping you safe was the first reason," he said, to which Dylan loudly cleared his throat. Joel laughed. "There may have been other reasons too."

Mia cocked an eyebrow at him. "Such as?"

Joel grinned wickedly as they made the turn onto his street. "Don't push your luck."

Thankfully, Joel was right. There were no waiting paparazzi gathered on his street or by the gates of his house. The luxurious Beverly Hills residence was blissfully quiet as they pulled up to the gates and waited for them to slide open.

Everyone in the car was silent, still checking the windows and mirrors out of the corners of their eyes, still expecting the media to make an appearance at any moment.

Joel drove the car through the gates and waited for them to slide shut behind him before pulling up in front of the house. Mia noticed Josh's car already parked near the front door.

Joel helped Mia down from the passenger seat and protectively guided her into the house while Niamh, Dylan, and Charlie went on ahead.

"Are you sure you're okay?" he whispered in her ear as they walked up the front steps.

The look in his nearly black eyes told Mia he wasn't just asking about her physical injuries.

"I'll be fine." She pulled her lips into a wry smile. "It's just a lot to take in."

He scanned her face with concern. "It's more than a lot, Mia."

"I know." She tried to continue into the house but Joel held her tightly in his arms.

"If this—" He gestured back at his house. "—staying with me is all too much, just say."

Mia shook her head. "No, it's not. I think it might be just what I need."

Joel's face finally creased into a smile and he placed a soft kiss on her lips before leading her into the house.

"Josh grinned as he wrapped his arms around Mia a little too tightly. Try not to break anything else while you're here."

Mia's eyes bulged in pain as Josh embraced her. Although she said nothing, Joel caught her expression. And Josh's playful comment. He punched Josh the arm.

Josh threw him a scowl. "All right, I'm just kidding. Really, I'm glad you're okay, Mia." He squeezed her shoulders. "We've been so worried about you."

Mia let go of Josh and, as she stepped down from her tiptoes, she saw who else was also standing in the room. Hovering by the side of the sofa, Luke watched Mia and Josh, quietly and awkwardly looking out of place.

"It's good to see you out of hospital," he mumbled quietly.

Looking from one set of dark-haired brothers to her own, Mia stepped toward Luke, "I'm glad you're here," she said as she stood back on her tiptoes to put her arms around Luke.

"It taken me long enough," he said hesitantly in her ear.

Mia held her brother for a moment longer, still in disbelief that he was standing in her arms. For so many years, she had thought he was gone, that he was no longer walking this earth. For so long, she had thought she was the last remaining member of her family, and here they were holding onto another. Mia was finally getting the reunion and the long-awaited hug with her brother she had dreamt of.

They said time healed everything, but Mia knew from experience that wasn't the case. Not a day had gone by where she had not missed her brother, her parents, and wondered how their lives would have turned out if they were all still together. If they had all still been alive.

At least now Mia could fulfil half of those wondering thoughts. She and her brother were reunited. Half of their family was together again, rather than a lone quarter. Strangely, Mia found herself wondering about Christmas. She now had part of her original family to spend Christmas with. She also wondered about Joel and his brother Josh, they too were half a family. Perhaps together they could sew their halves together to make a patchwork whole.

Looking over Luke's shoulder for a brief second as they parted, Mia's eyes drifted over the large dining table in the distance. What a strange, mismatched gathering they could have, she thought. "Come on." She motioned over her shoulder to where Joel, Josh, and her friends were watching her private reunion. "I've spent too long inside recently. Let's go sit in the sun."

ᑲᕼᑲ

The barbeque sizzled quietly in the corner, its delicious smells wafting through the warm, Los Angeles summer air over to where she sat.

Mia's chair was pushed close to Joel's and his arm was draped around her shoulders. His other hand was clasped around a cold bottle of beer, from which condensation was dripping down his fingers and onto the table in the heat. That bottle was currently jiggling in Joel's hand as he motioned with it while he chatted to Luke.

Mia's feet were curled up underneath her, and she rested her head in the crook of Joel's arm, contentedly watching her boyfriend and long-lost brother chatting like they were old friends.

Was this the norm? she wondered. Did you declare to the world you were a global rock star's girlfriend, only to be thrown from the road in a horrific car crash caused by his father hours later, then to wake up in hospital and be reunited with a relative you thought was dead, and come home to chat about American football scores over a barbeque?

No, Mia thought, that definitely wasn't the norm, but it was her norm.

She marveled over how recently she had lain in bed with Joel, waking up in his arms in his Beverly Hills mansion, and thinking how things like that didn't happen to girls like her. *How badly I have tempted fate.*

But she was a firm believer in fate. What would be would be. Life's twists and turns were all part of the road map to where she was destined to be and those twists and turns had led her to now.

And right now, everything seemed pretty good.

They had been to hell and back in a few weeks to get to where they were, but they were here, nonetheless, albeit slightly bruised and broken.

Mia smiled contentedly as she basked in the Los Angeles summer air in the arms of her rock-star boyfriend. She could hardly believe that Luke was alive and was back in her life. She sighed happily as she watched Niamh and Dylan together by the edge of the pool, still in the early days of their own relationship. Across the yard, Josh was teasing Charlie as he tended to the barbeque, threatening to flick pieces of uncooked chicken at her. Joel's dogs, Sonny and Diesel, were lounging in the sun by the table, one eye closed and the other on the barbeque, in hopes of catching falling scraps of meat.

The dogs ears pricked at the sound of someone making their way through the house and out to the back yard. Mia looked up to see Ruben walk through the French doors, shortly followed by Lyle, TJ, and Chad.

Joel tipped his beer at his friends as they walked across to the table. "Glad you could make it, guys."

"Good to see you're okay, Mia," Ruben clapped her on the shoulder before being swiftly pushed aside by Chad.

"Dude, you're alive!" he exclaimed before reaching down to hug Mia.

Joel paused, open mouthed at Chad for a moment, before shaking his head and carrying on with his conversation.

Mia simply laughed. "As charming as ever, Chad."

"Of course he is." TJ was also shaking his head and moving Chad aside to get to Mia. "I'm glad you're home," he said as he swiftly gave her a warm embrace.

Mia pulled back to meet his eyes. *Home?* She searched his eyes, and TJ winked in response before striding away to fetch a beer.

"You want another?" he asked, holding up a bottle.

"Sure," Mia replied.

She then noticed a girl loitering in the doorway of the house. Dressed in tiny denim hot pants, biker boots, and a tight white vest top was a girl with a dark Californian tan, a shock of short, dark hair, and a body to die for.

"Hey baby," Chad cooed, holding his hand out to the girl.

"Baby?" Mia whispered in disbelief.

Joel turned his head to look at Mia's disbelieving expression. "Uh huh," was all he said.

Chad introduced the girl. "Mia, this is my girlfriend Tara,"

"Hi, Mia, it's nice to finally meet you. I've heard so much about you." Her soft, delicate voice sounded musical.

"And you," Mia sat up in her seat, marveling that someone as simple as Chad had managed to bag himself this stunningly beautiful young woman. "I'm surprised we haven't met before," she added.

Tara wouldn't have looked out of place in Sixth String Studios, either working there or lining its walls in a photo from a glossy shoot. "I don't like to disturb Chad at work." She smiled, taking a seat beside Mia. "And, besides, I'm always so busy working myself."

"What do you do?" Mia asked.

"I'm a research scientist," Tara said.

"Really? Wow." Mia suddenly felt rather simple sitting next to this beautiful, educated scientist.

Chad grinned goofily as he took a seat beside his girl-friend. "I can't believe my luck either."

Me neither, Mia thought.

"They met in high school, in case you're wondering," TJ quipped from across the table as he sat down. "Been together ever since."

"Aww," Mia said, as the pair turned to stare dreamily at each other.

"Well, that explains a lot," Joel teased from beside Mia.

Everyone at the table fell apart laughing, much to Chad's dismay.

"Food's ready," Josh called from across the patio.

Charlie began piling the food onto plates and bringing it across to the table where Dylan and Niamh were squeezing into the remaining chairs.

"This place is incredible," Niamh gushed in Mia's ear as she scooted a chair between Mia and Tara.

Dylan followed at her side, and Mia noticed out of the corner of her eye that Tara looked rather pleased at having Dylan replace Mia beside her.

"I know." Mia smiled. "I guess I live in a pretty awe-some house, huh?" Niamh giggled and Mia hastily added, "For the time being, anyway."

"We'll see about that," Joel said from her other side.

"Since when were you listening?" she quipped.

"Always." He grinned in return, playfully nudging her arm.

Mia caught Luke's eye beside Joel and he threw her a re-assuring smile. "You okay?" he mouthed.

Mia nodded. "You?" she mouthed back.

He grinned, his smile reaching the corners of his crin-kling dark eyes. "Never better."

She felt as though she were drifting along on a cloud, dreamily bouncing along in her own little bubble. As strange as recent events were, at that moment, she couldn't recall ever feeling happier. Yes, she was battered and bruised. Yes, she had the shock of finding her long-lost brother. Yes, the world's media followed her every move. Yes, she didn't know if she had a job. Yes, half the world's female population wanted her boyfriend. Yes, his father had tried to kill her. But, at that moment, Mia felt finally, completely, at home.

She had been reunited with her brother, and somehow that didn't feel strange at all. Everything she had ever felt was suddenly calmed. Her emotions had found their tranquillity, their inner peace. The missing piece in her family had come home, and there was nothing strange about that.

She was sitting beside her best friend and the most beautiful, deep, caring man she had ever met, who just happened to be hers. She was surrounded by friends, old and new, in the blissful Los Angeles summer sun and, at that moment, another first Mia found herself feeling, it was that the first time in a long, long time she didn't have a care in the world.

Their strange little patchwork family was together again, with a few repaired seams and a few additional pieces, but together, nonetheless.

Yes, Mia thought, *life is pretty good right now. Ridiculously strange, but pretty good.*

Chapter 7

These pillows must have cost a fortune, Mia thought as she closed her eyes again.

Pillows this good didn't cost twenty dollars. They were worth every penny, though.

"Comfy?" a deep, rich Californian voice asked from somewhere north.

"Mmm," Mia murmured.

A low, hearty chuckle sounded and Mia opened her eyes to see California's most exquisite creation standing above her bed.

Or his bed? Their bed? Mia wasn't sure which to call it.

"How are you feeling?" he asked, a beautiful smile etched on his perfect face.

"Wonderful," Mia answered truthfully and Joel sat down on the bed beside her, snuggling his body up against hers on top of the duvet.

Mia nuzzled against his chest and sighed contentedly as Joel wrapped his arms around her body over the bulky duvet.

He smelled delicious, as always. Mia could have stayed there forever, wrapped in his arms and breathing in his scent.

"You need to get up, baby," he said softly into her hair.

"Why?" she groaned.

"You have a visitor," he said.

"Who?" Mia asked.

Joel rubbed her arm, hearing the worry in her voice. "It's only Luke."

"Oh," she exhaled, relaxing in his arms again, and smiled against his lips. "He can wait a few more minutes."

❧❧❧

"How are you doing?" Luke asked from the island in the kitchen where he sat with a large mug of coffee.

"Great," Mia replied, wondering when people would stop asking her that.

She didn't mind Joel and Luke asking, but it seemed that every time she saw someone they had to ask how she was. She wondered if there was a common code of practise for treating a near-death-experience patient.

Truthfully, she wasn't feeling exactly great. Okay would have been a better description. The ache in her healing ribs was slowly subsiding, day by day, and her repairing skull was still causing her pain. She was sleeping much more than usual, due to her medication, and was under strict house arrest. She was instructed by the hospital to take it easy and rest at home for the next few weeks to allow her body to continue to heal.

Everything possible had been done in the hospital over the previous weeks, and now Mia needed to rest at home until she was back to one hundred percent. The house arrest was as instructed by Joel Coben.

He hadn't wanted the media to intrude on Mia's recovery and portray it all over the world. This was a time for privacy and recuperation.

Mia had Joel, Luke, and her friends to help her get through the next few weeks, as well as daily phone calls from Sharon, and that was all the help in the world that she needed.

Joel was already near the Starbucks-sized coffee machine in his kitchen, clinking cups together as he waited for the machine to fire up.

"I'll get that," she said, coming up behind him and steering him by the shoulders to take a seat next to Luke.

"I don't mind—" Joel started.

"Hush." Mia squeezed his arm before going back to the coffee machine.

He had done everything he possibly could do for her since she arrived home from the hospital. As well as paying for her hospital fees, checking her out of her hotel and into his house, Joel had insisted on doing all he was able to for Mia while she recovered. As today was one of her better days, she wanted to do something for him instead.

Once she was sat back down with Luke and Joel and each of them had cups of coffee, Mia began to feel more awake.

She really hadn't wanted to get out of that seriously comfortable bed. At first, Joel had taken pity on her and her injuries, believing she was resting and had been catering to everything she needed. But after a few days, he had wised up and realized she could at least manage to get out of bed.

"What's your plan for today, lazy?" Luke teased.

Mia shrugged. "The usual."

She had been at Joel's house for almost two weeks. She was still under doctor's orders to rest and, therefore, hadn't returned to Sixth String Studios. She didn't know how to broach the subject. Did she just casually walk up at nine a.m. on a Monday morning and act as if nothing had happened? She had been due to have a meeting with Jackson the Monday after the accident, but as she had been unconscious in a hospital, that meeting hadn't taken place.

Jackson had sent her a very sympathetic email, telling her how sorry he was and how saddened he was to hear of the accident. He had briefly visited Mia in the hospital after she had come around, but he had only stayed for a few minutes as Mia had still been exhausted and pumped full of medication. His email went on to say he was pleased to hear she was recovering so well, and that he still wanted to meet with her once she was fully rested and recovered.

Some days, Mia felt well enough to go. She insisted she could go in to the studios, but everyone else had other ideas. Then, on other days, she realized they were probably right.

The guilt of abandoning the studio was what weighed most heavily on her mind. The guilt was what wanted her to get back in the studio, regardless of whether or not her body was ready.

"Actually, I had an idea," Joel said, placing his cup on the counter. "I need to go into the studio. Ruben has a few things he needs to go through with me, as I've been off for a few weeks."

Mia grimaced. That was her fault. Joel was supposed to be hard at work on his new album and had missed several weeks' worth of work due to her.

"Hey." He placed a hand reassuringly on her arm before continuing. "So I thought it would give you guys a bit of time to talk without me here."

Mia looked across at Luke and back to Joel again. She loved Joel dearly, really she did, but he was right. Having one-on-one time with her brother would give them both a chance to talk and to bond.

Though they had spoken for hours in the hospital, Mia had been pumped full of medication, in a lot of pain, and very confused. It had all taken place in a bit of a haze.

In the days that followed, she had remained in the hospital, gone through dozens of medical checks and more bed rest, before being allowed home to rest some more. Joel had protectively stayed by her side ever since, making sure she was okay.

But he was right, some time for just the two of them would give Mia and Luke the chance to talk properly, away from the rest of the world, which they hadn't yet had.

Joel stood up from his seat. "I better get going. Don't want to be on the wrong side of Jackson again." He winked at Mia, who had seen Jackson in a bad mood before. It wasn't pretty.

He leant over Mia and looped his arms around her waist, pulling her into him, still taking care to avoid her ribs.

This injury was really starting to get in the way of things. *More than just hugging*, Mia thought.

"I'll be back as soon as I can." He kissed her lips and Mia tried to hold him to her for as long as possible. Eventually, Joel chuckled and let out a heavy exhale. "I better go." He kissed her again. "Though I really don't want to," he whispered, quiet enough so that only she could hear him.

Mia smiled. "I'm not going anywhere."

"See you soon." He kissed her forehead. "Bye, Luke."

"See you later," Luke said from across the counter.

Mia suddenly felt a faint blush creeping across her cheeks as she remembered Luke had been watching her with Joel. The front door slammed shut somewhere behind them, and Mia heard the engine rumble away down the drive as Joel left. And just like that, she was left alone with her brother. Their first real time alone together, which Mia would be one-hundred-percent conscious for, since they had been reunited.

"He's a really good guy." Luke broke the silence, looking in the direction in which Joel had left.

Mia smiled. "Yeah. he is."

"We had plenty of spare hours to talk when you were in the hospital," Luke said. "He thinks the world of you, he really does."

That blush was creeping back across her cheeks again.

"You're a lucky girl, Mia." Luke's face creased into a faint smile. "Hang on to that one."

"I intend to." She grinned, suddenly feeling shy. "What about you? Is there anyone special in your life?"

Luke opened his mouth to answer then dropped his face to look at his mug on the counter. He fidgeted nervously with the cup in his hand, running his thumb back and forth across the rim. "Yeah, I guess there is." He smiled when he eventually looked back up. "I guess I haven't been as affirmative with her as I ought to have been. But seeing you and Joel together, seeing how good you guys are together, it's made me realize I want that too, that I should tell her more how much I appreciate her."

Mia nodded. "You should."

"I will, as soon as I go back," he confirmed with a nod.

"You're going back?" Mia asked, her hopes falling.

"Eventually, yeah." Luke's smile shifted slightly as his expression turned to puzzlement. It's my home, Mia."

Mia immediately realized she shouldn't have let those words slip out. She knew Luke was right. Koh Li Pe was his home. Just because they had found each other again didn't necessarily mean Luke would up and leave his own life to be with her. Would she do the same? No, probably not.

Though her life was its own tangling array of confusion, upping and leaving to a remote Thai island would not solve any of those things. Nor would she want to leave behind Joel, her friends in Los Angeles or Dublin, Mike and Sharon, or whatever was left for her at Sixth String Studios. It wasn't fair to expect someone else to do the same. Mia hadn't realized until that moment that they would have to find a way to make their reacquainted-sibling relationship work, despite the distance.

Plenty of people have family scattered across the globe, she thought. *They can make it work. This is perfectly normal. They also don't have a multi-millionaire rock-star boyfriend who readily pays for emergency travel expenses.*

"Do they have Skype in Koh Li Pe?" she asked with a bemused smile.

∽∾∽

Another blissful afternoon in Los Angeles, Mia thought

as she stretched out on the sun lounger by the side of the pool.

The scorching early July sun tingled against her bare skin as she lay in her bikini by the pool, still marveling from under her sunglasses at the luxury of Joel's home. People would pay thousands of pounds to stay somewhere like this. She actually lived in luxury...well, for the time being anyway.

Luke was stretched out beside her on the next sun lounger, one hand petting Sonny who was sprawled out beside him on the floor, the other enclosed around a cold bottle of beer. Mia wondered if Joel had an endless supply of beer. Those bottles seemed to just readily appear on a hot sunny day.

She felt her skin glowing warm with the baking heat, hoping that she would gain a Californian tan that would somehow resemble Joel's permanently brown skin. While she, thankfully, didn't have the translucent white Irish skin, Mia still felt pale when next to Joel's sun-kissed body. Hopefully, the tan would help to fade some of her bruises too. She absent-mindedly traced the edges of the largest bruise that still looked purple on the side of her ribs.

"How's it doing?" Luke asked as he watched her examine her injuries.

"Not bad. It doesn't hurt too much anymore," she said.

"All the rest is helping." Luke nodded. "And a warmer climate definitely helps your body, trust me."

He grinned and wiggled a very brown arm in Mia's direction. Yes, living in Thai waters had certainly changed her brother's complexion. His skin was so deeply tanned, Mia found herself comparing him to a worn leather handbag. His skin was weather beaten from the three years of spending endless days out on the Thai waters under the harsh sun. Those rays were even stronger when reflecting back from the ocean. *What a life.*

After eventually running out of steam asking the preliminary questions, which Mia realized she had asked most of in the hospital, they had turned their conversation to talking about their everyday lives.

Over the past few weeks, Mia now knew about the traveling Luke had done before he had landed in Malaysia, the wooden hut by the beach he lived in on the Thai island of Koh Li Pe, the fishermen he worked with every day, and the beautiful young Thai woman Nittaya who had stolen his heart. Mia chastised him for not making the most of what was right under his nose, after seeing a picture of the beautiful woman Luke adored. He now had strict instructions from his sister that, when he returned, he was to tell Nittaya how he felt.

"Life's too short to waste time," Mia added gravely.

"Yes, it is," Luke replied.

Their current and past situations were more than enough reminders to seize the present and cherish those they loved. Mia didn't want Luke to one day realize what he could have had with Nittaya.

Luke had also asked more than his fair share of questions. He knew about Mia's music, her upbringing in Kinsale, moving to Dublin, her friends there, working at Glen's, and how she ended up in Los Angeles. The rest he had already been brought up to speed with.

Since the time she had left the hospital, Luke had been a regular visitor to Joel's house. Joel was still insisting on paying for him to stay in a hotel. He had offered Luke a room at his house, to which Luke had politely refused, insisting Mia and Joel deserved their privacy.

In the times he had visited, they had been able to talk about most things, but not at great length or in great detail. Their day by the pool at Joel's house had allowed them to fill in the gaps, to add to the minor details, to polish the edges. Joel had been right, of courseThe day was exactly what they needed to cement their relationship back together, to fuse those retied sibling bonds.

How simply, Mia reflected, had their eighteen years apart so quickly been brought up to speed. One could condense the majority of their life into a few hours of conversation. And just like that, they were onto normal, everyday conversation.

"Have you tried exercising?" Luke asked, bringing her out of her reverie.

"No," she replied. "I haven't really dared to."

"Gentle exercise might help," he added, "like swimming?"

Mia turned to look at the enormous pool in front of them. "Really?"

Luke nodded. Taking a final swig from his beer, he stood up and held out a hand to help her from her sun lounger. "Come on."

Mia took his hand, feeling the strong, coarse fingers on her own lead her to the edge of the pool. When they reached the railings, Luke let go, walking beside her down the steps and into the water.

"Just take it easy," he instructed as they prepared to kick off. "Want to follow me?"

"Sure," she replied. Having someone pace her might help her not overdo things.

Mia soon surprised herself at how easily she found herself swimming several lengths of the pool. Her injuries were definitely on the mend. Her head felt fine today. Her bruises, for the most part, were fading, and her ribs weren't in much discomfort when she swam.

Luke was right. The gentle exercise up and down the pool was loosening up her body. Mia found herself wondering how much more physical exertion it could handle. Luke's face appeared from the water at the edge of the pool. "Joel should be back soon."

Mia tried to keep a straight face as she swan toward him. Were siblings thoughts always so in tune? She was too many years out of practise to know. She looked across at Luke's watch that he held aloft from the water for her to see. "He should."

As always, Joel had gone to the studio later in the morning. It was now early evening and as he was a creature of habit. He would be leaving the studio soon.

"I'll go shower and head off," Luke said as he began climbing the steps of the pool.

"You're not staying?" Mia asked as she followed. "You can stay for dinner if you like?" She cocked an eyebrow at herself. How strange inviting her brother to dinner sounded. She hoped she would get used to asking him that.

"No thanks." He shook his head. "I think you guys need your alone time too."

He grinned as he said it, rubbing his long hair with a towel then pausing, as if realizing it was his sister he was talking to. "To talk and stuff…" He trailed off, his cheeks turning pink under his dark tan.

Mia laughed out loud at his awkwardness. "Of course, to talk," she said as she picked up her own towel.

"If you're not too tired from swimming," Luke added with a grin, once he got over his embarrassment.

She shook her head. "Okay, too much information to be sharing with my brother."

"What?" Luke laughed, throwing up his hands. "I've missed out on years of teasing my little sister over boys. I've got some catching up to do there too, you know."

"I think we can skip that part out. And I've got to meet your girlfriend too," she added with a gleeful smile.

Luke snapped his head up, the pink embarrassment draining from his cheeks. "Oh, crap." He shook his head. "I guess this works both ways, huh?"

"Uh huh," Mia said with a smile.

He nudged her as he walked past. "Am I too old to race you to the house?"

"Never," she called before shooting past him and up the steps to the house.

෴

The simultaneous sounds of the front door opening and eight pawed feet skittering across tiles announced Joel was home.

Mia could hear him greeting his dogs and fussing over them before he appeared before her in the living room.

"Hey." His whole face creased into an adorable smile when he saw her waiting for him, "How are you doing?" he asked, leaning over her and kissing her eagerly.

She laughed breathily. "Much better now."

Joel laughed too as he sat down next to her on the sofa before placing his hands around her waist and pulling her onto his lap.

Mia snuggled up against the comforting contours of Joel's chest, his arms protectively wrapped around her body. She felt him rest his head against hers and relax back into the sofa, letting go of the stresses of the day.

"How was the studio?" she asked a pectoral.

"Fine." Joel's lips brushed against her hair, his words vibrating through her head.

Mia sensed something wasn't quite right with his answer. There was something in his voice that made her curious. "What is it?" she asked, trying to look up at his too perfect face. "Is Jackson mad? Did he say something about me?"

"No." Joel shook his head, trying to get her to nestle back on his chest again. When he realized she wouldn't settle without knowing what was wrong, he continued, "I just heard from the lawyer, that's all."

"Oh."

Mia paused. She had been trying to forget about the crash. Joel had been right, living with him had taken her mind off the world outside his gated mansion. She had loved living in her little bubble within the Hollywood one— a bubble that she shared with its finest resident.

Of course, there had been Luke too. becoming reacquainted with her brother had also given her much food for thought. There had been plenty of things to take Mia's mind off the drama of the accident weeks ago. It all still seemed so much of a blur to her, anyway.

"What did he say?" she asked hesitantly.

Joel didn't answer straight away. He gazed away across the room, his eyes contorted in a mixture of pain, anger, and confusion. Those nearly black eyes could say so much sometimes.

Mia placed a hand on his forearm. "Joel?"

His eyes were back on hers again. "He's being charged."

Immediately, Mia knew why Joel had looked so confused. This was his father, the man who had created him, raised him, and then abandoned him, betrayed him, and tried to kill him and those he loved. That was a lot for someone to try and process.

"With what?" Mia found herself daring to ask.

Joel shrugged, his eyes glassing over again. "Dangerous driving, attempted murder, a whole list of offenses."

"Is that what you want?" she asked.

Joel regarded her strangely for a moment and cocked his head to one side. "No one's asked me that," he mused, "I guess I don't know."

Mia rubbed his arm reassuringly. "It's okay not to know."

"I guess I do. I mean he tried to kill my friends, my brother, the girl I love." He sighed and rested his head on top of Mia's. "Every part of me is so angry with him. I could have lost you all. I'm furious, I hate him, I want to rip his fucking head off for all the things he's done. He doesn't love or care about me and Josh anymore. I would have killed him myself if I'd lost you or Josh that night." He paused and took a deep breath. "But at the end of the day, he's still my father. And some small part of me is sad that he's going to prison. Even though I know it's right, it's what he deserves, it's what I want and, hell, it's probably the best place for someone like him, it still makes me sad that our lives have come to this."

Mia looped her arms around his neck, pulling him into

her body. He rested his head on her shoulder, in the crook of her neck. This was her turn to comfort him. He had done so much for her recently. "It is the best place for him," she confirmed. "He can't hurt us or anyone anymore. You can move on, knowing he isn't around the next corner waiting for you."

Joel laughed into her shoulder. "Or waiting for my money."

Mia giggled. "And that too."

"And I know he can't try anything like that again." Joel pulled away from her shoulder to look her in the eyes. "That you'll be safe."

Mia found herself swimming in almost black irises. Black eyelashes tickled her skin as those irises came even closer to hers. There were so dark, so deep. It was more haunting than gazing up at the night sky.

In the space of a heartbeat, Mia had found herself lost completely in them before their eyes closed simultaneously and Joel's soft lips were on her own.

His slow, meaningful kiss quickly became deeper, more eager and yearning.

His hands were sliding up the back of her T-shirt, caressing her bare skin beneath. Her own hands were quickly doing the same, pulling the thin cotton over his head to reveal the familiar, sculpted beauty beneath it. Slowly, carefully, Joel peeled her T-shirt away from her chest, his hands more gentle than they needed to be, still ever cautious of her repairing body.

Mia felt her breath escape her lungs quickly as her bare skin was against Joel's chest, his naked arms were around her body and reacquainting themselves with her skin.

Their breathing was hot and heavy, their touches desperate and longing, both eagerly wanting to be reunited. "They said we should wait," Joel panted against her lips, begrudgingly pulling his mouth away from hers. "They said at least six weeks."

Mia was sitting in his lap, her legs straddling either side

of his hips. She gazed down into his black eyes, her hand still entangled within his mess of unruly hair, the other on his chest. "I can't wait six weeks," she breathed against his skin, making him close his eyes for a second.

His hands ran up her waist and across her back, pulling her body against his own bare skin. He was holding back, pleading with himself to do the right thing, although Mia could tell he didn't want to.

She ran a finger across his chest, outlining the definitions of muscle beneath her hand. One by one, she traced the edges of the muscles in his stomach before trailing her finger across the edge of his jeans and pulling at the button.

"Take me to bed, Joel," she said breathily against his mouth as the button of his jeans popped open in her fingers.

Joel let out a grunt of frustration before giving way to what he wanted just as much as she did. Running his long fingers across her back and down across her behind, he lifted her body up against him as he stood. Rising from the sofa, leaving behind their T-shirts and their medical advice, Joel carried her up the stairs to his bedroom.

Chapter 8

Los Angeles still looked the same. Mia didn't know why she expected it to look any different. The passing boulevards, palm trees, shops and restaurants, zillions of traffic lights, and busloads of tourists still went about their daily routines.

Joel's Escalade zipped through a yellow traffic light and automatically Mia checked the wing mirror. His hand was quickly on her thigh, squeezing in reassurance. "Relax."

"Sorry," Mia mumbled against the glass as she stared out at the familiar sights en route to Sixth String Studios.

She wasn't quite as over the accident as she thought she was. Living in her little bubble in Joel's house was all well and good. She didn't have to face the world, the media, or the daily prospect of entering a moving vehicle again when she was there.

But as Joel had reminded her when she had hesitated over getting into the car that morning, life went on and she couldn't hide away forever, as much as they both would have her liked to.

"I wish we could stay in here forever," he had whispered into her ear, hugging her tightly. "I really do, but that's not realistic, not yet anyway."

"Not yet?" Mia asked the tattoo on his collarbone.

Joel had squeezed her tightly before releasing her with an enthusiastic grin. "First, the world needs to hear your music."

She tried tugging at his T-shirt. "I could just play for you?"

He grinned impishly before bundling her into his car. "As much as I would love to say yes, the answer is no."

Three weeks after Mia had left the hospital for the safety of Joel's house, Jackson had finally called to ask how she was recovering and when she would be coming back.

Mia knew the call was due. She knew she was well enough to go into the studios for the meeting and face reality. She knew that if she were fit enough to be rekindling the physical side of her relationship with Joel, she was well enough for a meeting with a music industry exec. Something else which Joel had reminded her of, from the comfort of their bed that morning.

"Relax," he repeated again as they sat at another traffic light, his eyes seeing the worry on her face. "There's really nothing to stress over."

Mia tried to smile in return and failed. Joel's hand left her thigh and he entwined his fingers with hers. Mia wriggled her fingers as tightly as she could into his and held on.

Thankfully, Jackson had informed security Mia and Joel would be arriving that morning, so the waiting paparazzi were being kept well and truly under wraps as the Escalade pulled into the studio parking lot.

Joel jumped down from the cab and was immediately met by two waiting security guards who unnecessarily escorted him round to Mia's side of the car. Though he said nothing as he helped her down, his almost black eyes said everything.

Mia was torn between laughing at the hilarity of it all and crying at the frightening hoard of lunging paparazzi trying to get around the rest of the security.

Still gripping Joel's hand, she was shielded from the

press by Joel's body and the two burly security guards on either side of them whose services, thankfully, ended at the familiar sliding doors.

"Oh, my God, you're back!"

Another noise Mia was grateful to hear was the clattering of stiletto heels on the tiled floor and the chirpy Californian accent of Charlie barraging across the foyer to get to them. Mia was immediately engulfed in a bear hug—*a bear cub hug*, she thought, *given the size of Charlie.*

"I've missed your face around here," Charlie giggled as she finally let Mia go. "And you too, I suppose," she added with a cheeky hint of sarcasm before swiftly hugging Joel, who, to Mia's surprise, hugged Charlie back.

"I see Mia's working wonders on your social skills, bro."

Another friendly Californian accent told Mia that Josh was in the room.

Joel laughed as he released Charlie and clapped his brother on the back in a typical man-hug.

"Glad to see you're back, Mia." Josh grabbed Mia as soon as he had let go of Joel. Though both Charlie and Josh were regular visitors at Joel's house, Mia knew they were glad to see her back in the studios.

Mia also knew their relationship was going from strong to stronger. She had seen the way Josh looked at Charlie when they were together, the way they cuddled up together on the sofa in Joel's living room, the way they caught each other's eye, the private moments that only a couple truly in love share. Mia knew she and Joel showed the same signs. She was happy for Charlie that the same was happening to her.

"Seriously, don't be nervous," Charlie leaned in to Mia and whispered in her ear. As she pulled away she winked, not-so-subtly.

Josh nodded more subtly than his girlfriend had, and Mia wondered what they knew that she didn't. She looked up at Joel, whose arm was back around her shoulders, now the greetings were done, and he simply shrugged. At least he wasn't in on it too.

"Mia," a voice with an air of authority commanded from across the room, and the clipping of polished shoes on the ceramic tiles signalled Jackson was in the room. He smiled, ever professional, and shook Mia's hand. "Nice to see you back with us."

"Glad to be back," Mia said, without thinking, realizing she didn't know if, or for how long, she would be back.

"Are you ready? Do you want to follow me?"

Jackson motioned over his shoulder in the direction of the boardrooms and Mia knew it was time to face the music. *No pun intended*, she thought.

"I'll be right out here." Joel gestured to the foyer and, squeezing her shoulders, stole one final, reassuring kiss before Mia turned to follow Jackson.

Mia caught Charlie and Josh giving her a sly thumbs up as she turned away.

Jackson gestured into the room as he held the door open for her. "Please take a seat Mia."

"Thanks." Mia glanced around the ominous-looking boardroom, taking a seat on the opposite side of the table from where Jackson's papers lay.

She felt incredibly small as she wrung her fingers in her lap, hunching her shoulders in the large chair and glancing around the boardroom. There was an oversized table, fancy office chairs, and a larger-than-necessary screen on the wall with a projector overhead. She noticed the Skype icon flashing in the corner of the screen and wondered how many artists had Skype called this very room from some corner of the world on their tours. How many of her favorite artists had sat in this very seat, having the same conversation she was about to have?

"I trust you're recovering well?" Jackson asked as he sat down.

Mia smiled nervously. "Yes, thank you."

"I cannot apologize enough for what happened to you

Mia," Jackson began, holding up a hand when Mia began to interject, "although we are not responsible for the actions of Joseph Coben, I feel we must express our sincerest apologies at the failures of our security team and our driver as a result of the accident. Had they acted as they should have, with more care and attention, I feel the incident would not have taken place."

Mia fought the rising urge to argue every point he had just made. It was not the studio, or Jackson, or the security, or the driver's fault that Joseph had crashed their car off the road.

There was no one to blame but Joseph, and he was now safely inside a prison cell somewhere.

Instead, she chose to nod. "Thank you," she managed again. Now was not the time to argue with someone who may, or may not, be your boss and who may, or may not, be about to offer you the chance of a lifetime. Or to send your dreams crashing and burning to the ground.

Either way, now was not the time to argue.

"So, resuming to our original agenda," Jackson continued, looking down at the papers before him.

Mia noticed his light gray suit brought out his baby blue eyes, the contrast of his navy tie set off his blond hair and Californian tan. Even Jackson had time to get a Californian tan, Mia thought. He really was an attractive man and she found herself wondering if he had a girlfriend, not that she would ever dare to ask.

"How did you find your time here with us?" he began.

She immediately noticed he used the past tense. For several minutes they talked about Mia's three months at Sixth String Studios, how well she worked with her producers, the music they had created, the success of the Glasshearts' track, and how well Mia fitted in with the company.

"I notice you have built several...*relationships*...while you've been here," Jackson added, looking up at her from under his eyebrows, just the hint of a smile playing on his professional face.

"Umm…" Mia wasn't sure how to respond to that statement.

"Relax, Mia." Jackson finally let out a small laugh. "I'm please you've settled in so well. Joel is a great guy."

Mia tried to clamp her mouth shut, fighting the urge to allow her jaw to drop wide open. Did Jackson really just give his approval to her relationship with his biggest star?

"So, now that we come to the end of your contract," he continued, bringing Mia's attention immediately back to full focus.

He said *the end*, she realized.

Oh god, this was it. This was the end of her contract.

They were going to say, thank you for working with us, but no thanks. Thanks for the opportunity, but you're not quite right for us. Given your interwork relationships and all the media attention, we're going to have to let you go.

Mia could hear all the reasons why Jackson wouldn't want to keep her working with the studios. Each and every single one was running through her head on repeat. They were all so obvious, now that she thought about them.

Her dreams were about to come crashing down around her. Falling in love with Joel was about to cost Mia her dream job, the man of her dreams was going to lose her the dream career.

How ironic.

She would be on the next flight out of LAX that evening. She could just picture herself shame facedly packing her bags at Joel's house, him driving her to the airport, kissing her goodbye while the paparazzi snapped away outside the doors, Joel telling her they would find a way to make it work. Mia wondered if they could survive the distance and the dramatic differences in their lives. She would have to return to working at Glen's, where all her regular customers would ask her why she came back from LA and why she was still a barmaid.

She would be followed by the press, every girl that came into Glen's would look her up and down with a sneer before asking what on earth Joel Coben was doing with a barmaid from Kinsale.

"Mia? Did you hear me?" Jackson stared wide eyed across the table.

"Sorry?" Mia asked, shaking her head.

"Is it your head injury? Are you still not okay?" he asked, concern flooding his face.

"Sort of," Mia lied, too embarrassed to admit she had zoned out of the conversation.

"I said—" Jackson repeated slowly, holding her gaze to ensure she was paying attention, "—we would like you to continue working with us."

"Oh." Mia's voice came out several octaves higher than usual. Niamh would have been proud.

Jackson let out a small laugh again, pushing several pieces of stapled paper across the table to her. He gestured to the paper, holding out a pen to her. "We want to offer you a recording contract."

Mia took the pen from his hand, her eyes never leaving the piece of paper in front of her.

"I'll give you a few minutes to read that over. I'm going to get a coffee. Do you want one?" he asked.

Mia nodded, her eyes still on the table before her, her mouth now wide open.

Jackson let out a small chuckle to himself as he closed the door behind him.

Sixth String Studios
Offer of Recording Contract
Artist: Mia Ryan

Those words were not real.

Mia traced them with her finger, ensuring they really were inked onto the paper.

Gingerly, she lifted the top sheet of paper, and sure enough there was more.

Terms and conditions were inked across the paper, line

after line of jargon-filled sentences that weren't sinking into her brain.

Her eyes ran over the paper, trying to make the inky lines before her make sense.

> *Offer of a recording contract...signed for a minimum of three years...two album record deal...*

Mia blinked. Those words were real.

Two albums?

She was finally being offered a recording contract. Years and years of working endless shifts in bars, singing away hours on their tiny little stages, gigging wherever she could, hours writing music on the sofa of her little apartment in Dublin, hours of writing lyrics through her tears, playing her guitar until the tips of her fingers were so numb she didn't know what string they were on and they sometimes bled, endless emails of thanks-but-no-thanks, calls going unanswered, letters returned to sender, demo USBs and CDs returned in the mail, still in their original envelopes. It had all been worth it.

Her hard work had finally paid off.

This was it.

The moment people spent their lives dreaming of, some never even getting to see this day.

It was actually happening to her.

The pen felt cold and smooth in her hands, she thought it might slip from her fingers and splash ink all over the contract. Shakily, she put her hands down on the table for a moment, gripping the wooden edge for support. She took in a deep breath, trying to calm her racing thoughts.

The door handle clicked in the latch and without looking, Mia knew Jackson was back in the room. Shit, she should have signed the contract.

Long, muscular, tattooed arms were wrapped around her body from behind, their owner nuzzling into her neck before planting a huge kiss on her cheek.

"Congratulations, baby," a deep voice murmured in her ear.

That, Mia thought, was definitely not Jackson.

She turned as much as those arms would allow her in her seat to face their owner. Her eyes were immediately filled with nearly black voids, a distinct sparkle twinkling in their skies.

"I knew you would do it," he said. Mia didn't need to see his smile, the crinkling at the corners of his eyes told her his too perfect face was creased into an earth-shattering smile.

Mia wriggled an arm free and looped it around Joel's muscular back as he leaned in and kissed her.

The sound of a throat clearing from across the room reminded them both they were no longer alone in the room.

Mia begrudgingly opened her eyes and removed her lips from Joel's to see Jackson sitting back down in his chair across from her. Two steaming Styrofoam cups of coffee were on the table, and he pushed one toward Mia without looking up.

A low chuckle in Mia's ear brought her blushing face back to Joel's, and he kissed her again before letting her go, "I'm just out here—" He thumbed over his shoulder at the door. "Congratulations," he said again with a huge smile before turning on his heel and leaving the boardroom, nodding politely at Jackson as he left.

"Now." Jackson tugged at the lapels of his suit jacket, straightening himself and resuming the tone in the room to a professional one. "Do you have any questions about your contract, Mia?"

Mia glanced back down at the papers in front of her and shrugged. "I don't think so."

"Do you want some time to think over the offer?"

"No," she said, without hesitation.

"Great," Jackson said, gesturing for her to sign the contract.

Mia turned the pages and saw Jackson's initials in several places throughout the contract and a dated signature at the end. Placing her own initials beside his and signing her name on the line, Mia did the same in her own copy of the contract before handing one back to Jackson.

Jackson stood from the table and held out his hand to her. "Welcome to Sixth String Studios, Mia."

She shook his hand eagerly, her senses finally coming back to her. "I honestly can't thank you enough."

"We look forward to working with you," he added as he walked around the edge of the table to meet her at the door. "Congratulations, Mia," He placed an arm around her shoulder and in the simplest, most professional manner gave her a brief hug. "Welcome to the team."

"Glad to be joining." She grinned from ear to ear, the shock of the moment finally giving way to euphoria.

"I think there are some people out here who want to congratulate you," Jackson said with a smile as he opened the door.

Mia stepped through the boardroom door and was hit by a wave of applause, cheers, and shouts, and was immediately grabbed at the waist and hoisted into the air.

"Yeah, baby!" Josh cheered, one arm raised in the air in a fist and the other around Mia's waist.

Charlie was standing beside him, a bottle of champagne popping open as she cheered.

Seizing the moment, her professional guard down now that she was no longer in the boardroom with Jackson, Mia cheered and punched the air with Josh.

Her copy of the recording contract was firmly gripped in her hand, and she waved it high into the air for everyone to see.

Joel stood in front of them, holding a glass of champagne ready for Mia, as soon as his brother would set her down. His grin was still set in place, beaming from ear to ear with pride.

Raised aloft from the foyer, Mia saw TJ and Chad cheering and clapping a little farther behind, and even Ruben had come out of his studio hole to congratulate her. Joel's manager Lyle was at his side, clapping too. Dotted around her friends were other employees from Sixth String Studios whom Mia had gotten to know over the last few months, all who had turned out to congratulate her on her recording contract.

Josh whooped loudly before placing Mia on the floor beside him, hugging her tightly, and placing a larger-than-necessary kiss on her cheek. He beamed at her. "Congratulations, Mia."

"Thanks, Josh." She laughed along with him. She couldn't help it. His enthusiasm was infectious.

A loud, shrill shriek and a slender pair of champagne laden arms were then around Mia's body, pulling her into a waft of perfume and blonde-streaked cocoa-brown quiff. "I knew you would do it!" Charlie shrieked, nearly slopping champagne all down her neon pink dress.

Josh still grinning, nudged her in the ribs. "Well, actually, we did."

Charlie blushed brighter than the color of her dress, which was saying something.

"You what?" Mia exclaimed.

"We only found out this morning. I went to put some water in the boardroom for your meeting and Jackson had left the contract in there." Charlie giggled. "He made me promise not to say anything when you arrived."

Mia shook her head and laughed, placing her arms around Josh and Charlie's shoulders one last time before turning to the more handsome of the two brothers, who was waiting as patiently as ever for her attention.

Joel grinned, flashing his white teeth at her, his fingers placing a glass of champagne in her hand. "Congratulations again."

His other arm was around her waist, pressing her body against his, and, surprising Mia, he kissed her deeply, in the middle of the foyer, surrounded by studio employees. He let her go and laughed when several people wolf whistled and called across the room at their kiss.

"All right, all right," a voice said from behind their group, "my turn."

"Nice try, Chad." Mia giggled as Chad shoved his way through and grabbed her into a hug.

"I'm just messing. Well done, Mia. We're so pleased we get to keep you," he said, petting her on the head as he let her go.

She frowned, brushing her hair back down as everyone around her laughed. "Umm, thanks."

TJ shook his head at Chad, pushing him out of the way and in the direction of the champagne so he could congratulate Mia. His blond curls bounced on his head as he winked at her. "Didn't think you'd get rid of us that easily, did you?"

"Nope." Mia shook her head, laughing as she accepted his congratulatory embrace. "You guys are going to produce my album, right?" she asked when TJ released her.

"Who else is good enough to handle your music?" Chad said smugly.

"Of course, we are," TJ added, more politely.

"How long have you known?" Mia asked.

TJ shrugged, a sparkle gleaming in his eye. "Oh, only a couple of weeks or so."

"A couple of weeks?" Mia shrieked nearly as loud as Charlie and playfully slapped him on the arm.

"Yeah, man, no biggie." Chad shrugged and Mia resisted the urge to slap him across the head, right where his bruise from the crash was still healing.

Ruben clinked her glass in a congratulatory toast. "It's not like we could say anything."

"You knew too?" Mia asked.

He nodded, his fashionable glasses sliding on his nose as he did.

"Only us three and Jackson," TJ hastily added. "Ruben's head producer, so of course he knew too. Jackson asked us nearly every day what we thought. He had to reach a decision before your contract ran out. The crash just put things on hold a little while."

Mia shook her head, knowing they couldn't have said anything if they wanted to. It was still frustrating to know they had known all this time. "When do we start work then?" she asked her producers with an excited smile.

TJ raised his glass to her. "As soon as you want."

"Is this afternoon too soon?" she asked, her face bursting with an enthusiastic smile.

"Of course not." TJ placed his arm around her shoulder and hugged her again. "Here's to Mia," he added so everyone could hear, "may you have a long, successful career here at Sixth String Studios. Welcome to the family!"

"Welcome to the family!" a chorus echoed around her followed by several glasses clinking against hers.

As the sweet, bubbly liquid slid down her throat, Mia smiled to herself, feeling the familiar pair of muscled arms nestle back around her waist. Joel's body was pressed against her back and he leaned down to whisper in her ear, "Looks like you might be living with me for a while longer."

Mia could feel the smile dancing on his lips as he kissed her cheek.

Chapter 9

Being inside the booth instead of behind it was as surreal as Mia imagined it would be. TJ and Chad stared back at her from behind the thick pane of glass, their faces drawn in concentration.

Her fingers felt numb in the tips. She had played the same verse and chorus several times over, but she had played various parts of the same song dozens of times again that day.

Working with perfectionists definitely had its downsides. She was only at the beginning of recording her first album, but already she was wondering if her second album could be a live one.

Flexing her fingers before taking a sip of water, she prepared to go for another round.

She was tired. The day had been long, but better than she had imagined.

Though she was having a mini-moan to herself in her mind, realistically she loved being in the studio. It was all she had ever wanted. Hearing her own music finally being played back to her, the sounds of her own first studio album coming to life was incredible. This was what she had been striving for all these years.

She wondered when the day would come when she would wake up in her own bed in her apartment in Dublin, her alarm clock signalling it was time to get up and go to work at Glen's. She was sure she was still dreaming.

First the temporary contract, then falling in love with Joel, now her own studio album. Life was surreal right now. Mia flexed her fingers one more time just to make sure they were actually there.

"From the top, Mia." TJ's voice sounded in the booth when he pressed the button on the mixing desk in front of him.

Of course, Mia's time in the studio wouldn't be complete without her regular visitor appearing in their doorway whenever the recording light went on above their studio door.

Wearing a gray hooded sweatshirt, blue jeans, and black high top trainers, Joel looked tired. Beautiful, yes, but also very tired.

The last few months had been taxing on them both and now things were starting to get even more intense. Joel was still hard at work on his album, and now Mia was hitting the ground running with her own album. Not only were they both exhausted from work, but the press had increased their furor on the Mia-and-Joel saga now that Mia had gone from an unknown Irish songwriter to Joel's signed-to-the-same-label-girlfriend.

Any publicity was good publicity, Jackson had told her, when building up to an album release. And having Joel Coben on her arm was going to do wonders for the anticipation surrounding Mia's album.

Or so she was told.

"All right, Mia, that'll do for today," TJ said cheerily through the system when she finished.

Mia slid off her stool and took her guitar strap from around her neck before leaving through the door of the booth to her left.

TJ and Chad had begun packing up when she came through to the studio.

"You sounded really great today, Mia." TJ beamed. "We'll finish that one up tomorrow, I think."

"Great." Mia smiled back, pleased that her album was slowly coming together.

It was going to be a long process, but she was already loving the sounds that they had created for her album. It was better than she had imagined. Her two producers really were the best.

"See you tomorrow, Mia," Chad called from the door.

Mia spied Tara waiting for him in the corridor, which was a rare sight. She waved when she saw her. "Hey, Mia."

"Hey," Mia called back before Chad grabbed hold of Tara and his arms were all over her body.

Joel politely closed the door after Chad. TJ was shaking his head. "See you in the morning," he said over his shoulder before making a speedy exit from the studio and swerving to avoid Chad and Tara.

Mia giggled as Joel closed the door on Chad's wandering hands in the corridor.

"You sound great," he said, repeating TJ's earlier sentiments.

"Thanks, it's still a bit surreal." She scrunched her fingers in her hair in frustration and disbelief. "I'm exhausted, though. I had no idea it would be this hard."

He smiled down at her as he tugged at her hands and pulled her into him. "You're doing fine."

Mia nestled into Joel's sweatshirt and he rested his head on hers, both comforting each other in the silence. "You okay?" she asked. "You look pretty tired."

He let out a laugh. "I am."

Mia heard in his voice he was beat. "Let's go home," she said to the fold of his sweatshirt near his neck.

"I like the sound of that," he murmured into her hair before kissing her head.

Mia wasn't sure whether he meant the general statement or the sound of her referring to his home as theirs.

അരു

"Wake up, beautiful."

Mia's favorite sound in the entire world was speaking softly into her ear. Joel's voice. She would never tire of hearing that low, deep voice.

"It's time to go to work," he said.

Mia felt his words tickle against her cheek as he came closer before he kissed where his breath had touched her skin.

"What time is it?" she croaked out, snuggling back under the folds of the duvet.

"About ten a.m.," Joel said as Mia felt the weight of his body sit down beside her on the bed.

"What?" she shrieked, instantly awake and sitting bolt upright in bed.

A strong pair of muscular, tattooed arms was soon around her body, pulling her into their owners' chest. "Relax." He laughed. "It's Saturday."

The realization hit Mia and she elbowed the chiselled body that was pinning her in place.

"Ouch." Joel laughed as she squirmed in his hold.

"What the hell did you do that for?" She feigned being mad, but turning in his arms to look at his face, Mia's face instantly cracked into a smile. She couldn't be mad at him, not when he looked so perfect.

"I needed you awake," he murmured into her ear before tracing her cheekbone with a pattering of soft kisses.

Mia made an agreeable noise, all too easily distracted by the feeling of Joel's lips on her skin and the feeling of his body against hers. She snuggled up closer to him and his arms snaked around her waist, pulling her out of the duvet and into his lap.

He smiled wickedly just as his lips reached hers and pulled away teasingly. "But not for the reason you're thinking."

"What?" Mia was instantly crestfallen. Her hands were still on his wonderfully sculpted chest, her eyes staring longingly at the thin layer of material that covered what lay beneath. This was not the wakeup call she had imagined.

"I need you to get dressed." His eyes, still full of promise, closed as he briefly touched her lips with his before he pulled away too quickly.

This *really* wasn't the morning Mia was hoping for.

"Why?" She tried, and failed, to keep her voice from sounding like a whine.

Joel chuckled to himself. The low sound resonated from his chest under Mia's hands. She traced a finger along the outline of the hard, rounded muscles beneath the material, hoping to change his mind. Long, dark eyelashes fluttered against her skin as Joel finally caved and kissed her on the lips. Mia felt the glee surging in her chest at her success as strong, gentle hands caressed her waist before trailing across her body.

She began to smile against Joel's kisses and felt his own lips do the same as his hands flowed across her hips and down her thighs. Mia's smile quickly vanished when those hands wound underneath her legs and lifted her effortlessly from the bed as Joel stood up.

She let out a small squeal, as he rose before carefully setting her down, standing, on the floor beside the bed.

"What the—" she asked, feeling somewhat rejected as Joel untangled himself from her, putting his recently exploring hands now on her shoulders.

"I really need you to get dressed and come downstairs," he said with a teasing smile, stooping so that his eyes were level with hers.

Mia pursed her lips, fighting the urge to smile, despite her rejection, as his nearly black eyes were so full of happiness and still tinged with promise.

He was up to something, she realized. This was no request to come downstairs for breakfast.

"What are you up to?" she asked, entwining her hands with his long fingers.

"That's why you need to come downstairs—" He grinned, flashing her a Hollywood white smile. "—so that I can show you."

She narrowed her eyes, trying to read the tantalising expression that his features were wearing. So full of promise and giddiness. His eyes were alive and dancing, his lips curled into a playful smirk. How could a girl say no to that face?

"And then maybe we can come back up here," he whispered into her ear before repeating his trail of kisses down her cheek and leaving a long, lingering kiss on her lips.

"Okay," Mia said breathlessly, "I'm getting dressed."

A low laugh escaped Joel's throat as he watched her sprint across the bedroom into the bathroom and slam the door behind her.

Mia wondered if there was an Olympic record for the fastest woman to wash, brush her teeth, and get dressed.

ℰ✑ℰ✑

"Are you sure they're closed?" his deep Californian accent was in her ear, one of his hands was clamped around her eyes, the other securely around her waist, guiding her body in the direction of the front door.

She laughed. "Yes!"

"Okay, okay." He let go of her waist and Mia heard the door opening before her.

"Joel?" she asked, still laughing.

"One second." He was laughing too. His hand now took hers, guiding her through the doorway and onto the top step in front of his house.

Mia smelled the fresh air, the warm morning sun on her

skin from the Los Angeles day outside. She heard the traffic rushing by in the distance, the sounds of a neighbor nearby splashing in their swimming pool, the birds singing some-where in trees overhead. She marveled in what she what she would have paid no attention to now that one of her senses was taken away. In temporarily losing her sight, she realised she was noticing things she would otherwise have turned a "blind eye" to.

"Are you ready?" Joel said as he came to a stop, standing behind Mia again.

"I think so," she said, wondering what on earth Joel had brought her outside for.

He wrapped his arm around her waist again, pressing his body into her back and rested his head on her shoulder. Mia leaned back into the secure, familiar feeling of his body as he lifted his hand from her eyes.

She squinted in the harsh morning sunlight, adjusting her eyes to Joel's driveway before her as he whispered into her ear, "Surprise, baby."

The bright Californian sun's rays bounced off the metal-lic paintwork of the brand new Range Rover Sport on Joel's driveway.

Mia's throat let out a choked gasp.

"I figured you could use a car," he said, his voice still playful but now slightly wary.

She felt his hand leave her waist and reach into the pock-et of his jeans before he dangled a key in front of her eyes.

"Do you like it?" he asked as she reached up and took the key that was blocking her view.

She nodded, still staring at the car on the drive. Should she be mad? Should she scream and jump up and down? It was an obscenely grand gesture, that was for sure, and an expensive one at that.

But she couldn't be mad at Joel. She saw the meaning in his gesture, the wanting to surprise her, and the look on his face when he wanted her to get out of bed and come and see what he had done.

"It's…" She trailed off, still looking at the black metallic paintwork glistening in the morning sun. She felt Joel's body tense against her. "Gorgeous," she breathed, letting out her held breath and laughing.

Joel laughed too, the tension immediately evaporating from his stance. "Just like you then," he said as he wound both arms back around her body and kissed her cheek.

She turned in his arms, her eyes reluctantly leaving the beautiful brand new car on the driveway to look at the even more beautiful man who had bought it for her.

"Thank you." She caressed his cheek with her hand before entangling her fingers into his thick mess of hair as she kissed him. "But why do I need one?" she asked, reluctantly breaking their kiss.

Joel laughed against her body. "I just figured you could use one." He shrugged. "We're not always at the studio for the same time, we don't always work the same hours. If I have promo stuff to do or other things, this means you can come home whenever you want."

"Home?" She found the question leaving her mouth before she could stop it.

Joel chuckled again. "Yes." He kissed her softly. "Home," he said against her lips with a smile.

Mia knew she was grinning from ear to ear. "I like the sound of that."

Joel laughed again, his hands smoothed over her back, pulling her body flush against his before kissing her again.

"Come on." He took hold of her hand. "Let me show it to you."

He pulled her away from the house and down the steps toward the car which was parked beside his own. It wasn't quite as huge as Joel's Escalade, but it was an impressively sized car, nonetheless.

Everyone in Los Angeles drove everywhere. Nobody walked. They would drive from one block to the next. Only tourists walked everywhere.

Locals all drove hugely oversized jeeps too, or the fancy,

sporty things Mia sometimes saw parked outside Sixth String Studios.

Mia knew Joel would have wanted her to blend in with Los Angeles. He wouldn't have bought her something outlandish. If she was constantly being followed by the press, it made her an easy target. And after the accident, Joel was bound to buy her something that resembled a tank as opposed to a six-gear two-hundred-mile-per-hour machine.

She pressed the key fob as they approached the car, and Joel pulled open the driver's door. He gestured and held it open for Mia to climb inside. "After you."

"Wow." She laughed, looking around the plush leather interior of the car.

The car smelled that new, fresh off the production line smell. The dashboard shone—all its controls pristine and untouched. An array of dials stared back at Mia from underneath the built-in SatNav and MP3 system.

"Do you like it?" Joel asked again, one arm propped on the frame of the car.

She giggled, feeling like a child at Christmas who had opened every present she had asked for and more besides. "I love it."

Joel nodded, relieved, and smiled to himself as he watched Mia relax into the driver's seat, familiarising herself with everything in the car.

"You look so small sitting in there," he mused.

Mia felt it. She did feel small in the enormous car. But in a way, that made her feel safe, knowing she had so much space around her from the outside world.

She patted the empty passenger seat beside her. "Come and sit with me then."

Joel's lip curled into a brief lopsided smile. His eyes twinkled back at her before he shut the driver's door and climbed in to the back seat behind Mia.

"The studio's please, driver," he called from seemingly far away behind her.

She laughed as she watched him sprawl across the large, empty back seats.

"Don't be getting used to this," she called, turning in her seat.

He winked as he reclined into the plush leather. "I've chauffeured you around. I think you need to return the favor."

"And get your feet off my car seats," she teased as Joel rested his feet across the backseat.

He grinned, flashing her his white smile again. "Shut up and drive."

Mia let out a mock disgruntled sound and looked around for something to throw at him. "Joel Coben you..."

"You what?" he teased.

She pursed her lips as she tried to think of a response and ended up laughing instead. "I mean it, get your feet off my seats." She reached over the driver's seat and tried to swipe his legs but found she couldn't reach. "Stupid too-big car," she mumbled as Joel laughed at her.

Hoisting herself out of her seat, she clambered through the gap between the front seats to where Joel was still lounging in the back of the car and laughing at her.

"I can't sit like this but you can climb all over it?" he asked, still grinning.

She stooped down, pulling his legs off the back seat and plonking herself down beside him. "My car, my rules."

"Any other rules I should know about?" he asked, sitting up next to her and sliding his arm around her.

She smiled as he slid his other hand under the hem of her shirt. "I can think of a few."

"And what are they?" he said breathily against her neck, making her shiver.

"I..." Her voice trailed away as he kissed along her throat and across her cheek before taking her lips.

In one swift motion, he lifted her shirt over her head and tossed it onto the floor of the car. Then his hands were on her bare skin.

He grinned, his dark eyes, almost the color of the paint-work outside, sparkled under his brows as they scanned her body. "I think you need to show me."

"Okay," was all she could manage before his kiss, hungry and eager, devoured her every sensation.

Chapter 10

I'm getting too used to this, Mia decided, as she pulled up outside the restaurant in her Range Rover.

She had too quickly gotten used to driving everywhere in Los Angeles and had relished in her new found independence. When she wasn't working in the studio on her new album, she could drive herself home, to wherever Joel was, to the store or, like now, to visit her brother.

Luke's tourist visa would expire at the end of September. Ninety days was all she was given with her brother and the first week of that she had been unconscious.

Luke understood Mia had a lot going on in her life—her relationship with Joel, the media attention, writing material for her first album, and trying to build bridges with her long lost brother managed to rapidly fill the following weeks of Mia's life quicker than she had imagined.

Dylan and Niamh had flown home at the end of July. They had stayed for as long as they could before having to go home and return to their lives in Dublin and their jobs at Glen's.

Mia knew Glen would have allowed them to stay as long as they wanted, but she knew the guilt of taking advantage of his offer would weigh heavily on them both and the need to return to normality and paying of bills soon won out over the Los Angeles sun.

Mia missed them already. Her time with Niamh had felt too short. Dealing with everything after the crash—her injuries, the media, and Luke—had turned the few weeks she had been in LA into a bit of a blur, and Mia found herself wishing she had made more of her time with Niamh.

She had no idea when she would next get to visit Dublin and see her friends again.

Mike and Sharon, of course, still phoned as much as possible. They hated not being able to be there for Mia after the crash, to help her through her injuries and, of course, to meet Luke. As soon as she could find a few days spare in her schedule, Mia promised she would fly home to see them and everyone at Glen's.

She had no idea when those few days would be, though. The pressure of writing and recording material show-stopping enough for a debut album was overwhelming. With the added pressure of the already-mounting media speculation about Mia and their relentless pursuit of her relationship with Joel had the label sweating about her album release date.

The sooner the better, they had repeatedly told her.

So one Friday afternoon when TJ and Chad had to leave the studio early for a meeting, Mia found herself with an earlier finish than she had expected.

Knowing Joel would be working for a few more hours still, she had called Luke and arranged to meet him in a Beverly Hills restaurant for dinner.

Joel was always reminding Mia to make the most of the time she had left with Luke before their relationship would become mostly Skype-based and reuniting for holiday gatherings.

Luke nodded approvingly at Mia's Range Rover from across the parking lot as she approached him. "Nice car."

She turned to stare admiringly at it before greeting her brother with a hug. "Yes, it is."

"Present from Joel?" he asked, his eyebrows nearly vanishing into his long, dark hair.

She grinned. "How did you guess?"

Luke stared to and from Mia and the car, shaking his head. "They say Hollywood changes people."

Mia knew he was kidding. She could see the tell-tale hint of a smile in the corners of his lips as he spoke. "Yeah, yeah." She nudged him. "Come on, I'm starving."

"People here actually eat?" He feigned surprise as he walked with her into the restaurant.

She laughed. "Only occasionally."

Luke had only been in LA for a few weeks, but already he seemed clued up on the citizens of the city. It wasn't hard, though. People in Los Angeles definitely fit their stereotype.

Never before had Mia felt so self-conscious about the way she dressed, the way she spoke, the way she did her hair or make up and particularly over what she ate. Hollywood was *the* place to be if you ever wanted a sharp look in the mirror. Mia had never felt so inferior in all her life. Hollywood was home to the most beautiful, most stylish, most athletic, and thinnest people in the world. It was no wonder everyone here was a wannabe something or other. The city was a mass-producing factory for magazine-ready people.

"Coconut water?" the waitress asked, holding aloft an iced jug of something.

"Sure," Mia replied politely while Luke eyed the jug sceptically, as if it were about to crawl involuntarily down his throat.

He sniffed over the edge of the glass before taking a hesitant sip. He immediately wrinkled his nose and pulled a face. "I think I'll have a beer."

The waitress threw him a disgruntled look before disappearing to fetch his drink.

"It's the latest health craze—" Mia shrugged as she pointed to the glass. "—or so I'm told."

"I'll pass, thanks." Luke shook his head. "I'm used to

drinking coconut straight from the tree. I've no idea what that shit is."

Mia giggled as the woman at the next table turned up her nose in disapproval. Introducing Luke to Los Angeles reminded Mia of the *Crocodile Dundee* movies. He was so alien to it all. He was used to a much simpler way of life. Granted, he had spent the majority of his youth in Ireland but for the past few years he had lived on what sounded like a desert island. Los Angeles would come as a culture shock to anyone, let alone someone who had lived on a beach for the last few years.

Mia had recently spent an entire Sunday showing Luke how to use Skype and reacquainting him with an email address so that they could keep in touch when he went home.

"*Beer*, sir." The waitress returned and placed a little too much emphasis on the word *beer* before taking their order and disappearing again.

At least Luke looked the part, Mia thought, as he took a sip from his drink. He was dressed in dark jeans, trainers, and a white T-shirt—an outfit so effortlessly simple that Mia had a sneaking suspicion it had something to do with Joel Coben. Outfits that cool didn't fall off a fishing boat in Thailand.

Once back on familiar ground, they chatted effortlessly about Mia's week in the studio, how Joel was, Josh and Charlie, and even Ruben, who Luke had formed an unlikely friendship with. Mia had been surprised to learn they been for a few drinks in the last couple of weeks, had exchanged email addresses, and were going to keep in touch when Luke went home.

Of course, Luke wanted to know everything about Mia's car and asked if he could take it for a drive. Living on a remote Thai island clearly didn't take away all the allures of modern society. *Boys, ultimately will be boys*, Mia thought.

"Excuse me, are you Mia?" A female voice interrupted Mia's conversation with Luke about the unnecessary amount of Starbucks in Los Angeles.

Instantly Mia's guard was up. She turned, eyeing the woman warily. There were only a handful of reasons someone in LA would know her name. This woman clearly wasn't an overzealous Joel Coben fan, nor did she look the type to hang around the Kibitz Room on an open mic night. That either left the options of an ex-conquest of Joel's or a media representative of some kind.

Dressed in skin-tight black jeans, sky scraper heels, and a chiffon cream blouse, the woman oozed every inch Los Angeles. Of course, her skin was tanned, her light brown locks, kissed with highlights, were wrapped in an elegant bun, with not a strand out of place and her nails were freshly manicured. She held a brand new Blackberry in one hand, and her other was around the strap of a tan leather Miu Miu bag.

Resisting the urge to wrinkle her nose in jealousy at her immaculate appearance, Mia replied, "Yes."

"Rebecca Calder." She let go of her bag and placed the Blackberry into her left hand, holding the other out to Mia. "Pleased to meet you."

Mia quickly glanced at Luke whose face looked equally torn between confusion and lustfully admiring the woman before him. Mia shook the woman's hand, raising her eyebrows in a question.

"I apologize for interrupting." Rebecca gestured to the table. "I wondered if I may speak with you for a moment?"

"Are you the press?" Mia asked bluntly.

"No." Rebecca smiled as she shook her head. "I'm not. I'm an executive from Sky Records."

"Oh." Mia swallowed. Instantly she regretted the coconut water. It didn't mix well when churning nervously with risotto.

Rebecca gestured to an empty seat at their table. "May I?"

Mia nodded, immediately wishing Joel was with her. He would know how to handle this woman. He would have cleared her off by now and they would be continuing with their dinner. Instead, Mia felt her meal churning in her stomach as she watched Rebecca take a seat.

"Again, I apologize for the intrusion, but you're a hard girl to pin down, Mia," Rebecca smiled a tight, professional smile. "I've been trying to get hold of you for a few weeks now."

"Oh, really?" Mia asked.

Luke said nothing. He sat back in his chair, sipping his beer and observing Mia and Rebecca, taking it all in. In many ways he reminded her of Joel, sitting there, scrutinising the scene before him from under his hooded dark brown eyes.

"Yes, after you went into hiding after the accident, I've had trouble tracking you down," Rebecca continued. "Your label wasn't too particularly helpful in the matter."

Mia stared at her for a moment. She had tried contacting the studio? But Charlie hadn't said anything? Mia pictured Charlie perched at her desk, her neon blue talons slamming down the phone to Rebecca's dainty French manicured ones.

"Yes, Jackson Miller can be quite the curt man when he wants to be," Rebecca quipped, the spite clearly in her voice. The edges of Luke's mouth curled up into a smile from around his glass as he took a sip.

So she had gone straight to the top. Mia knew Charlie would have said something to her if Rebecca had phoned the reception desk. Mia should have realized Rebecca would have higher contacts than the front desk at Sixth String Studios.

"I imagine only when he needs to be," Mia replied, with her own tight lipped smile.

Rebecca paused, as if taken aback. "I see you are not a woman to be trifled with, Miss Ryan," she resumed, a politely admiring smile now on her face.

"No," Mia said.

"Then let me get straight to the point."

Mia nodded. "Please."

"I understand you've recently signed a recording deal with Sixth String Studios?"

Mia paused for a fraction of a second. Remembering that the press had somehow found out about her recently signed deal, she replied, "Yes."

"And you're happy with the offer they have made you?"

"Yes," Mia added more warily.

"Well, Mia, Sky Records have had their eye on you for some time now. We wanted to make you an offer a while ago, but due to the accident, this was somewhat postponed."

Mia said nothing, allowing Rebecca's words to sink in. Not only one, but two of the biggest recording studios in Los Angeles had been keeping an eye on her? But how? Jackson had seen Mia in Dublin. How on earth had Sky Records heard her music?

"A member of our team heard you perform at the Kibitz Room," Rebecca added, seemingly reading Mia's mind, "and you peaked the company's interest."

"I see," Mia managed.

"We were wondering if you would consider an offer from us?" Rebecca asked, smoothing a non-existent flyaway hair back down on her bun.

"What kind of offer?" Mia asked.

Rebecca pulled a face, her elegant features curling into the briefest of amused smirks before her professional demeanour was back in place. "A recording contract, Mia," she explained.

Luke's hand came to a stop on the table, abandoning his beer glass.

Rebecca still seemed completely unaware he was sitting there.

"I—I—don't understand," Mia stammered, "I've signed to Sixth String Studios."

"So I understand, Mia," Rebecca continued, "but we are extremely keen on signing you to Sky Records. We cannot express our interest in you as an artist enough. We are prepared to do whatever it takes to sign you to our company."

Mia felt the color leaving her face. She couldn't say anything. She stared into the space between Luke and Rebecca, searching her mind for answers.

"Mia, we have the best lawyers in Los Angeles prepared to take you out of their contract. We have found smaller loopholes in larger contracts than theirs, and we are sure we can easily navigate you out of their deal."

"You haven't even told her what you're offering her," Luke pointed out.

Rebecca turned to look at whatever was sitting across from her, as if suddenly aware there was a human being there. She cast an eye over Luke, her eyes lingering a moment longer than they should have, Mia noticed. Luke was an attractive man, there was no doubt about that. His tall, muscular build had been well defined from years of labouring away on the fishing boat and his dark complexion was emphasised by his deep tan. There were freckles on his arms and highlights in his dark hair that the sun had brought out. He certainly pulled off the rugged appeal, Mia thought.

Rebecca smiled, less professionally, at Luke. "I realise that."

Mia cleared her throat and brought Rebecca's attention back to the conversation at hand.

"I understand you may need some time to consider our offer, Mia," Rebecca explained as she pulled a folder out of her Miu Miu handbag, "but we are prepared to give you as long as you need."

She stretched her long, tanned arm across the table to hand Mia the folder. Taking it from her, Mia opened the cover and blinked. Twice.

Sky Records
Offer of Recording Contract

Mia felt a strange sensation of déjà vu as she stared at the second recording contract she had seen in the space of a month.

"I am sure you will find our offer extremely generous," Rebecca explained as she turned the pages of the contract with a manicured nail. She tapped one of those nails at a paragraph on the page and Mia read where she indicated.

"But—I—You?" Mia sputtered.

"As I said." Rebecca smiled knowingly. "We are making you a very generous offer."

Mia stared back down at the type her eyes struggled to read. There were so many zeros. "Really?" she said in a strangled voice, losing all her earlier composure.

Rebecca nodded, a satisfied smile on her perfectly clear complexion. "We will give you as much time as you need, Mia. We do hope you will consider our offer, and we hope you understand the generosity of it. We don't take making such decisions lightly. This kind of offer doesn't happen very often."

Mia nodded. Her eyes were still fixed on the paper.

"Call me when you're ready." Rebecca deftly placed a business card on the table beside Mia and rose from her seat.

Without another word, she was gone—quickly striding away in her far-too-high heels across the restaurant and into to a waiting car outside. Mia felt the whole operation seemed a little CIA.

Luke got up from his seat and crouched down beside Mia. He whistled loudly. "Wow," was all he said when he read the page Mia had read several times over.

"I know," she replied.

"Are you signing?" he asked.

"I have no idea." Her voice sounded so small. "What do I do?"

"Only you can figure that out, sis." He patted her arm. "Take your time, though."

Mia nodded.

"Are you going to talk to Joel?"

Mia nodded again.

"The studios?" he asked.

Mia knew he meant Sixth String. She shook her head. "Not yet."

"Hmm," Luke mused as he read the page again. "It's not every day someone offers you several million dollars."

Chapter 11

Mia ran a hand through her long hair in frustration. "I have absolutely no idea."

Joel pursed a face at the page in the folder. His shoulders were hunched over with his head bent down to the table. Mia stared admiringly at the muscles in his arms that were being shown off in his vest, the inkings on his skin trailing over the contours of his body.

Joel mimicked her action by running a hand through his hair. Damn, he was so perfect. She was sure her hair looked like a bird's nest after a hurricane, but Joel running his hands through his hair only made him look sexier. You either had it or you didn't.

She drummed her fingers on the table, half lost in staring at Joel and the other half lost in a swirl of numbers.

Joel tapped a finger on the paper. "Let's just hope the press don't find out about this."

"Mmm," Mia agreed.

Right at that moment, the press was the last thing on her mind. The fact that another huge record label in Los Angeles was offering her a seven figure deal, something she had joked about with Charlie only weeks ago, was what was at the forefront of her thoughts.

That and her too perfect rock star boyfriend, but he was a given.

"Does Jackson know?" Joel asked.

Mia shrugged. "She said she had tried calling him a few times. I don't know if she went into specifics."

After Rebecca left, Mia had driven straight across to Sixth String Studios to find Joel and tell him what had happened. Mentally thanking Joel's unsociable recording hours, she found the studios nearly empty when she arrived. Avoiding awkward conversations with Charlie and Jackson, Mia had been able to go straight to Joel.

"Don't worry about it," he said finally, looking up from the table, leaning back in his chair, and fixing Mia with his almost black eyes.

"Is that it?" she asked.

Despite the seemingly intense situation on their hands, Joel made it sound effortless.

"Yep," he said, taking her hand in his. "Don't worry about it. You'll know what to do."

Mia giggled and shook her head. She *didn't* know what to do. She was confused, overwhelmed, flummoxed, and downright shattered. Los Angeles was hard work.

"Focus on your album, that's all that matters," he said, stroking the back of her hand with his thumb.

He tugged gently at her hand and Mia immediately, knowing what he meant, got up from her seat and crawled into his lap. Joel sighed heavily as he wrapped his arms around her, kissing her head. "It's a lot to take in—these last few months—huh?"

"Mmm hmm," Mia agreed, suddenly feeling homesick. Joel had a way of reading her every thought before she even thought them herself.

He seemed to confirm what her subconscious mind she knew. How did he do that?

"Things are only going to get worse," she said with a deep sigh beneath her cheek.

"Why?" she asked in a small voice.

She already knew the answer, but somehow felt the need to hear those words aloud.

"Your album will be released, you'll go on tour, the press will write more about you and me. When your fan base grows, you'll have your own fans to deal with, this is just the beginning."

Speaking like a wise old musician, Mia thought.

Joel had been in her position years and years ago. He had signed his recording deal a long time ago. He knew what was coming. He knew what the press was capable of at their worst. It was what had forced him to shut down the way he had.

The fact that Joel was on her arm, anyway, was a huge contributing factor in the furor Mia was about to face—something that they both knew.

"There will be more like this." He gestured to the contract, now lying abandoned on the table. "Some will be real, others won't. Just remember where you started, remember who you are, and why you came to Los Angeles in the first place. Don't lose sight of the Mia who got on that plane in Dublin. She's the girl that got you where you are. Don't get distracted by the bright lights and big numbers. They'll all disappear as fast as they came if you let them."

Mia fell silent, listening to Joel speak about the things he had to learn the hard way, his thumb still tracing an imaginary pattern on her hand.

"That's the Mia I fell in love with, the feisty girl who told me I was acting like a total ass, the girl who showed me how to be myself again. I'm not saying you're not her anymore. I know you are, but I've seen so many people walk through those front doors and walk out a different person. I don't want that to happen to you. People come to Los Angeles, chasing the dream, and they forget the person who dreamed that dream in the first place. Los Angeles is a scary place, full of big expectations and big let downs. There are a lot of people offering you fifteen minutes of fame for fifteen lines on a piece of paper. You need to read between those lines, Mia. It's up to you to remember what you really came here for."

Mia allowed Joel's words to sink in for a moment before she answered. The silence in the room wasn't tense, it was expectant. Like she did, he already knew the answer. He just needed to her it spoken aloud.

"This," she said and reached out to trace her finger across the strings of the guitar propped against their chair.

The strings resonated under her fingertip, the sound tinkling into the air around them.

"There's your answer," Joel whispered into her hair.

♥♥♥

"It happened again," called a musical Californian accent from across the foyer as Mia walked through the doors.

She looked up to see Charlie waving a magazine in the air above her head. Charlie had folded it over to reveal a one-page article a few pages into the magazine.

JOEL COBEN'S NEW LOVE SIGNS TO SAME LABEL

Mia shook her head as she took the magazine from Charlie's mint-colored fingernails. The picture of her and Joel taken before his appearance on *Coffee with Kelly* was by the side of the article.

Mia tossed the magazine back at Charlie. "I'm surprised it's taken them this long."

It was harmless. There was nothing in the article, for once, that was malicious, fabricated, or slanderous. It was just another useless gossip magazine that was a few weeks behind its competition with the news of Mia signing her deal.

"Don't worry about it." Charlie flicked her hand in dismissal and threw the magazine into the trash can behind her desk.

Mia smiled to herself, remembering Joel had said the

same thing a couple of days ago. "I'm not."

"Anyway, girl, I haven't seen you for days." Charlie grabbed Mia's hand on the desk and pinned her in place. "You're either holed up in there—" She gestured to the studio. "—or holed up with him." She gestured a mint-colored talon in the direction of the magazine. Mia knew she meant Joel.

"I know, it's been a crazy few weeks, I'm sorry." Mia exhaled. "Lunch?"

Charlie pursed her candy pink lips. "I was thinking something a little more exciting than lunch."

❧❦❧

Mia tugged at the hemline of her dress. "Are you sure about this?"

Charlie's reflection winked at Mia in the mirror across the room. "Absolutely."

Charlie was adding the finishing touches to her ever-perfect quiff of cocoa-brown hair, the blonde highlights flashed through one side were out in all their glory tonight.

"Two seconds," she called as she added another coat of mascara to her eyelashes.

Mia rolled her eyes. She preferred the more natural approach to make-up, but Charlie was the complete opposite. She had her hair done, nails painted, eyelashes on, eye shadow applied, lipstick on, and was dressed to the nines. It was who she was. Mia wouldn't have had her any other way. All Charlie's colors simply emphasised her exotic beauty, showcasing her as the bird of paradise she truly was.

That bird of paradise had gotten halfway to turning Mia into one too.

Reluctantly agreeing Charlie could do her hair and make-up in exchange for raiding her wardrobe for the night, Mia had been bronzed, glossed, and mascaraed within an inch of her life.

She turned in the mirror again and admired what she saw, admitting to herself that Charlie had done a pretty good job.

Charlie grinned, her phone in hand. "You look stunning."

"Thanks." Mia shrugged. "So do you."

Charlie flashed a smile as the shutter sounded on her camera phone.

"Charlie!" Mia exclaimed, realizing Charlie had been taking a photograph of her.

"I'm sending it to Joel," Charlie cackled. "He needs to see how hot his girl looks tonight."

Mia rolled her eyes again, wondering how many more times Charlie would be taking her photo that night.

"Come here," Charlie beckoned Mia over to pose beside her in the mirror.

Mia posed and the camera flashed. "Can we go now?" she asked.

"Yep," Charlie said with one final glance in the mirror and one more adjustment of her quiff. "Come on." She laughed, grabbing Mia by the hand and pulling her out of the door of her apartment.

The streets of Los Angeles came alive at night. The tourists vanished and the socialites came out to play when the sun went down. The boulevards lit up, the music resonated through the air, and the streets buzzed with energy as young Hollywood took to the streets to party the night away.

It was a world away from the nightlife in Dublin that Mia was used to. "Are you sure this looks okay?" she asked for the hundredth time as they queued to get into the bar.

Charlie raised an eyebrow at Mia. "Do I have to tell you again?"

"No, I'm just not used to wearing this, that's all."

Mia had reluctantly given up her skinny jeans and converse trainers for a red Herve Leger bodycon dress that had been stashed in Charlie's bulging wardrobe.

How one small person managed to fit so many clothes

into such a tiny apartment, Mia would never know. Her closet was rammed with varying designer labels, high street purchases, and vintage store bargains. Dresses, jackets, jeans, skirts, and tops all flowed out from the closet and into the drawers. Piles of accessories littered the tops of cupboards and her dresser, shoes spilled out from the bottom of the wardrobe and onto the floor where they lay abandoned by their owner.

"How on earth did you get all this stuff?" Mia had asked astonished at the sheer volume of stuff Charlie possessed.

"The label gets free stuff all the time," Charlie had replied nonchalantly. "Designers are always sending things for the artists to wear, half of the time they never want it, so I get to keep it."

"The perks of the job," Mia had mused as she picked up a pair of Louboutin shoe boots.

"They look amazing with this." Charlie had grabbed the red Herve Leger dress Mia was now wearing from somewhere in the back of her closet and thrust it into her hands with the boots. "Oh and this too." She rummaged some more before pulling out a beautiful, butter soft leather jacket.

"Armani?" Mia asked incredulously.

Charlie wiggled her painted nails at Mia. "I've done a bit of modelling in my time," she said with an impressive tone. "I bagged a few freebies then too."

Mia had stared again at the mass of clothes and accessories. "This is incredible."

"You will soon have all this and more besides," Charlie said. "Once the designers start seeing you on Joel's arm more often and your music is released."

"Perks of the job," Mia had repeated with a giggle—

"Hey, Charlie, didn't see you there," the enormous bouncer said, pulling Mia from her memories. He reached down and hugged the tiny person that was Charlie. The difference in their sizes was incredible.

"Hey, Dave," she said, greeting him in return.

He gestured back at the long line now snaking down the block. "You should have come to the front."

"I didn't know you were working tonight," she said.

"Who's your friend?" he asked, pointing at Mia.

"This is Mia," Charlie said, introducing her.

"Nice to meet you, Mia," Dave said with an approving glance at her outfit.

"And you," Mia replied politely.

"Hey, she's Irish," he said to Charlie.

Charlie rolled her eyes. "No shit."

"You fancy getting a drink with me after?" Dave suddenly asked.

"Dave!" Charlie snapped before Mia could reply. "She's Joel Coben's girlfriend," she added, quieter so only they could hear.

"Oh, shit." Dave let out a low whistle. He wiggled his eyebrows at Mia as he lifted the rope and allowed them into the bar. "Joel's a lucky man."

"Thanks," Mia replied, dashing past him before he could ask her out again.

c∽c∽c∽

Mia fumbled with the fob on her keys for the gates to Joel's house. The combination of the darkness and the alcohol in her system made the simple action of pressing a button so difficult.

"Mia? You got it?" Charlie called from the taxi behind her.

"Yeah," Mia shouted, the gates finally coming to life and siding open.

"All right, see you Monday." Charlie slammed the door shut and waved.

Mia waved back as the car pulled away and the gates slid closed, encasing her in her familiar, safe little bubble. She carefully tottered one foot in front of the other up the driveway, balancing one hand on the hood of her car as she passed for support.

One step, two, three, four.

She counted the steps up the front of the house before she reached the front door, fumbling again momentarily with the keys before letting herself into the house. As she closed the door behind her, she realized hers was the only car in the driveway.

She shook her head, a little too harshly for her current senses to cope with, before turning off the alarm and kicking off her heels in the hallway.

Mia heard the sounds of pawed footsteps at the top of the staircase as she began to climb up and saw Sonny waiting with a wagging tail to greet her. She reached down to pet him when she eventually reached the difficult summit at the top of the stairs.

The cold marble beneath her sore feet was soothing after hours of dancing in Charlie's high heels. Her bare feet padded across the landing and onto the plush carpet of Joel's bedroom, which her tired feet also relished the feeling of.

Mia pouted her bottom lip when she saw the bed was empty.

Aside from a snoring Diesel anyway.

She unzipped her dress and placed it over the back of a chair. Plonking her bag down on the chair, Mia fumbled inside to find her phone.

She was relieved to see a text message awaiting her attention when she did.

STILL AT THE STUDIO. BE HOME SOON. HAVE FUN XXX

Mia smiled as she read Joel's text. Then she saw the time on her phone three-eleven.

Joel never stayed that late at the studio, was her last thought as she slumped down on the bed, tossing her phone on the nightstand and pulling the covers over her head.

Sometime after that, her brain registered the sound of the bedroom door opening and closing followed by the feeling of someone climbing into bed beside her and a muscular arm curling around her body.

Chapter 12

*M*Y AFFAIR WITH JOEL COBEN.
NEW LOVER PARTIES ALONE.
The headlines stared angrily back at Mia.

Twenty-four hours after she had woken up in Joel's arms—when he had sleepily reassured her he was in the studio, making the most of the time to himself to work on his album while she went out with Charlie—the headlines had landed.

Mia's own face stared back at her from the cover of the newspaper, arm in arm with Charlie as she walked down a street in Los Angeles, both of them dressed to the nines and looking pretty good, if Mia thought so herself.

Beside that picture, was one of another face Mia recognized. Lucy.

At the start of her relationship with Joel, Lucy had sold a tell-all story to a gossip magazine, claiming she had shared a wild night of passion with Joel at his house. Lucy had described Joel's house to the media, each and every description Mia had later found out to be false, proving she never saw the inside of Joel's house.

Lucy's long, blonde hair and curvaceous body were once again plastered across the press in all their glory.

"What the hell is that?" Joel asked, nearly ripping the newspaper in half as he yanked it from Mia's hand.

Mia said nothing, allowing him to read the story.

Charlie sat back down in her seat, suddenly looking as small as she really was. She turned her attention to the emails on the screen in front of her, trying to make herself look as invisible as possible.

This is another test, Mia reminded herself, this was exactly what Joel was talking about.

But still? He hadn't come home until the early hours. He could have been anywhere while she was out with Charlie. Tis time, Lucy's story was entirely plausible.

Mia could feel the hurt rising in her chest. Her eyes threatened to sting with tears already. She wanted to snatch the newspaper back and whack him over the head with it until he explained himself.

Joel's dark eyes narrowed as he read the article.

Mia folded her arms across her chest, hugging herself.

Joel finished reading the article and snapped his head up. He glowered at Charlie. "Does he know?"

Charlie made a small squeaking noise in surprise before answering. "I don't know."

"Fucking hell," Joel spat before storming away across the foyer in the direction of the elevator. Mia knew Jackson's office was upstairs, and she guessed that was where Joel was headed.

He hadn't given her another glance, she realized.

Charlie patted tried to grab Mia's hand soothingly. "Don't worry about it."

"Why does everyone keep saying that?" Mia snapped before storming away in the direction of the privacy or her own studio.

 espço

"Mia?" TJ tugged on her arm, motioning for her to take off her headphones.

Mia already knew who would be there. TJ flicked his eyes in the direction of the door behind them. She glanced over her shoulder, seeing who she had guessed would be standing there, she snapped her headphones back in place and resumed her work. She saw TJ shrug his shoulders. Over the noise of the music in her ears, Mia heard the studio door close again.

An hour later, the sleeve of Mia's T-shirt was tugged again.

"What?" she snapped angrily, turning in her seat and seeing a shocked expression on Chad's face. "Sorry," she replied before looking at what he had wanted her attention for in the first place.

Chad nervously pointed over his shoulder at the door.

"Mia?" Jackson stood in the doorway, his face like thunder.

"Yes?" she replied with less aggression in her voice.

"A word? Please?" He gestured into the corridor behind him.

Shit, Mia thought as she got up from her seat and left a confused pair of producers in her wake.

Jackson held open the door for Mia, who when seeing was in the corridor, tried to turn around again.

"No," Jackson said as he gave her a shove out of the door and slammed it closed behind him.

Feeling childish, Mia folded her arms across her chest, not wanting to look Joel in the eyes.

Jackson stood between them, his hands on his hips, looking slightly dishevelled.

"Do you want to explain to me why I've spent the last three hours of my life on the phone to media lawyers?" he snapped immediately.

"Me?" Mia squealed.

"Yes, you," he replied, jerking his head. "This idiot here—" He thumbed in Joel's direction. "—has had me spend my entire bloody morning filing a lawsuit against some shitty newspaper."

Mia swallowed. "And that's my fault?"

"Yes," Jackson snapped again, "because before you came on the scene, this idiot wouldn't have anything to do with the media. Now that your face is printed there beside his, he's suddenly learned every fucking libel law there ever was!"

Mia narrowed her eyes at Joel. Why was she being told off for his actions? She suddenly felt like she was back at school, getting a telling off in the corridor from the headmaster. This was not the Los Angeles she had pictured.

"I'm sorry," she said, regaining her composure, "but I don't see why this is my fault."

Jackson let out a heavy sigh. "Because you're the reason this soppy bastard has had my staff trawling the CCTV footage of this place to prove to you he was where he said he was the other night!"

Mia opened her mouth in shock. "Really?" she squeaked.

"Yes!" Jackson said, exasperated. "Thankfully, it will probably come in useful for the lawsuit. Which you're paying for by the way," he said to Joel.

Joel nodded, his hands still in his pockets.

"There's an email coming through to you with a CCTV file attached to it," Jackson explained. "Don't make me do this again, or I'll put a ban on co-worker relationships!"

Joel let out a snort of laughter.

Jackson snapped his head up at him before sighing and letting out a laugh. "I don't think I'd have many staff left if that was the case, huh?"

Joel grinned. "Nope."

"What I actually came to say—" Jackson turned his attention back to Mia. "—before I got carried away, is we need you to speak to the lawyer who's waiting upstairs."

"Okay," Mia found herself saying.

"Now, I am not your relationship counselor." Jackson shook his head, still laughing. "Sort it out, you guys. You're better than this shit."

"Yes, we are," Joel said affirmatively.

"Tell *her* that, you soppy bastard." Jackson laughed, slapping Joel hard on the shoulder as he passed. "Upstairs in five minutes, Mia," he called out over his shoulder.

When he was out of sight, Joel turned back to look at Mia. "Mia," he began, taking a step toward her, his hand outstretched.

"Don't." She shook her head and his face fell. She paused, not meaning to, at the expression on his face. He looked heartbroken. His eyes were swirling black holes in that moment, torn and broken. She reached out, took his hand, and stepped into his arms. Pulling his head down to hers, she kissed him firmly. "Don't ever do that to me again," she said.

"Huh?" he asked, breathless.

"Don't walk away from me," she explained. "Just talk to me, tell me. That's all I needed to hear. I don't need any of this. You freaked me out when you walked away from me."

"I'm sorry," he said, the light slowly coming back into his dark eyes. "I panicked, I was mad."

"I know," she said, feeling her own anger ebb away. She knew he was true to her, she knew he was hers, she didn't need a lawsuit or CCTV footage for that, she just needed him to say it to her.

"I'm sorry," he said again. "I wanted to teach her a lesson, I wanted to prove that I'm serious about you, about us. They've said whatever they wanted about me before, but now that we're an *us*, it's different. They can't keep making this crap up, saying what they want about you. And I'm not going to stand by and watch the world hurt the woman I love."

He really was hers, she thought as she listened to him. A man who spent his life under the media spotlight was prepared to stand in it and fight for the woman he loved. There was no bolder declaration than announcing to the world that they were an *us*.

He pulled her body against his, his hands tightly around her waist, and brought his eyes down level with hers. She could stare into those eyes forever. She would never tire of looking at that face, of staring into his soul through those nearly black eyes.

"I love you," she said against his lips, before reminding him in more than one way that she truly did.

℘℘℘

A blinding flash of lightbulbs and the sound of dozens of shutters going off could be heard as Mia stepped through the studio doors and walked across the car park, hand in hand with Joel.

"Joel, why did you file a lawsuit?"

"Mia, why have you taken him back?"

"Joel, are you a cheat?"

"Joel, Lucy or Mia?"

"Mia!"

"Joel!"

Their shouts sounded over and over again, each one more obscene and absurd than the last.

The press had begun following Mia and Joel everywhere since Lucy's story broke, and then even more so when they learned Joel had filed a lawsuit. This was the kind of story they lived for. They thrived on the stuff. The scandals and tribulations of others' lives were what made the Hollywood bubble keep turning.

Mia and Joel were just another set of cogs in the machine. They just needed to ride out the storm together until it passed and someone else was the hot story.

In Hollywood, that could last a day or two. Sometimes, one story fell by the wayside as soon as something more interesting came along. Sometimes, it lasted for weeks. Mia prayed for a busy news day at TMZ.

Wherever they went, they were followed. Mia saw them dashing into their cars from her wing mirror and following them out of the parking lot and through the streets of Los

Angeles. The thought made her nervous. Cars chasing theirs through the traffic made her fidget in her seat. The accident was still raw in her mind. The sight of cars weaving dangerously in her mirror reminded her of how quickly things could go wrong.

"Relax." Joel's hand was on her leg, his eyes still in the rear view, watching what she was.

"I can't help it," she replied.

Only the day before, the press had been waiting outside their house for them to leave for the studios. As Joel had pulled out of the driveway, the flashbulbs had gone off and dazzled Mia in the passenger seat. There was a swarm of them gathered at the gates, desperate for a picture to prove she and Joel were still together, despite Lucy's claims.

Joel had yet to make a formal statement. He refused to do so. Mia knew he never would. It would only add more inches to the column if he released a statement explaining why he was doing what he was.

The press had obtained the details of the lawsuit, and that was more than enough to keep them going. Lucy was surprisingly silent after receiving details of the charges against her and the newspaper. Mia wondered how her modeling career would pan out now that she was being labeled a liar.

Any press was good press, she remembered someone telling her and Lucy was probably writing a tell-all autobiography and signing up for a calendar shoot right at that moment. Mia also remembered Joel's words of wisdom about fifteen minutes of fame and was immediately grateful for being on the right team.

She knew she and Joel were right to hold their silence and that, together, they could face any backlash from the press. They would take on the media in court and they would win.

"This isn't even the eye of the storm," Joel muttered beside her, glancing up at another weaving car in the traffic behind him.

Mia took hold of his hand and allowed his fingers to curl around hers.

No, it wasn't. This was only the beginning, but together they would face the storm head on.

Chapter 13

In the wake of Joel's lawsuit against both the newspaper and Lucy, both parties suddenly fell very quiet on the Mia and Joel front.

The newspaper issued a brief, and very small, apology in the corner of one of its pages the following day. Mia could only shake her head when she saw the pint-sized article on page twenty-one. Nobody was going to take any notice of that. The story had been front page news the previous day, the damage had already been done, and nobody read those tiny articles anyway.

Lucy's management declined to comment, and she mysteriously deleted her Twitter account in the aftermath of the scandal. Thousands upon thousands of dedicatedly loyal Joel Coben fans had taken to the social networking site to vent their frustrations and brutally honest opinions of Lucy directly to her account.

Mia was grateful that day she wasn't on Twitter. She knew both she and Joel were better off without it. Their names and accounts would only have been mentioned or targeted in the thousands of tweets that flooded the site.

Mia reminded herself of the Joel she had met only a few months ago at Sixth String Studios, the Joel who wanted nothing to do with the media, the Joel who hated giving interviews unless absolutely necessary, and the Joel who had absolutely no involvement with social networking. Joel's management ran very professional Facebook and Twitter pages for Joel's music, but unlike many other celebrities, Joel himself steered well clear of the site.

The lawsuit, however, was still going ahead. Mia had given a very brief account to the lawyer who had been waiting upstairs in Jackson's office yesterday, and the newspaper was being charged.

Despite her own lack of social media presence, her name was appearing everywhere. Her phone was constantly beeping in her pocket with friends from home telling her where they had seen her face this time.

NIAMH: *YOU'RE ON THE CELEB PAGES OF THE SUN! AND YOU'RE IN HEAT MAGAZINE! :) XXXXXX*
DYLAN: *DUDE, YOUR FACE IS EVERYWHERE?! X*
GLEN: *HOPE EVERYTHING IS OK MIA, YOU SEEM TO BE GETTING A LOT OF PRESS COVERAGE THESE LAST FEW DAYS.*
BEN: *WHY AM I SEEING YOUR FACE IN FHM MAGAZINE? KINDA WEIRD :/*
SHARON: *CALL ME. WORRIED ABOUT YOU. XXX*

Mia turned her phone on silent. She would answer them later and eventually get around to calling Sharon. As she scrolled through her settings to turn off the vibrate mode, her phone announced she had yet another message.

LUKE: *SOME REPORTER KEEPS CALLING ME. HOW DID THEY GET MY NUMBER?*

Mia frowned at her brother's message. She had no idea how the press had gotten hold of Luke's personal details, but frankly it was worrying.

The last thing she needed was her friends and what little

family she had left being dragged into this concocted story.

She massaged her temples with her free hand.

This was only the beginning, as Joel had told her, and things would only get worse from here on out. Once her album was finished and released, her face would be appearing in every magazine and newspaper and on every gossip website.

It was a lot to think about.

Mia tried not to picture how many people these publications had the potential of reaching. She had flashes of a folded newspaper on a train seat, a newsstand with her face on every cover, the newsagents near her flat in Dublin had her name on the A-board outside, a girl reading a glossy magazine on the bus with Mia's face on it...the possibilities were endless. That was without even beginning to think about the internet and social media.

Mia let out a heavy sigh and tossed her phone back onto the table. It lit up as it landed on the wood with a soft thud and Mia saw the tell-tale flashing icon of an email landing in her inbox.

From: Rebecca Calder
Subject: Recording Contract
Message: Hi, Mia, Have you had chance to give our offer any further consideration yet? Regards, Rebecca

Mia instantly regretted picking up the phone.

When would she need a manager? Or an agent? she wondered. Surely this was their job to deal with all this kind of thing? Mia simply wanted to focus on her music, to write songs and play her guitar, to stand behind the glass and sing into the microphone and listen to TJ and Chad work their magic on her album.

And a little downtime with Joel too.

The studio door opened and closed behind her with a soft click, and Mia tossed her phone back down on the table. TJ had gone to fetch a much needed caffeine fix that would hopefully kick start Mia's brain into the creative process once again.

The studio door's lock clicked into place shortly afterward, and Mia sat up in her chair, wondering why on earth TJ would lock the door. She froze as she turned, feeling all the blood draining from her face as she looked up into Mediterranean-esque features staring back at her.

"What do you want?" she asked sharply.

His lip curled into a smile. It was not one that she liked the look of. Something about Adam immediately put Mia on her guard. She remembered how he had invaded her personal space when she had only just met him, the way he stood just a little too close, the way his lips had been centimetres from hers, and the way his breath had touched her skin. She shuddered at the thought.

Despite the opinion of millions of female fans, Mia couldn't see the appeal in Adam Morgan. She could practically hear the hysterical shrieks of millions of Glasshearts fans as she thought those thoughts. She could hear the catcalls, the hisses, and the insults hurling her way. But all Mia wanted to do was scratch her skin or take a running leap into the nearest shower.

"You," was all he said.

His voice was low and quiet, his tone deep and seductive, but it paled in comparison to Joel's. His voice lacked that same empathy, his tone was deep but meaningless, the seduction in his voice failed to match the leer in his eyes.

"No, you don't," Mia said firmly, shuffling back in her seat. "Get out of here, Adam."

"Do you know how many girls would kill for this opportunity?" he scoffed, flaying his hands up and down himself in appraisal.

Mia pulled a face. "I'm not one of them, sorry."

Her voice was low and steady. On the outside, she appeared calm and controlled, but inside, she could hear her heartbeat pounding loudly in her chest.

Her nerves crashed and toiled and her blood was pumping so fast she could hear it in her ears. Adam scared her. That was the simplest way she could put it.

He cocked his head to one side and took a step toward her. "But you will be."

Knowing she needed to get out, Mia gripped the arms of her chair and pushed herself out of it.

He moved in a flash, instantly closing the distance between them, slamming his hands over hers on the arms of the chair, knocking her back down into her seat.

"Adam, *move*," she spat.

She writhed in her seat, desperately trying to get out of his hold.

"I said, you will be." His breath was on her skin again, his lips against her cheek as he spoke. "And I always get what I want."

His knee dropped between her legs, pinning her in place in the chair, his hands held a death-like grip around her forearms, clamping her to her seat.

"Get off me!" she yelled.

He chuckled. "No one can hear you." His nose trailed across her cheek and down her neck, inhaling the scent of her skin as he went. "This room is completely soundproof, remember?"

Whatever blood was remaining in her face drained away completely. An icy chill washed over Mia as the realization of his words hit her.

"I always get what I want, Mia," he repeated, "and I want you."

His breath was hot and clammy in her ear, his lips pressed against her skin as he spoke, the stubble on his chin scratched at her cheek as he trailed his lips across her face.

He drew in a breath, long and slow before clamping his lips against hers.

Before she had been frozen in place, both petrified and mortified at what was happening.

In hindsight, you always find yourself thinking what you should have done straight away, what you would do if you were faced with the situation again. If someone had asked Mia before Adam had locked her in that room, what she would have done if someone had done what he was now doing, she would tell them how she would run from the room, kicking him in the balls as she went.

But hindsight and anticipation were no good when the moment had passed, Mia now realized. What she should have, or would have done were no good now that her adrenaline had frozen her in place only moments ago.

When faced with a surreal situation, most people often found themselves blanking out what was happening. When faced with a moment you often only dreamed of or worried about, your brain shut itself down in disbelief, only to find afterward how much you kicked yourself over what you should have done.

Mia felt the scream in her throat struggle and suffocate as she tried to let it out. The repulsive taste of Adam crawled over her lips as he continued to attack her mouth against her will.

His strong hands still held her own tightly on the arms of the chair, despite struggling, pulling and tugging against him, they were not budging. His body now leaned over hers, his weight pinned her in place, and he pushed against her, letting her know exactly what he wanted from her.

"I want you, Mia," his breath was heavy and ragged, "don't fight with me, baby," his shudder inducing smile was back in place as he leered at her.

Seeing her chance now that her mouth was free, she screamed at the top of her lungs, "*Joel!*"

Adam's eyes narrowed. "Shut the fuck up," he snapped. "No one can hear you, anyway."

Mia noticed his face pale slightly and began to wonder if the room really was soundproof enough to blanket her screams. "*Joel! TJ!*" she screamed again.

"Quit it!" Adam snapped, releasing her hand of his grip and clamping his hand over her mouth.

Mia wriggled and pulled against him, wrestling with his

hand over her mouth and pulling at his arm to free her voice again.

"You're gonna shut the fuck up." His faint southern accent that was laced with Californian tones sounded in her ear. "And you're gonna enjoy this."

His other hand let go of her arm and clamped around her thigh, jostling her body as he angled against her hips, his hand running where it shouldn't.

Disbelief quickly turned into panic and the adrenaline coursing through her veins finally began to kick in. Now, both her arms were free. She elbowed all her might against Adam's face and instantly felt the spray of blood on her cheek.

"You fucking bitch!" she heard him cry out as her elbow collided with his face.

Shoving her hands into his chest, she forced his body off hers and, as he stumbled in shock, she slid out from underneath him, dutifully remembering to shove her knee in his groin as she did.

He collapsed into a heap on the floor, groaning and clutching his crotch, his nose still bleeding down his face.

The door handle to the studio was rattling as someone tried to get in from outside. Mia dashed toward it, and yanked it open, charging out into the corridor.

She immediately collided into the chest of someone else and her ears were met with a cry of surprise, followed by the sound of two polystyrene cups landing on the floor. A loud, splashing noise told her coffee had just landed everywhere.

"Mia? What the hell is going on?" TJ gasped. Immediately seeing the panicked look on her face he placed his hands on her shoulders. "What's wrong?"

"Adam—" she stammered. "He—he tried—"

All her bravado from elbowing his face, kicking his crotch, and shoving him to the floor had dissipated as meekly as the pools of coffee puddles now seeping into the carpet.

"Don't believe a word she says," came a sniffle from the door as Adam appeared wiping his bloody nose.

"Excuse me?" TJ asked.

"She came onto me, locked me in there, and forced herself onto me," Adam continued, his eyes now glassed over.

All his false bravado was now firmly back in place.

"Mia?" TJ turned aghast before spinning back to Adam. "That's bullshit, man, Mia wouldn't do that."

Adam shrugged. "It's true. I told her politely I wasn't interested and then this happened." He pointed to his face.

"Are you fucking kidding me?" Mia launched at him. TJ's hands were instantly back on her shoulders, pulling her away from Adam.

"Sweetheart, I already told you no once today," he said patronisingly.

"You bastard!" she yelled, hearing footsteps coming across the foyer. "*You* came into my studio! *You* locked the door! *You* came on to me!"

Adam shrugged at TJ. "Chicks always take it bad when I turn them down."

"Don't talk shit, Adam," TJ snapped.

"You assaulted me!" Mia yelled even louder.

"What the hell is going on here?" Jackson appeared behind TJ's shoulder, along with Cole, who Mia hadn't seen since she started and several other employees. Most of who were wearing suits.

Great, Mia thought, *all the company big shots have turned out to see this*.

"Jackson, man, this girl's crazy." Adam gestured at Mia with his thumb. "She just forced herself on to me."

"No fucking way."

Mia immediately recognised Joel's voice and saw his messy dark head of hair as he shoved his way through the big shots.

"Joel," she began, grabbing his arm.

"It's okay," he said to her and Mia saw in his eyes what was meant for her only.

She saw immediate understanding there. Joel was on her side. *Us against the storm*, he seemed to be saying silently.

His fingers squeezed hers tightly, letting her know he was there, that he believed her already.

"Dude, you need to have a word with your girl," Adam sneered at Joel.

"*Dude*," Joel mocked, "the only one I need to have a word with is *you*."

"Hey, man, don't take it out on me. I already told these guys, she came on to me."

"Oh really? And what the hell were you doing in her studio?"

"I—" Adam began, his cocky demeanour vanishing, "I needed to borrow something."

"And what was that?" Joel asked, his eyebrows rising in question.

"A—" Adam began again, but was unable to finish his sentence.

Jackson intervened. "Guys, what the hell is going on here?"

"He—" Mia jumped in and pointed at Adam before anyone else could speak. "—came into my studio, locked the door, and forced himself on to me. He assaulted me, Jackson."

The small space in the corridor fell silent.

The angry, confused atmosphere suddenly plummeted several degrees.

Mia felt Joel's hand flex and tense in her own.

A flush crept across Jackson's face, his colleagues behind him stared open mouthed. No one spoke for a moment.

"That's bullshit," Adam replied, "I already told you what happened."

"Oh, really?" Mia snapped, "is that why my arms are red? From where you pinned me to the chair. Is that why my face is grazed with your stubble? Is that why there's probably a bruise on my thigh where you pinned me down? And another where you grabbed me?"

Adam was silent.

"Is that why you're the one with the bloody nose? Because *you* turned *me* down? Or because I hit out at you, trying to get away? Because you were about to do a whole lot more than assault me?"

In a flash, Joel released Mia's hand, and his fist collided with Adam's already bleeding nose, sending him hurtling to the ground once again. Joel was then lost in a flurry of bodies as people scrambled over him to pull him away from Adam. Yells and cries sounded as people grappled with one another to pull Joel and Adam apart.

"All right! Stop this now!" Jackson yelled.

Joel emerged from the tangle of suits and nosebleeds seemingly unhurt. Others adjusted their ties, their jackets, and massaged various body parts that had been hurt in the scuffle.

"Somebody better tell me what's going on. Adam, what the hell were you doing in there?" Jackson asked.

"Nothing, man," Adam answered, shifting his eyes to the ground.

Mia ran her hands through her hair in exasperation. Karma was a bitch sometimes. Only minutes ago, she was complaining she had a lot to deal with, already stressed about Joel's lawsuit with the media and Lucy, her own media coverage, her brother, her friends back home, still recovering from the car crash, and having a debut album to write and record, *and* another studio vying for her attention. Life clearly thought she could handle a little more drama.

"*Nothing?*" Mia meant to yell but it came out sounding more like a squeak. "You call that *nothing*?"

"Somebody better start talking," Jackson warned.

"Jackson, I told you exactly what happened," Mia said. "That was the truth."

"Was it?" he asked Adam, his eyes warily casting over Joel who was being held back by Cole.

Mia wondered who would win in a fight between those two. Cole was definitely the silent but deadly type.

Adam shifted his eyes around the corridor, not wanting to answer.

"Adam?" Jackson snapped.

Adam looked up from the floor and Mia saw within them a calm, cool surface beneath. The man thought he was invincible. He was sticking to his story, she then realised.

"Sort of. She came on to me, though. It was mutual, man."

That time it was Mia who needed holding back.

☙❧☙

"I really think you ought to call the police." Joel gripped Mia's shoulders, focussing her gaze entirely on him.

"No." Mia shook her head, that was the last thing she needed right now. That was the last thing any of them needed right now.

"He's right," Jackson agreed from across the room, "though I've no idea what's gotten into you, Joel."

Joel released his hold on Mia and turned to face Jackson who was perched on the edge of his desk.

Jackson's suit jacket lay abandoned and strewn across his desk, his tie was so loosely pulled down it almost touched his navel and his lack of fastened buttons were giving Simon Cowell a run for his money.

He was stressed.

"Why's that?" Joel asked.

"Lawsuits, police, all of this just isn't like you," Jackson explained. "Before you wouldn't bat an eyelid. You would have strode over Adam lying in the corridor and locked your own studio door behind you. You wouldn't have even read the newspaper, let alone sue both the model and the publication. It's just not like you."

Joel said nothing. He glanced away from Jackson back to Mia. That was his explanation.

Embarrassed that she was ultimately the cause of so

much drama, tension, and stress in the studios, Mia looked out of the window.

Behind the tinted black glass, the sun shone fiercely down on Los Angeles, the glare from windows of nearby buildings reflecting back at Mia through the slanted blinds. The heat radiated from the rooftops of those below the studios, and not a puff of a cloud littered the ocean blue sky.

A forgotten, wilted plant and a once-shiny VMA in need of polishing were all that lay on the window ledge of Jackson's office. Around the room hung various pictures, landmark editions of bestselling albums, and more forgotten awards. *What kind of artist owns so many awards they donate them to the studio*, Mia wondered.

Mia found herself surprised when her eyes drifted over Jackson's desk and saw a framed picture of Jackson standing with a beautiful blonde woman and a small boy.

They were the American dream—the picturesque family, the blonde Californian picture of happiness. Mia never heard Jackson speak about his wife or son. She then realized she hadn't heard that much about Chad's girlfriend Tara until she met her. Perhaps Mia was so wrapped up in her own bubble, she was missing the minor details in the lives of those around her.

She reminded herself to pay more attention in future, to remember the world still turned on its axis, regardless of what was going on in hers.

"*That's* why," Jackson said, breaking the silence.

Mia looked up into his tired eyes. He was watching her staring at his family photograph.

"Sorry?"

"That's why," he repeated pointing at the photograph and back to Joel. "That's the reason he's changed his ways. He's turned all mellow and love-struck. The things that would usually pass him by are now affecting him. The things he turned a blind eye to are now staring him in the face. You've given him a reason to sit up and take notice, Mia."

Mia blinked in surprise as she listened to the usually professional and reserved Jackson peel away a few layers of his outer shell.

"This man right here," he said and pointed at Joel, "has changed so much in these past few months. I won't lie to you. He was a pain in the ass until you showed up. He was moody, he was quiet, he was rude and, frankly, the guy drove me insane. I wouldn't go as far as saying he was difficult to work with, but he didn't make my life easy that's for sure."

"And it is now?" Mia found herself asking.

She hadn't meant to ask, the words had simply come tumbling out.

Surely, Jackson's life would have been far easier if Joel was still his quiet, moody, and even rude old self? If Jackson didn't have to spend his days dealing with lawyers and pissed off models, trawling through CCTV footage, and breaking up scuffles, he could be getting on with business as usual.

Jackson laughed softly to himself. "No," he said, staring at his shoes. "No, it's not. But it's far more entertaining."

He looked up at Mia and smiled. She smiled in return. Joel had turned silent beside her. She knew he was taking it all in. Joel never missed a beat.

"If you had any idea how many days, weeks, and months passed with the same old story happening in these four walls," Jackson continued. "I'd bore you to death with the details. It's been a long time since I had some real rock and roll drama like this to deal with. You've shaken things up around here, Mia, that's for sure."

"I didn't mean to—" she began.

Jackson waved her off. "I like the change. I miss the days where no two were the same. Where we had fresh and exciting things happening all the time. Where rock stars would brawl in the hallway, where the media clamoured outside the doors, where people would come spilling out of the studios at all hours. Those are the things that inspire music. The best and worst parts of life as a musician are what inspire the greatest songs. Not a mundane, nine-to-five routine. People showing up Monday to Friday to write music doesn't make hits. These things do. Things had turned a little stale around here until you showed up."

"He's right," Joel added quietly.

"Not that I enjoy being your relationship counselor or trawling through twenty-four hours' worth of CCTV footage, but the rest of it keeps me on my toes." He winked at Mia, who laughed in response. "I know these last few weeks have been crazy," he went on. "They've been hard, they've been confusing, and they've even been life threatening, but I'm a believer in fate, and everything is sent to us for a reason. Without getting all philosophical on you, you're only dealt the hand you're able to play."

Mia nodded and saw Joel beside her doing the same.

They knew Jackson was right, despite the ups and downs of the past few weeks, despite all the craziness that had been thrown their way, they had pulled through it all together with only a few cuts and bruises. *And five days unconscious in hospital*, Mia reminded herself.

Even the accident blurred into the tangle of events that had happened in the past few weeks. How did something as life-changing, as dangerous, and near-death-like blur into the rest of your life? *When you lead one as strange as mine,* Mia realized.

Reluctantly, Mia had told Jackson everything about the last few weeks. She had filled in all the gaps and cracks, even the one about the second recording deal offer. Jackson had ruffled a little, at first, when Mia had told him how much Sky Records were offering her, but he calmed eventually. He had seen more things in his time with the company to be fazed by a little competition.

Poor Jackson was turning into their life coach in recent days, Mia thought.

"So what I'm trying to say," Jackson continued, "is I think you guys may need a little time. Don't worry about all of this." He gestured to the studios. "This isn't going any-where. I have people here to deal with the media, with the lawyers and everything else. Mia, if you're serious about not wanting to press charges against Adam?" he asked. Mia shook her head. "Then I'll respect your decision. You guys have got a lot on your plates right now. All this will blow over in a few days or so. Trust me. I've seen it happen many times before."

Joel laughed softly. "It's true."

"Joel, you know what I'm getting at here?"

Joel nodded. "I certainly do."

Chapter 14

J oel?" Mia groaned. "Where the hell are we going?"

"Just wait and see."

His hand entwined with hers and lay contentedly in his jean-clad lap. His messy dark hair was blowing softly in the wind that blew in through the open window. One hand was on the steering wheel, and he was relaxed and leaning back in his seat. Wearing his aviator sunglasses, Joel looked happy and content. And also like he was posing for the pages of a supercar advertisement. *Introducing Joel Coben, the new face of Ferrari.* Mia could see the glossy page unfolding before her along with an image not too dissimilar to what she was now seeing in person.

"Can I at least have a clue?" she tried, to which Joel smiled and shook his head, causing his already tousled bedhead hair to jostle in the wind.

Mia tried to scowl at those nearly black eyes masked behind aviator sunglasses and failed. The glimmer of a smile crept about his features and made them come alive. They danced more than the hair that played in the wind.

He lifted his thumb off the steering wheel and pointed in the direction of the highway they were driving on. "You'll see a clue in a moment."

They were still in Los Angeles. Only minutes ago, Joel had driven them from his house, having instructed Mia to pack a bag for a few days and meet him downstairs in ten minutes. That was all he had said before ushering her into his car and heading out of the gates and onto the highway.

Mia hung her hand out of the open window beside her and let her mind drift along in the breeze as they sped along the highway. The interstates surrounding the outskirts of the city were a terrifying network of twists and turns, a maze Mia was glad she didn't have to navigate.

Joel, however, had grown up not far from the city and swapped and changed lanes with ease, barely batting an eye at the confusing lanes and exits around him.

"But that's..." Mia's voice trailed away from her as a large Virgin Airways jet flew over the highway and descended somewhere in the horizon.

"An airport," Joel finished her sentence for her, never taking his eyes off the road.

Mia laughed and nudged him with her hand that was still clasped in his. "I know that."

"So there's your clue," Joel said calmly.

"That's my clue?" she asked.

Joel nodded.

"The airport?"

Joel nodded again.

Words failed Mia as she watched Joel navigate the car off the highway and toward the terminals of LAX before them.

Plane after plane appeared from the clouds behind them, descending from the sky like a conveyor belt. As soon as one plane touched the ground, another appeared at the rear of the queue—a stairway of planes formed in the sky.

The efficiency of the system amazed Mia.

Every now and then, Joel would glance out of the corners of his sunglasses, checking Mia's face for signs his plan wasn't going according to...well, plan.

Not that it wouldn't. Mia had no intention of resisting. She was just a little taken aback by it all.

When Jackson had suggested they "take a few days," Mia didn't think this was quite what he had imagined. Leaving the country, in the midst of recording two hotly anticipated albums, was not the usual recording protocol at Sixth String Studios.

Joel pulled the car up to the valet and instantly hopped out of the car and around to Mia's door. She noticed he pulled the hood of his sweatshirt around his head as soon as he climbed out of the car.

Sunglasses still in place, he offered her his hand to help her down from the car. "I'll get those," he called out to the valet who was opening the boot of the car. "Are you okay with this?" he asked.

Mia nodded. "Sure."

Truthfully, she was. She loved surprises, and she loved to travel. She liked to think of herself as spontaneous too. It was just that the combination of all of the above with her world famous rock star boyfriend was not something a girl from Kinsale was used to doing.

Mia then realized this was about to become the norm for her. This would soon be her life. A nonstop whirlwind of touring, airplane journeys, tour bus rides, and being ferried to and from venues was about to come her way.

"Come on." Joel balanced one bag on top of the other before wheeling them with one hand and taking Mia's again in his other, still managing to tip the valet driver as he passed. He strode through the sliding doors and one of Mia's favorite sights lit up before her eyes.

Airports.

Something about them made her stomach flutter with anticipation. The eagerness for the journey ahead, the curiosity about those around her, and the reasons behind every journey about to take place were why airport terminals fascinated Mia.

They were a hub of human activity, a perfect spot for people watching, and ultimately a great place for inspiration.

Mia could almost feel the notebook in her bag burning with desire to be written in.

"Good afternoon, sir," the check-in girl chirped from behind her desk.

Joel smiled politely as he lifted his sunglasses from his eyes. "Afternoon."

Mia tried to stifle a giggle as the girl nearly dropped the passport in her hands. Glancing to and from the passport to the real life owner before her, she blushed as scarlet as her lipstick as she realized who she was checking in.

Joel handed over Mia's passport, ignoring the girl, who was now blushing profusely and her hands shook as she took the document from his hands.

"Thank you, sir, have a wonderful flight," she croaked out once their bags were checked and their boarding passes printed.

"Thank you," Joel replied politely.

"The first class lounge is through the doors on your right," she said and pointed with a quivering finger.

Joel thanked her again, and Mia nodded politely, not trusting herself enough to open her mouth.

"The Joel Coben Effect," Mia muttered to herself, albeit loud enough for him to hear.

He tilted his head to her and flashed her a lopsided grin around the corner of his hood, which was now back up. "I seem to remember a similar effect on you not so long ago," he quipped, nudging her gently.

"You wish." She giggled, looping her arm through his as they entered the first class lounge together.

"Good afternoon, sir, madam." A man greeted them as they walked through the doors. "May I see your boarding passes?"

"Sure." Joel handed him the tickets, angled just enough so Mia couldn't see the destination printed on them.

She mentally kicked herself for inwardly giggling at the blushing girl at the check-in desk and missing an opportunity to find out where Joel was taking her.

"A pleasure to have you and your companion flying with us, Mr. Coben," the man said, blushing slightly less than his female colleague. "If you would be so kind as to follow me, I will show you both to the VIP lounge."

"Thank you," Joel said again.

Still hanging on to Joel's arm, Mia followed suit as the man led her and Joel through another set of doors and into an even swankier, more luxurious lounge than the first class area she had been standing in moments before.

"If there is anything you need, my colleagues and I will be more than happy to assist you." He stopped just short of bowing to Joel as he left the room.

Mia exhaled as she looked around the room. "Wow."

Small, but yet exquisitely luxurious, the room resembled a living room in a penthouse apartment. This was a far cry from the plastic chair benches in the departure lounge where you jostled for a seat between the old couple eating sandwiches out of cling film and the mother with the baby that screamed constantly for your entire three-hour wait.

There was not another soul in the VIP lounge. They had the plush leather sofas all to themselves.

Joel dropped their hand luggage onto the nearest sofa and pulled Mia along to one closer to the window.

She wondered where the VIP lounge staff were. Though the man had told them his colleagues would be happy to help, not one of them was visible in the lounge.

Mia was sure they must be hiding somewhere nearby. There had to be someone to cater to the every whim of the rich and famous as they waited for their first class seats to whichever exotic location they were flying to.

Joel came to a stop before the window and stood quietly, watching the planes landing and taking off. One taxied into a gate so close to their window, the plane looked as though it were headed straight into the room.

"I love airports," he said quietly, pulling Mia in front of him and wrapping his arms around her waist.

"So do I," she said with a smile. "I love wondering where everyone is going. Not that I'll see much of that in here, mind you."

"No, that's true." Joel chuckled. "I do miss that. This is just so much easier. It's not worth the hassle of waiting in the main lounge. I don't think they'd even let me walk in there if I tried."

Mia laughed. "No, I don't think so either."

She watched an AirBus come gliding toward the runway before touching the tarmac with a gentle nudge. They made it look so easy, she thought as she watched the enormous aircraft navigate into its designated gate.

Joel's hands were clasped over hers at her waist, and she realized they were empty. He had stashed the tickets somewhere she couldn't see.

"Joel, where are we going?" she tried again.

A low chuckle sounded in her ear. His breath tickled against her skin before he nuzzled into her hair. "Guess," he whispered.

Mia sighed for a moment as she thought, "Hawaii?" she tried. Hawaii was only a short flight from Los Angeles and she certainly wouldn't mind spending a few days in paradise in a bikini with Joel Coben. That was the stuff dreams were made of.

Joel laughed again. "No."

"Canada?" she asked. That was kind of close by.

Joel laughed and kissed her cheek. "No."

"Mexico?"

"No."

"Barbados?"

"No."

"Brazil?"

"No."

She sighed. "I have no idea."

Thinking quickly, she let go of Joel's hands and ran hers

back across his hips toward the back pockets of his jeans.

He laughed and instantly grabbed her hands gently. "Do you give up?"

She giggled as she struggled against his hands. "Yes."

Joel let go of her hands and beat her to it. Sliding the boarding passes out of the back pocket of his jeans, he placed them upside down in her hands. He said nothing as she turned them over. He simply kissed her cheek and rested his head on her shoulder as she read the print on the tickets.

From: Los Angeles, LAX
To: Dublin, DUB

The departure location stared back at Mia. Those three little letters made her world turn on its axis once again.

"Dublin?" she asked quietly in disbelief.

Her voice sounded barely a whisper in the empty room. Joel had heard her though.

She felt him nod his head on her shoulder.

She stared back down at the tickets, just to check they were still there. She needed to make sure she hadn't misread them.

But Joel had nodded. The tickets were still there.

This was actually happening.

Joel was taking her home.

Chapter 15

Mia cast her eyes over Joel's sleeping face beside her. His eyes were closed, his face nestled into the pillow, and his messy hair ruffled around his face.

He still looked perfect. He looked so happy and so calm. She didn't want to wake him, but she didn't want him to miss the view either.

In a few minutes, the plane would begin to descend from the sky and Mia's homeland would materialise beneath them. Soon, the endless green fields and valleys of Ireland would appear as they coasted their way toward the beautiful city of Dublin.

"Joel?" she whispered quietly, leaning in to him so not to wake anyone else in the first class cabin.

"Mmm," he mumbled sleepily before opening his eyes.

"We're nearly here." She smiled to herself as his eyes opened wider, slowly coming to life in the dull light of the cabin.

It had been late in the afternoon when they checked in at LAX and early evening by the time their plane had taken off from the runway in Los Angeles. Mia mentally did the math and figured it was now six a.m. in Los Angeles and three p.m. in the afternoon in the land below their plane.

By the time they got off the plane, found their bags, and hailed a taxi into the city, the evening would be approaching. And Glen's Tavern would be opening, Mia mused with a smile to herself.

Joel sat up in his oversized chair. The blissfully comfortable chairs were worlds apart from the cramped seats in economy. One of the many perks of flying first class, Mia decided, as Joel peered over her shoulder to watch what she was already seeing from out of her window.

Due to the generous spacing between the large first class seats, Joel couldn't see what Mia was eagerly waiting to show him. So, ignoring the scowls from the flight attendant, he got up and perched on the arm of Mia's chair. Mia was sure anyone else would have been ordered back to their seat immediately, but as the first class air hostesses had spent the last several hours vying for Joel's attention, Mia was sure they were turning a blind eye.

Slowly, the plane descended from the sky. The cottonball clouds beneath them rose, as the plane drifted down, and floated past their window. The last few wisps of stray cloud cleared from their window, and Mia felt her heart soar as she recognised the green landscape materialising beneath them.

"It's beautiful," Joel whispered in her ear.

Mia nodded. She could feel her eyes prickling with moisture as her emotions soared at the prospect of visiting not only those she loved, but the land she loved too. Mia was fiercely proud of her Irish heritage. No amount of time spent in Los Angeles, or anywhere else in the world, could take away that pride. She could practically hear the familiar Gaelic tunes as the wheels began to lower beneath them in preparation for landing.

"Sir, I need you to return to your seat please?" the air hostess snapped at Joel, disturbing their admiring reverie.

The air hostess had finally given in to protocol and was now looming over Joel until he returned to his seat. The seatbelt light had been switched on long ago, and Mia knew she had let Joel break the rules for long enough.

Joel obliged, sitting back down in his seat and fastening his seat belt. "Sure."

Once he had done so, the air hostess returned to her own seat in preparation for landing. Mia could see her still eyeing Joel from the front of the cabin.

Joel then leaned over as far as his belt would allow him to continue watching what had Mia so fixated. He smiled at her, his eyes crinkling at the corners. "I can already see why you love it so much."

Mia smiled in return, thinking of the conversation they shared on the sand in Hermosa Beach several weeks ago when she had told Joel all about her homeland and the love she felt for it. Joel had listened intently to everything she said before expressing his own desire to see the country.

Now it was finally happening.

When they had sat on the beach that day, Mia never imagined she would get to show Joel her beloved city so quickly. It had been one of those wistful conversations, full of ifs and buts and one day's. Mia felt her heart do a little flutter at the thought of taking Joel back to Dublin. Thousands of idle little daydreams she had had were about to come true.

The rooftops of Dublin materialised in the distance as the plane cruised closer to the land. Mia tried to recognise some of the buildings she saw before they disappeared as the plane turned in to the airport to land. She felt the anticipation in her stomach bubble and swell as the plane grew closer and closer to the land. With a sharp bump the plane touched down on the tarmac, the breaks slowly pulling the large aircraft to a stop as it turned into the taxiway.

Mia refrained from bouncing up and down in her seat in excitement, barely containing the urge to yank open her seatbelt and rush toward the doors and down the steep metal staircase that was now being steered into place.

A ping sounded over their heads and, immediately, Mia

heard the frantic sounds of the passengers behind them in economy leap from their seats and begin to jostle their baggage out of the holds above their heads.

"Let's go," Joel said with an eager grin, rising from his seat, as Mia did.

Mentally thanking the perks of flying first class for the umpteenth time that day, Mia calmly exited the plane behind Joel and the other first class passengers as the stampede of economy flyers waited not so patiently in the next cabin.

Mia practically danced her way down the corridor as they approached passport control and, seeing the virtually empty lobby before them, let out a small squeal of glee.

Joel shook his head and laughed at her excitement as they went their separate ways through passport control, Mia breezing through IRE nationals while Joel had to queue a few moments longer with the other international first-class passengers.

Another perk of flying first class was that your bags were the first off the plane, so you were out of the airport and in your taxi by the time the economy passengers were filtering through passport control.

Mia's heart fluttered again when she heard the thick tones of the taxi driver's Irish accent as he asked them where they were headed.

Joel held out an upturned hand to Mia, who realized he was giving her the option of where she wanted to go first. She paused for a moment, glancing at her time zone adjusted watch, before giving the driver the address of her flat in the city.

"We could head there first," she explained to Joel as they clambered into the back seat, "drop our things off before we head out."

Joel nodded, a musing smile playing on his features. Mia knew he was glad to see her so happy. Both Jackson and Joel had been right. Taking a few days was just what she and Joel had needed. Taking a few days in Ireland was *exactly* what Mia had needed.

Mia sat back in the plastic faux-leather seat of the taxi, the kind of seat covering that peeled away from your clothing as you got up from it. She stared longingly out of the window at the motorway before them that promised to take her back into the city she loved.

Los Angeles was incredible. Mia would readily admit that, but nothing in the world compared to the feeling of going home. Particularly after a long period of absence.

"Are you happy? Do you like the surprise?" Joel's deep Los Angeles accent jolted Mia out of her musings.

Though his hand was entwined with hers in her lap, her eyes were fixed on the passing stretch of motorway and the green fields beyond. She had almost forgotten he was sitting there, *almost*. One couldn't quite forget the nearby presence of a globally famous, drop-dead gorgeous rock star.

"Of course." She grinned from ear to ear. "More than happy. I just wasn't expecting this," she explained, pointing out of the window.

"Where did you think I was taking you?" he asked.

"I have no idea, really." Mia laughed. "Somewhere a short plane ride from LA?"

"I nearly hired the jet, but I didn't think you would approve," Joel said with his eyes sparkling. Black diamonds in a hand crafted piece of jewellery would never catch the light the way his eyes did, Mia thought.

"The jet?" she squeaked. "There's a *jet*?"

"The company has one, yes." Joel laughed. "But not me personally."

"Of course you don't," Mia replied with a hint of sarcasm.

"That's not a Dublin accent," the taxi driver called over his shoulder to Mia, interrupting their conversation.

Mia giggled quietly when she saw Joel squint in concentration as the driver spoke. He was going to need subtitles over the next few days.

"No, it's not. I'm originally from Kinsale," she replied.

"Ah, Kinsale, lovely place," the driver said, "been there more than a few times meself."

"Yeah, it's a quiet little place, not much going on."

"That's why you moved to Dublin, eh?" he said, grinning at her in his rear view mirror, "bit more going on for you young ones?"

"Yeah, something like that." Mia laughed as Joel scrunched up his face again in concentration. "Don't worry, not everyone's accent is so broad," she whispered to him when the taxi driver fell quiet at the next set of traffic lights.

"Thank God," Joel muttered.

જીજીજી

Locking the door behind them, Mia tried not to shake her head in disbelief. The last time she had locked that same door, she had been carrying a few more bags and a plane ticket to Los Angeles. How much had changed since then. She certainly hadn't expected to be arriving with Joel Coben the next time she opened that door.

Mia had shown Joel around her tiny flat in Dublin, trying not to blush as she realized how different it was to the life he was used to. Joel, of course, never batted a long-lash-laden eyelid at any of it. He took everything in with a smile, kind words, or that deep brooding stare of his that Mia knew meant he was analyzing everything he saw.

Due to the time difference and eleven hours of sitting in the same place, they had both slept for most of the flight to Dublin, so after dropping their things off at Mia's flat, showering, and changing their clothes, the last thing either of them wanted to do was sit down again.

"There's somewhere I want to take you," she said as they prepared to leave.

Joel grinned, taking her in his arms and kissing her deeply. "Now, I wonder where that could be."

"Or maybe we could just stay here," she said, her breath coming deeper than usual after his kiss.

"Tempting offer." Joel's smile creased up one side of his face into that lopsided smile that Mia loved so much. He leaned in and kissed her again, pulling her body against his and lifting her off the ground momentarily.

She laughed as he set her down again. "Make me leave now, before I change my mind."

Locking the door behind them, Mia briefly wondered if she had made the right decision. Joel's offer certainly was appealing.

They descended the stairs and stepped out onto the street, Mia pausing to admire the view she was so used to seeing. Despite the gray sky overhead, Joel had his sunglasses back on and a hood pulled up over his head. Mia knew it wouldn't be long before he was recognized. They had been stopped four times already since getting off the plane.

"Do want me to grab a taxi?" she asked hesitantly, watching as several black cabs went whizzing past.

"No," he said, "we came here to see the place, for you to see your home again. Let's walk."

Mia raised an eyebrow at him, still unsure if this was such a good idea. "Okay."

Surprisingly, they made their way through the early evening crowds of Dublin fairly effortlessly. They strode hand in hand along Grafton Street, even stopping to listen to a few of the busking musicians who were ever present along Dublin's famous street. They mingled inconspicuously amongst the tourists and locals that gathered around the buskers to watch. Mia smiled to herself as the familiar sounds of her beloved city drifted into her ears, the sounds of the Irish buskers on the streets soaking back into her veins. How she had missed them. The sounds in Los Angeles would never quite compare.

Even Joel, with all his years' experience touring the world and making multi-million-copy-selling albums was

impressed and awed by the music he saw and heard along
the streets of Dublin.

There was something about the raw authenticity of hearing the buskers that couldn't be found anywhere else in the
world. The guitars strummed out into the evening night, the
Gaelic accents sang soulfully, their words drifting into the
twilight skies.

Los Angeles was where dreams came true, but Dublin
was where Mia's dreams were born. The streets of the City
of Angels were filled with try-hards and wannabes. Everyone in Los Angeles was trying to get somewhere, trying to
be someone else. Nothing in Los Angeles was ever good
enough. Everyone wanted something more than they already had.

Back on home soil, Mia could appreciate the raw sounds
of the music she loved. These guys weren't vying for a record deal or hoping they would be spotted by Simon Cowell
out to lunch. They were simply happy to share their music
with the crowds. All they wanted to do was perform, to
make music, and this is where they lived that simple dream.

"This is what it's all about," Joel said quietly to her, as
they watched a five-piece band play acoustically to a huge
crowd, "stripping it all back, just the music and the raw love
for it."

"I couldn't agree more." Mia smiled up at him. He had
seemingly been reading her thoughts again.

Knowing they were on the same wavelength was both
surreal and comforting.

"You ready to show me where your magic happened?"
he asked.

Mia looked up at her own reflection staring back at her
from his mirrored sunglasses and grinned at herself. "I can't
wait."

Having only been recognized twice on their way down
Temple Bar, Mia was relieved she had gotten to Glen's
Tavern with Joel so effortlessly.

Word would soon spread that he was in the city. She

knew how fast social media would announce his presence in Dublin to the world.

Pushing open the front door, Mia felt more like she was coming home than she did when she had opened the front door to her flat. The wood paneling was still the same, the place still smelled the same, Ben and Dylan were still charming the crowds behind the bar, and the Poison tribute act were once again warming up the crowd for the evening.

Mia took Joel by the hand, noticing his puzzled look as he took in the band on the stage, and led him toward the bar. She spied Glen perching on a bar stool talking to a regular customer and sneaked up behind him.

"I see you're hard at work as always," she said in his ear.

"Jeysus." He jumped in his seat in surprise, spinning around to face her, startled at realizing who was there. "Bloody hell, Mia! What the devil are you doing here?"

"It's nice to see you too," she teased as he got up and embraced her warmly.

"No, love, it's just a surprise that's all!"

"I know, we're only here for a few days," she explained.

"We?" Glen asked. As he asked, he glanced over her shoulder. Immediately recognizing who she was with, he spluttered and blushed. "Jeysus! Bloody hell!"

Mia laughed. "Glen, I want you to meet Joel. Joel, this is my boss and good friend Glen."

"It's a pleasure to meet you." Joel held out his hand to Glen, who shook it, a look of utter disbelief plastered on his usually tranquil features.

"I'm a huge, huge fan," Glen managed at last. "I saw you last time you toured here, fantastic, absolutely fantastic."

Joel smiled politely. "Thank you, I appreciate that."

"Bloody hell, it's Mia!" Ben called from behind the bar, flinging open the hatch with a loud bang and dashing over to see her.

"Hey, stranger," she said as he hugged her tightly. "I've missed you guys."

"Missed *us*? You've been in LA. We've bloody missed

you, though," he said, letting her go, the dimples in his cheeks rising as he grinned at her.

"Missed having someone to pick on, more like," she teased.

"Well, something like that." Ben shrugged with a mischievous glint in his eye, "Dyl! Look who's here!" he called toward the bar, interrupting Dylan who was serving a gawking group of Chinese tourists.

Dylan thrust the change into the Chinese girl's hand, who snapped another picture of him on her giant camera before turning to her friends and giggling.

"Mia! How the devil are ye?" Dylan called in his broadest accent.

"Not bad, Dylan. How's life treating you?"

"Aye, grand." He hugged her before clapping Joel on the shoulder. "You doing all right, Joel?"

"Yeah, great thanks," Joel said, man-hugging Dylan in return.

Mia laughed at Ben's open-mouthed reaction to Dylan casually greeting one of the biggest rock stars in the world.

"Joel, this is my friend Ben," Mia said, gesturing to the gob-smacked Ben.

"Nice to meet you," Joel said, shaking his hand.

Ben nodded in return, still staring open-mouthed at Joel.

"*Mia!*"

That high-pitched shriek could only mean one thing. Niamh had worked her way back across the bar and spotted who had arrived. The teeny body that belonged to the giant pair of lungs flung itself around Mia, nearly toppling her over.

Dylan laughed as Mia regained her composure. "That's my girl."

"I've missed you," Niamh said, squeezing Mia even tighter.

Mia laughed, trying to manoeuvre out of the suffocating hold. "I've missed you too."

"You guys want a drink?" Glen asked, sliding behind the abandoned bar.

Mia looked at Joel who nodded in agreement. "Sure."

Mia took Glen's recently vacated bar stool and Joel sat down beside her. One by one, her friends reluctantly returned to work, with Glen promising he would keep the bar open for them to catch up once the customers had left.

Sipping on her drink and soaking up the familiar atmosphere of Glen's, Mia whiled away the remaining hours the bar was open by talking to Joel and listening to the changing line up of artists on the stage. She intermittently caught up with her friends, between them serving customers and clearing tables.

As Joel draped his arm around her shoulders, she leaned into him, relaxing in his arms to the sounds of an acoustic guitar and a lone voice through the microphone. Jackson was right. This was exactly what she had needed. She needed to come home again, to feel what made her feel human again, to remind her why she went to Los Angeles in the first place.

She did feel at home. Despite having a world-famous rock star boyfriend by her side, she felt back where she belonged. And for several precious hours, neither she nor Joel was photographed, questioned, followed, or asked for an autograph. For several precious hours, neither of them thought about lawsuits, libellous models, ostentatious rock stars, six-figure record deals, or hounds of paparazzi.

For several precious hours, they were simply Mia and Joel.

Chapter 16

As Joel pulled the car to a stop, Mia opened her eyes and looked around her. It was night time and, by the looks of things, they had been driving for a few hours. Dusk had only begun to settle when she had closed her eyes, leaning her head on the passenger seat headrest.

Joel had a habit of organising things when Mia was asleep, she was quickly learning. Another thing she was learning was that she must be a really heavy sleeper. She had woken in her own bed in Dublin, her head still pounding from the night before, to find Joel dangling a set of car keys in front of her face, shortly followed by a large mug of coffee.

She was worried he had gone and bought another car, but Joel quickly reassured her he had only hired one for the few days they had left in Ireland. Once Mia had gotten out of bed and ready, and after they had seen her friends again for lunch, Joel had taken her for a drive out of the city and into the Irish countryside that she admired so much.

She loosened out the kinks in her neck and sat up straight in her seat, undoing her seatbelt. "Where are we?"

Joel smiled in the low light. "Somewhere only we know."

"That sounds perfect." Mia smiled back and Joel caressed her cheek with his palm, kissing her once before getting out of the car and coming round to open her door.

"After you." He held out his hand to Mia, gentlemanly escorting her from the car.

Mia giggled as Joel held her hand aloft before bringing it to his lips and kissing the back of it.

"I've missed this," he said softly as he brought his face down to hers, his arms now around her waist.

"What?" Mia asked.

"Us," he replied, a trace of a smile lingering on his lips, "just us. Just you and me. No media, no studios, no one. Just us."

"*That* sounds perfect," Mia reiterated.

Joel allowed his smile to break across his full lips before bringing them down to hers. 'I've missed us.' His lips traced the edges of hers as he spoke. "I'm sorry it's gotten so crazy recently."

"Ssh," Mia hushed him, running her hand up his neck and into his hair before gently pushing his head down.

She felt his body relax against hers and his deep, tense breath escape him as he kissed her. Their hands didn't rove across each other's bodies. They were tightly clinging to each other's waists, holding them close together.

Mia smiled against Joel's lips as she broke their kiss, threading her arms up and around his neck, taking a moment to marvel at the beautiful man before her and that he was all hers, grateful that, for tonight, she didn't have to share him with the world.

"Come with me." He tugged one of her hands free and stepped away, leading her around the front of the car.

Finally averting her eyes from the beauty before her, Mia stopped to appreciate the beauty that surrounded her.

Joel had parked the car close to the edge of a cliff. Trees were on either side of the path but they cleared as they neared the cliffs edge.

Beyond the cliff, Mia could see and hear the ocean. The

familiar sound of its waves lapping against the shore reminded her of home.

Far below them, farther along the coastline, was a small town, its few lights twinkling in the distance.

Mia looked again.

The way the land rolled down to the coast, the scattering of houses up the coast before the clustered town at the bay. She would recognize that sight anywhere. No matter how long ago she last saw it, it would forever be etched into her mind. She could close her eyes at night in Los Angeles and picture every last contour of that hillside. She could close her ears to the sounds of the Los Angeles highways and the nightlife beyond her window and imagine every last crash of those waves against the shore. Some things were never forgotten.

Mia could never see this place again and still be able to remember every last detail.

Kinsale. The pretty little town in the distance sparkled its night-time lights back at her. It seemed to be winking in response to her unasked question.

Joel stood quietly beside her, his eyes watching as she stared across the bay at the town. He knew she knew. He was just waiting for her to say it.

Peeling her eyes away from the sight before her, she saw an almost identical one staring back. The dozens of little lights from the town in the bay were reflected back in Joel's eyes, the near blackness a mirror image of the night sky.

"You drove us to *Kinsale*?" she marveled.

Joel nodded. A glimmer of a smile crept across his face. "I thought you could use a day or two back here," he added.

"Oh, Joel." She sighed, pulling him back to her. "It's perfect, thank you."

Joel finally smiled fully, showing Mia his beautiful features in all their glory. He motioned back to the car. "Come here."

"What—" Mia didn't get to finish her sentence.

Joel sat down on the car bonnet, sliding himself across

the smooth metal before patting the space beside him for Mia to join him.

Mia let out a small laugh before climbing onto the car and sliding across to his side, where he wrapped his arms around her body and lay back against the car windscreen.

"But I'd like to keep you to myself for a while longer first," he said as she rested her head on his chest.

"That's quite all right with me," she said to the curve of his pectoral muscle.

She lay in the crook of Joel's shoulder, his arms around her body and his fingers twirling around her hair.

They both were quite for a while, appreciating the silence, the remoteness of it all. They had only the stars for company. An endless black abyss stared back down at them both as they lay against the windscreen. Thousands upon thousands of twinkling stars littered the black sky above the sleepy little town of Kinsale, a sky that was a few shades darker than the eyes of the man beside Mia, eyes that were fixed upon their near mirror image above him.

The night around them was quiet. The only sounds Mia could hear were the waves hitting the shore in the distance and the rhythmic rise and fall of Joel's breathing beneath her cheek. This was why they had boarded that flight out of Los Angeles. Peace and quiet, stillness and tranquillity. No media, no madness, no nothing. Just each other's presence and comfort and the endless expanse of the night before them.

And, for now, the quiet and the solitary company of the stars was all they needed.

Mia had no idea how long they stayed like that—laying in each other's arms and staring at the night sky. It was, in a way, their own form of meditation.

They could have stayed that way for hours, or maybe just minutes. After what seemed like forever, she untangled herself from Joel. She sat up on the car bonnet and hugged her knees. Her back felt stiff from laying against the windscreen for so long.

Joel stayed where he was, his hand simply left her waist and trailed to her lower back as she sat up, still letting her know he was there with her.

Her quieted thoughts were beginning to run away with her the more she sat and pondered. She sighed, staring out across the endless expanse of midnight blue. "I'm confused Joel."

Somewhere out there the dark night sky met the ocean on the horizon line, but it had grown too dark to distinguish one from the other. The ocean reflected the darkness of the sky and the scattered stars were reflected back on the water's surface. It was impossible to tell where one ended and the other began.

"I know," he whispered softly.

"I finally felt like everything was falling into place. I had my place at Sixth String Studios, I felt like I was making friends and settling in, I had you—" She smiled down at him. "—and then the accident happened and everything seems so different since then."

"You still have all of those things," Joel reminded her, "and more besides."

"I know." She sighed again. "I can't quite explain it. I know I haven't lost any of those things. It's just that things have been so manic recently. With Adam and Lucy and then Sky Records and everything else that's happened, it just feels like a lot to deal with."

"I know. It is a lot for anyone to deal with, especially in such a short space of time."

Mia knew he understood. He was just prompting her along, allowing her to continue rambling.

"I mean, don't get me wrong, I finally got the deal I wanted so badly, but then someone else goes and offers me something bigger. I was happy with the contract I had. Why do they have to go and throw something else into the mix?"

Joel laughed up at the night sky. "I'd take that as a compliment."

"I know, I do." She laughed too. "Really, I do. I guess it

just tainted the contract I'd already signed, it made me question what I already had."

"Which is only natural," Joel reassured her, his palm caressing her back.

"I guess so. And then there's Luke. I mean, it's not every day a long-lost brother you'd thought was dead shows up in your life."

"No, it's not. That'll take some readjusting. You guys need to build bridges you never had, you need to try and forge a relationship with a virtual stranger that you should have had your whole life."

Mia nodded. "I've waited so long for him to come back into my life, for so long I've been hoping and praying, and now that he's here, I've no idea what to do. Don't get me wrong, I wouldn't undo what has happened. It's just taking some getting used to." Mia glanced back at Joel and he smiled up at her reassuringly. She turned back to look at the ocean and Kinsale as she thought aloud, finally letting it all out. "The uncertainty over him was what defined me, and most importantly my music. I feel at a loss with my music now that I finally have what I've been writing about back in my life."

"You'll figure it out, Mia. You couldn't keep rewriting about the same thing, time after time anyway. You'd need some fresh ideas. You're a talented woman. You'll know what to do."

Mia sighed. Joel was right. He was always right.

"But Sky Records?" she began, her mind switching to ramble on another tangent, "and Adam? Lucy? The media?"

"Don't even begin to worry about the last three on that list." Joel sat up beside her and kissed her cheek. "We're here to forget about those, remember?"

"I know, I'm just venting."

"I know, that's what we came here for. To forget about it, to let it all out, and to help us along with it," he soothed. "It's all part of the process. You've kept things bottled up for so long, I think you need to talk about it. There's no need to think about Lucy, that's been taken care of. Adam won't be bothering you again, I'm pretty sure he learned his lesson. The media are always going to be in our lives. They'll come and go with intensity when there's a new story. It's just part of our job description. It's a pain in the ass at times, but they're a direct link to our fans, and they're the people who keep us where we are."

"That's true," Mia agreed.

"I know I was a total jerk about all of this stuff before I met you, but you've made me realize I had my head up my ass for too long," Joel confessed, making Mia laugh. "I couldn't ignore the media forever. They have their pros and cons, but ultimately, our fans like to know what's happening and to read about us. If it's done in the right way, then it's the best tool there is. Too many celebrities, myself included previously, are ignorant to the media and the fact that it links ourselves with our fans and, at the end of the day, the fans are what matter the most. They're the people who buy our music, who come to our shows, and support our dreams. Without them, there would be no studios, no recording, no tours, no nothing. We just have to accept that the connecting link is a bit of a temperamental one."

Mia laughed, smiling to herself at Joel's wisdom. He was right, of course.

"But I don't think you need to worry about Sky Records. It's only playing on your mind because of the monetary value. It's made you question what Sixth String offered you. There will always be offers on the table. They come and go with each new success. I've been offered more lucrative contracts than you can imagine. They're always coming up with something else. You just need to stay loyal to those who gave you your break in the first place. As long as they're taking care of you and your music, you have no reason to switch sides. Just remember all those people who turned you down originally. Sky Records could have been one of those. They only want you because they've now seen the finished product someone else saw the blueprint for. I think you already know what you're going to do. You've known all along really."

Mia turned her head to look at him. There was so much depth to this man.

And he understood how deep her own soul was. She knew he was thinking the same as he gazed back at her, his eyes analyzing hers, piecing together the picture of the soul within.

She nodded. She knew, she already knew. They both knew. That, she realized, was what they had come here for. For clarity, for reassurance, for solidity in their decisions.

Joel nudged her playfully. "Besides, we couldn't be rivals anyway."

Mia laughed and lay back down on the bonnet of the car, staring back up at the night sky, feeling calmer now that she had vented her frustrations. "No, we couldn't," she said as he lay beside her. "I hope you realize just how much money I'm turning down for you."

Joel pointed at his chest. "For me?"

"Yes, you," she teased, "I couldn't record an album without your face showing up in the doorway every five minutes."

Joel nuzzled in closer to her. "Ah, you'd miss me too much."

She ran her hand through his ever messy hair. "Yes, I suppose I would eventually miss this face."

"Even if it's costing you a few million?" he asked.

"Even if it's costing me a multi-million dollar record deal." she laughed as he kissed her.

"I'll write you a check," he said against her lips, pulling her body closer to him.

The last thing she saw before she closed her eyes was Joel's face staring lovingly down at her, silhouetted by the night sky and Mia's own, personal stars were shining back at her from within his eyes.

Chapter 17

Dawn was beginning to peak over the Irish vales, the soft glow of morning light rising from the rolling hills toward the ocean where the first tinges of sunlight were peaking from the horizon.

Mia cracked open the passenger window and took a huge inhale, feeling the cold, crisp air fill her lungs and whip about her face as it rushed in from the ocean. Seagulls cawed in the distance, their seemingly eternal presence and raucous noise hovered about the bay.

No matter where you went in Kinsale, there were seagulls. That constant cawing and shrieking was something Mia didn't miss in Los Angeles. Dublin also had its fair share of the pesky birds, but nothing compared to Kinsale. Dozens of them were soaring about the coastline, searching for their morning meal in the early light of dawn.

Mia and Joel had lain on the bonnet of the car talking and stargazing until the early hours, sometimes dozing in each other's arms before rousing on the cold metal beneath them.

Mia could feel the ache in her back from lying on the car's hood for a few hours. She would be grateful to see her own bed at the end of the day. She didn't think she could make it until that evening. Jet lag was still reigning over both her and Joel. They hadn't had chance to sleep off the time difference between LA and Dublin yet.

The car coasted down the slow incline of the hill. The sleepy town of Kinsale was beginning to rise for the day as they approached. Few cars passed them on their route into town. The early morning commuters were still brushing their teeth in the comfort of their little houses at this hour of day.

Mia watched as the first fishing boats of the morning began to sail out toward the horizon where the sun was rising higher.

What a sight to behold.

Those fishermen must have the best view in Ireland right now—the sleepy town behind them coming to life in the rising light and the sun peaking above the horizon line before them on a tranquilly calm ocean.

Mia's eyes froze for a moment as she watched the fishing boats, reminded immediately of Luke. She wondered what his morning view would look like back home in Koh Li Pe. Was his view just as idyllic as what she was now seeing? Probably even more than this, Mia realized. The paradise islands would look spectacular in the light of dawn.

She wondered when she would get a chance to visit Luke in his adopted home, to experience his life, and meet the woman he adored. She wondered if he would let her come out on the fishing boat with him, to gaze out across the waters of the Malacca Strait as she was now doing from the Irish coast.

She had previously wondered when she would get to do what she was now doing with Joel and realized that Luke would probably be showing her around Koh Li Pe sooner than she imagined.

Joel drove slowly through the small town to reach their destination on the other side of Kinsale, his eyes scanning everything he saw.

The shops were still closed, their owners and customers

not yet risen for the day. The pubs were locked up, their landlords and patrons only recently having vacated for the night.

Soon the small town would be awash with summer tourists that crawled the narrow streets hunting for touristy gimmicks in the little souvenir shops before searching for the nearest pub to drink a pint of Guinness and eat a bowl of Irish stew.

Joel chuckled to himself at the sight of a large leprechaun statue outside one of the shops. Mia hated the damn thing, with its bright green hat and neon orange beard. All day long the tourists would stop outside and pose for a picture beside him before heading in and buying all nature of things adorned with shamrocks and Guinness's. It kept the town afloat, she had to admit. Without the tourists, there would be very little still surviving in Kinsale.

"Left here and straight up the hill," she said to Joel as they reached a traffic light.

Joel nodded, still staring out of the windscreen at everything he saw. He had stopped the car for a moment when she pointed out the pub she used to work in, the place that had given Mia her very first stage to perform on.

Joel had paused, gazing all meaningful at the little place, and Mia knew he was picturing her performing inside there. He was taking in every detail of what made her the person he knew today. He dropped the car into a lower gear as they climbed the steeper incline toward their destination. She felt her heart flutter with familiarization when she could see a light on in the distance.

She gave Joel his last few brief directions and gradually the car came to a stop outside the little house that overlooked the Kinsale town and the bay beyond.

Mia was truly home.

There was no feeling in the world that compared to the feeling she had for this little house overlooking the bay. While she had lived in Dublin for a few years, Kinsale was still her hometown and always would be. Nothing else would ever replace the spot it held in her heart. The stirring in her soul, the butterflies in her stomach, the comforting feeling, and eagerness to see everything that was familiar and safe all danced around her as they had approached the house.

Joel smiled knowingly. "You're finally home."

Of course, he knew what she was thinking. They were so in tune, sometimes it scared her.

She nodded, staring back at her second most comforting, familiar feeling in the world.

Joel's eyes.

Their never ending depths, the radiance in those nearly black abysses, quietened her soul like nothing else. She felt she had seen them before somewhere. Her soul recognized them, perhaps from a thousand lifetimes before this one. She knew they were connected, that they knew one another in a way that needed no words.

Entwining one hand in hers and squeezing tightly, Joel placed his other hand on Mia's cheek, pulling her toward him and kissing her tenderly on the lips.

It was all she needed, that simple reminder that he was hers, that he was with her one-hundred percent of the way. And she was his. No matter what the world might throw at them, they would always be together.

"Let's go," he said in barely a whisper, his hand still on her cheek and his eyes taking one final, deep stare into her soul before he got out of the car.

Mia shook her head a little. How did she manage to get someone like Joel? How did she end up this lucky?

"You coming?" he said with a twinkle in those glimmering eyes, a playful smile on his features as he held the door open for her.

"Of course." She laughed as she got out of the car, her bones still aching from sitting for so long in one place or another recently. She sighed as she stretched her arms above her head, trying to release some of the aching and tension. "I think we should go for a walk later."

"Sounds good to me," Joel said as he stared up at the hills behind the house.

"But first there's some people I want you to meet," Mia said as she held out her hand to him.

"I'd love to," he said, taking her hand.

Rekindling her emotions of coming home, Mia felt giddy as she saw the light on in the kitchen. She resisted the urge to run up the driveway and straight through the front door. Knowing someone was awake in the house made her eager to get home. It just wasn't the same arriving home to an empty or sleeping house.

Sharon and Mike had always been early risers. They didn't believe in wasting half the day sleeping. Weekends were the same as any regular day. Mia knew they would be sitting in the front room with their morning coffee watching the seven a.m. news, as they did through the week before Mike went to work for the day.

Mike was a joiner, a man who believed in real men's work and grafting long and hard for a living. Mia smiled comfortingly at the sight of the garage beside the house and the two cars parked outside. Mike had long ago turned the garage into a workshop and virtually everything in the house was handmade. The kitchen, the cupboards, wardrobes, coffee tables, even bed frames were all handmade by the man of the house. Men like Mike were a dying breed, Mia thought sadly.

Sharon was a midwife. A woman with seemingly never-ending love for children had found contentment in her ideal career. Mia knew the job suited her perfectly. Sharon adored children and working with them. Bringing them into the world gave her the biggest sense of fulfilment she could ever ask for. It was Sharon's purpose in life.

She had even talked about fostering children when Mia had left home, her desire for more children reignited now the house was empty again. Mia wondered if she had had any luck in persuading Mike to start again with the fostering process. They had tried it years ago, not long after Mia had left for Dublin, and had fostered two young sisters, but their plans were put on hold when Sharon had been taken ill for a while.

Her and Joel's footsteps were faint on the paving stones beneath their feet. Mia knew Sharon and Mike wouldn't hear them coming up to the house. She hadn't wanted to tell them she and Joel were coming. She had wanted to surprise them. It was early Sunday morning and Mia knew she could have a whole day with her adoptive parents before they returned to work in the morning.

Her knuckles rapped softly on the wooden front door, something else which Mike had hand crafted.

Mia heard the clink of a cup settling on the coffee table followed by shuffled footsteps hurrying toward the front door.

She turned to briefly look at Joel standing beside her on the front step, his hand still securely in hers. He smiled reassuringly back at her, but Mia could have sworn she saw a flicker of nerves cross his features. Joel Coben was nervous about meeting the parents, Mia mused and had to try desperately to contain a little giggle of glee.

The clicking of a bolt sliding back followed by a key turning in the lock snapped Mia's attention back to the front door just in time.

"Mia!" Sharon squealed loud enough to wake up the whole bay.

She dashed over the front step, so eager to greet Mia that she practically fell into Mia's arms.

Mia was immediately reminded why her adoptive mother and her best friend got on so well as she was gripped in a vice like clamp, her ears still ringing from her greeting.

She hugged her back, inhaling her familiar scent and the comforting smell of home drifting in from the open door. Mia found herself letting go. Her tension evaporated, her stresses vanished as she squeezed Sharon tighter. No, she reminded herself, nothing in the world compared to coming home.

"Oh, love, I've missed ye so much," Sharon gushed, relief outpouring from her voice and tears of happiness running down her face as she pulled back to take a look at Mia.

Mia felt her own tears begin to fall down her cheeks as she stared back at Sharon's familiar, yet watery eyes. "I've missed you both too."

"I'm glad you're home, Mia," came a deeper Irish voice from the hall behind them.

Mia looked up to see Mike standing in the doorway, watery eyes and all at the sight of her arriving home.

He was closely followed by a four legged friend who came careering through the front door faster than Sharon had.

Mia reached down to pet their retriever Max, who greeted Mia with overly enthusiastic tail wagging and licking of her hand before bounding across to Joel to sniff out the newcomer.

"Me too," she said, reaching up to Mike to hug the strong, safe embrace that only came from a father figure.

A heavy, strong hand patted her on the back as he held her before he let her go and took her hands in his. Mia felt the rough, calloused palms of a man who had worked his entire life in her softer ones. The years of hard labor could be felt in his hands.

His tired eyes crinkled as he smiled. "It's so good to see you."

"And who's this?" Sharon asked from behind them.

Mia turned on the step to see Sharon smiling appreciatively and inquisitively at Joel who had taken a step back to allow Mia a moment with her family.

Mia chuckled to herself. Stepping back down she introduced Joel. "Sharon, this is Joel. Joel I'd like you to meet my adoptive mum, Sharon," she said smiling to herself at the blush now creeping across Sharon's face.

Here we go again, Mia thought.

"It's lovely to finally meet you," Joel said, holding out his non-dog-drool-covered hand, much to Max's dismay.

"Oh, away with ye." Sharon dismissed his hand, pulling him in for a hug. "It's grand to finally meet you, love."

Mia laughed as Joel was grabbed and hugged enthusiastically by Sharon. No amount of schoolgirl blushing was going to deprive Sharon of her Irish hospitality.

Mike simply shook his head and rolled his eyes, a knowing smile on his face.

Mia laughed again as Joel was released, looking a little dishevelled. Now she knew how to make a world famous rock star blush, just bring him home to your parents.

Mike held out his hand to Joel. "Nice to meet you, kid."

"And you, sir," Joel replied as Mike shook his hand, clapping him on the back.

Mike thumbed over his shoulder in the direction of the living room. "Come on in you lot, get out of the cold."

"You're letting the bloody heating out, in other words, he means," Sharon muttered after Mike as she followed Mia and Joel into the house.

Mia giggled to herself at the familiar sound of Mike and Sharon's marital bickerings. "You know you're home."

Joel laughed beside her, a smile on his features as he took in everything he saw inside Mia's childhood home.

The TV continued with the news in the corner of the living room. The sofas looked as inviting as ever. The coffee stain near the table, where Mia once spilled her drink which Sharon had desperately tried to cover up by repositioning the furniture, was still there. Mia's childhood pictures were on the mantelpiece. Mike and Sharon's wedding photo hung in the corner of the room. The light from the spectacular view outside the kitchen window fell into the room the same way it always had. Everything, Mia saw, was the same.

It was as if she'd never left.

She half expected to see herself stumbling down the stairs still half asleep in her pyjamas in search of the source of the coffee smell that wafted up the stairs every morning.

"Do you both want a drink?" Sharon asked as she bustled into the kitchen and restarted the coffee machine.

They would both end up with a drink regardless of their answer, but Mia and Joel both replied that they would.

"Come sit down," Mike said as he returned to his favourite chair. God forbid if anyone else ever sat in that chair, Mia remembered fondly.

Mia sat down in the middle of the sofa and sank down into the cushions, resting her head temporarily on the back she closed her eyes, grateful to be home.

Max did an obligatory lap around the living room before settling at Mia and Joel's feet, tilting his head back and panting heavily as they petted his head.

It was the simple things like these that she missed— sitting in the front room, drinking coffee, with Sharon and Max's never-ending affection—that left a void in her life. Life had gotten so busy recently. How had she allowed herself to stay away from home for so long?

"Just like always," Sharon muttered as she stepped over Mia's outstretched legs to sit beside her.

Mia laughed as she opened her eyes to see Joel on one side of her and Sharon on the other.

"Never was a morning person, this girl," Sharon said to Joel, gesturing at Mia.

"Because of my job!" Mia explained.

"If you say so." Sharon rolled her eyes. "Being a teenager, more like."

Mike winked at Mia from across the room, staying as silent as ever. He knew better than to get involved.

"Anyway." Sharon swiftly changed the topic, patting Mia affectionately on the knee. "How are ye, love? It feels like you've been gone for ages."

"It does," Mia agreed.

"But you're doing okay? You're still enjoying Los Angeles?"

Mia knew there would be an endless stream of questions directed at her while she was home. She sighed heavily. "Yeah, things have just been a little hectic recently."

"You said so on the phone." Sharon nodded. "What's

wrong, love?"

"Nothing's wrong, I guess. We just needed to come home for a few days." Mia smiled, remembering what Joel had told her earlier.

He was right, nothing was really wrong.

"You've had a busy few months, Mia," Sharon agreed with a smile. "A few days home will do you good."

"Hmph," Mike grunted from across the room.

Mia looked over at him and laughed. He knew all too well how interrogating Sharon could be.

Sharon rolled her eyes. Mia wondered if she would throw the cushion at him, like she usually did.

"But something's changed." Sharon's face darkened. "Something's brought you home for a reason."

Mia let out a deep exhale, Sharon knew her too well. She looked at Joel for support and he simply raised his eyebrows above the rim of his mug and shrugged. She should have known. "We just needed a couple of days to cool off. There was a lot of media around us, and we decided we could use a bit of breathing space. But other than that, I'm fine, I guess, great, in fact."

Mia smiled, putting aside the recent troubles they had. She had to admit life had been good to her.

"Are you sure, love?" Sharon asked, "It's perfectly normal not to be fine. You've had a lot going on and especially after the crash. Oh—"

Sharon's eyes welled up again and she began to fan herself to stop from crying.

Mia reached over and hugged her tightly.

"I was so worried about you. I could only watch it on the TV—it was heart breaking. Niamh and your friend Charlie phoned me all the time, but it's just not the same."

"I'm sorry," Mia sniffed.

"Oh, love." Sharon hugged her again. "It's not your fault. I just wish we could have been there with you. Joel, of course, was extremely generous in offering to fly us out. We can't thank you enough for that, Joel."

"Don't even mention it," Joel said quietly.

Mia knew Joel had offered to fly her adoptive parents out to Los Angeles after the crash but both Sharon and Mike wouldn't hear of it. Mia wondered if they'd thought of Joel's offer as an apology for his father being the cause of the crash. She knew the thought played heavily on Joel's mind. She could see his thoughts going into overdrive behind his dark eyes.

"How are you now, are you recovering well?" Sharon asked.

Mia shrugged. "I'm fine."

"Five days in and out of consciousness isn't fine, Mia," Mike's deep tones said from across the room.

"I know, I know," Mia agreed quietly, realizing how feeble her response had sounded. Her adoptive parents had been through hell on the other side of the world while she had been intensive care for five days. "I'm feeling much better," she added. "The first few days were tough but I was resting at Joel's house for a couple of weeks, and I'm back at work now. Joel's been taking great care of me."

Mike nodded at Joel. "Good. Thank you, Joel."

Sharon glanced across at Joel. "This can't have been easy for you either, Joel."

"No, it hasn't," he admitted. "But it's nothing compared to what Mia went through."

Everyone fell silent for a moment.

Sharon was still hugging Mia. Eventually she released her and held her at arm's length to analyze her. Mia knew she was looking for more than the physical signs that she was well again.

"You're coping well with all this press attention?" Sharon asked.

"Sort of," Mia said quietly.

"I saw what happened with that girl in the magazine." Sharon gestured to a copy of *Heat* magazine on the coffee table. "She said some awful things."

"Why do you buy that crap?" Mia sighed. "Yes, she said

a lot of untrue things, but that comes with the job description, I guess. There will be more like her. The media are always going to print things that aren't true."

"They will," Joel said beside her.

Sharon gave him a sympathetic smile.

"But aside from all that, life is good. I really can't complain. I got my recording deal, I've made some great friends, and I have Joel. Life is good right now."

Sharon opened her mouth to congratulate Mia on her recording deal. Though she'd already heard over the phone, Mia knew Sharon would be eager to congratulate her in person. it was what Mia had strived for years for. Sharon and Mike had been there through all Mia's years of hard work.

Instead, Mike butted in first. "So Joel's your boyfriend?" he asked bluntly.

Mia paused open mouthed, only a father could ask that.

Joel laughed, answering for her. "Yes."

"Hmm," Mike said, a contemplative look on his face.

"Mike…" Sharon warned.

"I said nothing." He held up his hands in surrender at her and Mia and Joel laughed.

"I'm sure you're taking very good care of our Mia," Sharon said to Joel.

"I am indeed, I promise," Joel said.

Sharon looked back at Mike and shook her head. He would be chastised for that later. Mia recognized that look.

"So tell me about Los Angeles, your friends, the studios. I want to hear everything," Sharon said again eagerly. "And we still need to celebrate your recording deal!"

Now that she had seen Mia was okay, all seriousness was forgotten, and Sharon was back to her usual self. It was easy to forget they hadn't seen each other since Mia left for Los Angeles a few months ago. Sharon had only heard snippets of Mia's life through long distance phone calls. Now that she was here, Sharon was going to want to hear the whole story again in detail.

Mia cast a quick glance at Joel. This was going to be a long day.

෧෧෧

There's no place like home and certainly no place like your own bed, Mia thought as she opened her eyes. Jet lag and endless quizzing from Sharon after a long night had eventually worn Mia out. By lunchtime, she was ready for a nap. Mike had taken Max for a long walk down by the beach, and Sharon began preparing dinner while Mia and Joel had crashed out in her room.

Mia thought her insides would burst from laughing at the look on Joel's face when Mike had suggested they sleep in separate rooms. It took him more than a moment to realize Mike was joking. Poor Joel, Mia thought, there really was nothing like your parents to embarrass your boyfriend, no matter who he might be.

After sleeping for a little longer than a couple of hours, Mia had opened her eyes on the familiar pillows of her own bed. She was still nestled in the crook of Joel's arm, the duvet hastily thrown on top of them, and they were still in their clothes from when they had instantly fallen asleep.

Earlier, Joel had begun looking at the pictures in Mia's room, the things on the shelves, books in the bookcase, and her old guitars on the rack before she had pulled him away from rummaging in her things and onto the bed. Neither of them had been in the mood for anything other than a long sleep, but Mia had wanted Joel to fall asleep with her, not to leave him poking through her childhood things as she slept.

A gentle kiss on her forehead told her he was now awake, probably awoken by her own stirring in his arms.

"Sleep well?" he asked groggily.

"Mmm," Mia murmured, snuggling back into his arms.

He let out a low chuckle, wrapping his arms tightly around her and pulling the duvet around them both so that they were in their own little cocoon.

"I don't want to get up," she mumbled again.

"Me neither," he whispered, resting his head on hers.

"We need to, though."

"No, we don't." Joel gripped her tighter, so she couldn't leave him.

Mia laughed, looking up into his tired eyes. Somehow they still sparkled, their almost blackness as radiant as ever, despite his lack of sleep. Mia doubted she looked anywhere near as good.

"We need a shower." She sighed, knowing she really did.

"Together?" Joel brightened.

Mia laughed. "I wish we could."

Joel's face fell playfully. "Please?"

He could pout well, Mia noticed. How could a girl refuse that look? Seeing his pleading face, she almost pulled him from their cocoon and into the bathroom, regardless that Sharon was downstairs.

"Maybe tomorrow, when they're at work?" she suggested, feeling like a teenager sneaking around the place all over again.

Joel immediately brightened again. "Sounds good to me," he said before kissing her deeply, a promise of what was to come.

His body was tightly pressed against her and his arms caressed her waist as his lips explored hers. Mia wound her legs around his jean-clad hips and heard a moan escape Joel's throat.

She closed her eyes and wished, for a few minutes, that they were back in her flat in Dublin or Joel's Los Angeles mansion.

The alluring, tingling feeling of his hand on her bare skin as his fingers traced up under her shirt and up her back only emphasised her desire to be alone with him. She allowed him to lift her T-shirt up over her head, and his hands caressed her bare skin. A deep exhale from his throat as his lips were against hers told her he felt the same.

Reminding herself of how teenage she already felt, she whispered, "How quiet do you think we can be?"

A devilish smile crossed Joel's face as she spoke and her hands tugged at the button of his jeans.

"Quiet enough," he whispered, an irresistible glint filled his eyes as he pulled the duvet up over their heads.

Chapter 18

Her nostrils flared involuntarily in her sleep. The sensation as familiar as it has always been, the delicious scent filled her nose and stirred her eyelids open in the early light of the morning.

Beside her in the entanglement of sheets, Joel lay sleeping peacefully, his senses undisturbed by the aroma that had stirred her. A soft morning light drifted into the room from under the curtains. Mia reached over and lifted the corner back to see the world outside her childhood bedroom.

Kinsale was as sleepy as she always remembered. The bay far down below the coast was coated in a thin veil of morning fog. The faint lights from houses and cars were pinpricks shining through the blanketed mist.

Farther out to sea, Mia could see the fishermen making their daily commute to work across the tranquil ocean. The little boats bobbed across the duck-pond-like water, slowly making their way toward the horizon.

Mia thought again of Luke and wondered when she could call him. It had been a few days since they had spoken, and Luke was still in Los Angeles, waiting for her return. His tourist visa would expire soon, and Mia wanted to see him as much as she could before he went home...well, between recording her album, she reminded herself.

The light spilled into the room and across the pillows. Mia quickly released the curtain and let it fall back into place, not wanting to wake Joel. She knew he was sound asleep. His shallow breathing told her he was out for the count. She was still feeling the effects of jet lag, traveling, and emotional exhaust, but her familiar routine was calling to her.

There was some other emotional turmoil that she needed to get out of her system, and the person she needed she would find with the source of the alluring aroma.

Pulling the duvet higher over his bare chest, Mia took a moment to admire Joel's naked chest. She still wondered how on earth a girl like her had managed to get a man like Joel Coben. Men like him didn't grow on trees, that was for sure.

There were the thousands of regular, run-of-the-mill-type guys and then there were the few exceptions in between. Joel was an in between, a one-in-a-million, catch-him-if-you-can-type of guy. How did a girl filter out the millions of masses to find the one that was right for her?

Somehow, Mia had managed it. Somehow her one in a million was sleeping peacefully in her childhood bedroom, his hair its usual unruly mess on his head, his long eyelashes resting on his cheeks as he slept. Mia ran a hand as lightly as she dared across his thick dark hair. No matter where she moved the strands, they still fell stylishly around his face. She wondered if she ruffled his hair, would he still look good? But then she thought better of it.

Trailing a hand down his neck, across his collarbone, and onto his toned chest, she traced the outline of his muscles before running her finger over the scripted ink across his collarbone. In long, swirling script, a text so ornate you had to be as close as she was to read it, it said, *Not All Who Wander Are Lost*.

Mia smiled to herself, picturing the man Joel was when he had had that tattoo inked.

She wondered if he ever felt alone still, if he ever felt as lost as she sometimes did. But not anymore, she reminded herself, looking at the exquisite man before her who was all hers.

Tucking the corners of the duvet under his chin, she quietly lifted herself from the bed and tiptoed across the room to the door. She stole Joel's hooded sweatshirt from the back of a chair before closing the door silently behind her, taking one final glance at his face nestled comfortably in her pillows. Once on the landing, she shrugged herself into his sweatshirt, zipping up the front over her pyjamas and pulling the hood over her head to snuggle up inside the warmth of the fabric and the comforting smell of Joel and his aftershave that mingled into the cotton.

Max was waiting for her at the bottom of the stairs, his long shaggy tail wagging eagerly as she padded toward him on the carpeted stairs. His front paws jumped up on the first steps and Mia could hear his panting breathing as she approached.

"Hey buddy," she cooed quietly to him, hoping he wouldn't bark and wake Joel up.

Max sniffed her hand and shoved his nose into her palm as soon as she was within reaching distance, desperate for some affection.

"Come on, let's go find Sharon," she whispered to him, ushering him toward the kitchen.

Sharon startled when Mia walked into the kitchen. "You're up early?"

Mia shrugged, peering over at the bubbling coffee pot on the counter. "Old habits die hard."

"It won't be a minute," Sharon said. "Sit down, love."

Mia heaved herself into the wooden chair at the kitchen table, plonking herself down in the first chair she reached.

"You still tired?" Sharon asked.

"Mmm," Mia mumbled, immediately regretting her decision to get out of bed and leave Joel. She really wasn't awake properly.

"Sleep well?" Sharon asked, sitting a large mug of black coffee in front of Mia before sitting in her own seat.

"Mmm," Mia said again over the first gulp of coffee.

Sharon laughed. "So come on, out with it?"

"Huh?" Mia asked.

Sharon laughed again. "English, love."

"Sorry," Mia said, finding her voice now that caffeine was flooding into her system.

"There's a reason you're awake so early and especially as that fine young man is still in your bed." Sharon raised her eyebrows with a smile. "And it's not just for the pleasure of my company."

"Actually, it sort of is," Mia said. "I've been wanting to talk to you, just you."

"I thought so."

"I mean, I love Joel, I really, really do, and of course Mike is like a father to me, but sometimes I just need a girl-ie chat."

Sharon smiled. "Girls need their mums."

Though Mia had never called Mike and Sharon her mum and dad—she had always felt she would be abandoning the memory of her own parents if she did—the two were like parents to her. Mike and Sharon were the closest thing she had.

"We do," Mia admitted, knowing Sharon would appreciate the confirmation.

"So tell me, what's on your mind?"

Mia sighed. "A lot of things."

"Go on?" Sharon prompted.

Mia ran a finger around the edge of her mug, watching the wisps of steam rising and disappearing into the air as she thought hard. "I just need to let it all out," she said with a meek laugh.

"I'm all ears," Sharon said, placing her hand over Mia's on the table.

Mia felt her guard wobble and falter before falling to the ground completely. It was hard work keeping up a front to the world. Bottling everything in was what Mia thought she did best with her feelings, only letting them out in the form of her music, but finally unscrewing the lid on that bottle to Sharon made her realize she was reaching the brim.

Mia knew she could tell Joel anything. Anything she could say to him, she knew he would sit and listen to her with a fixed gaze and a listening ear, quietly contemplating as she poured forth everything she needed to. He would understand, he would offer advice, and he would hold her when she had finished. But sometimes a girl just needed her mum. No one else in the world would do. Not even a drop-dead gorgeous, world-famous rock star boyfriend.

Mia sighed again when she eventually finished. "So I just feel a bit exhausted."

"I can imagine," Sharon replied. "Joel did right in bringing you home. I think you needed it."

Mia nodded.

Sharon smiled. "He knows you much better than you think."

Mia grinned back. "He does."

"But you left something out of all that rambling," Sharon said sombrely.

"What?"

"Luke."

"Oh."

Mia had only briefly touched on the subject of Luke. She had spoken to Sharon many times on the phone since the accident about Luke turning up at the hospital. She had told her everything Luke had told her about his life since leaving care, their catching up when Mia left hospital, and everything in between. But, somehow, Mia had only scratched the surface on how she felt about having her brother back in her life.

"Are you all right, Mia?" Sharon asked with a deep stare.

Mia stared back into Sharon's blue eyes. Eyes that couldn't be more different from her own emerald green ones, but still they were so familiar. They knew her too well. "I think so," she said. "I don't really know what to make of it. I guess I've waited all my life for him to come back. I never knew what had happened to him, I spent years searching for answers, and now I finally have those answers, I don't really know what to do with them."

"I think you do, love."

"What's that?"

"Write music."

Mia smiled. "I suppose you're right."

She had always turned to song writing, no matter what was happening in her life. Writing it all down and expressing it through her music was what made Mia who she was. It was her coping mechanism.

"But this is going to take some time," Sharon continued. "You can't just expect him to reappear after all this time and for everything to be okay. You're practically strangers. You're not little children anymore. You're not the separated siblings you were all those years ago. Don't rush things, that's all I'm saying."

Mia stared back at her.

"Just don't go charging into this head on, don't expect that lost bridge to spring back into shape. If you try to put that bridge up too soon, cracks will appear and things will go wrong. You need to give it time to strengthen and grow. Don't go asking for miracles, Mia."

"I know," Mia said, her voice small in the quiet of the kitchen.

"I know exactly how much you've missed him, and I'm sure he's missed you, but don't take things so quickly that you rush them. You can't expect that kind of relationship to forge overnight. Take it slowly, get to know each other again. It will seem strange, love, having this person in your life that you've searched for so long for."

"It does," Mia admitted. She still expected Luke to disappear as quickly as he had arrived. "I guess he got caught up in everything else that's happened," she continued, "with the crash, the record deal, Adam and Lucy, even Rebecca, the media—I guess Luke got caught up in all that some-where along the way."

"He was bound to. You've had a tough few months," Sharon said sympathetically.

Mia laughed. "I guess so."

"And don't worry about everything else, love, Joel's right. That will all blow over soon enough. You'll be yes-terday's news before you know it."

"Thanks!" Mia teased.

"You know what I mean. I mean, the gossip mill. You're career on the other hand—"

Mia waved a hand in front of her. "Okay, okay."

"What? I was just going to say how great you're going to be, and how proud we both are of ye."

"Thank you," Mia said, "but I don't want you jinxing anything, I've barely even started."

"It's the start of something great, though. I can just feel it, Mia. You've got the luck of the Irish on your side," Sha-ron said with a cheeky wink.

Mia laughed. "That's so cheesy."

"But it's true, I can just feel it. Big things are coming your way."

"She's right," said a deep voice from behind her in the kitchen.

Mia turned to see Joel leaning against the kitchen work-top in pyjama bottoms and a rumpled T-shirt. "How long have you been standing there?" she said, surprised.

Sharon shrugged before Joel could answer. "Oh not that long."

"I came looking for my sweatshirt, actually," he teased and Mia fidgeted with the edges of the sleeves.

"Sorry," she said. "It was the first thing I grabbed."

Joel laughed, a low chuckle, and came over to sit beside her at the table. "Yeah, right."

He ran a hand through his hair and Mia watched as the unruly strands fell around the edges of his face. Out of the corner of her eye, she noticed Sharon watching Joel too. It was hard not to. He just looked so good.

"I better be going to work," Sharon said a little too quickly and jumped up from the table. She clattered around in the kitchen cupboard before producing another mug and swiftly filling it with coffee, placing it in front of Joel before she left. "I'll see you both later on. I'll be back after my shift."

Mia stood up and gave her a hug as she left. "See you later."

"Bye," Sharon called over her shoulder from down the hall.

The front door opened and closed with its usual thud, and that noise told Mia she and Joel were alone in the house again.

Mia let out a deep exhale, stretching her arms over her head. It felt good to let everything off her chest, to hear a familiar voice and a sympathetic ear letting her know she wasn't going crazy, after all.

"You okay?" Joel's voice sounded thoughtful.

"I'm great." Mia smiled. "This trip was a good idea."

Joel smiled back. "I'm glad you think so."

He held out a hand to her and Mia walked back across the kitchen to where he sat, his eyes looking up at her from under his messy hair.

Curling his long fingers around her hand, Joel pulled her gently into his lap. Mia tucked her feet underneath her and nestled against his chest, feeling his toned arms wrap securely around her body.

Joel brushed a strand of her hair out of her face and lightly kissed the top of her forehead.

"What do you want to do today?" he asked.

"I've no idea," Mia said, wondrous that they had an entire day free from commitments and the prying eyes of the media to themselves.

"How about that walk you were telling me about?"

Chapter 19

This place is so colorful," Joel mused aloud as they strolled hand in hand through the little town of Kinsale.

Mia smiled up at him. "It is."

Many of the shops, buildings, and even houses in Kinsale, were painted bright colors. The deep red bookshop on the corner of the street they were now passing always caught Mia's eye. Neat little rows of houses and shops painted alternating blues, yellows, greens, and even a few pinks stared back at them from the gaps of opening side streets.

Mia had wanted to walk along the beach and up into the hills around Kinsale, but Joel had insisted on seeing more of the town where she grew up.

Unsurprisingly, there were few people walking the streets so early on a Monday morning. Mia knew that, in a matter of hours, there would be a few more hundred tourists dawdling through the little narrow streets and along the seafront. She was eager to show Joel the town, but also keen to drag him onto the beach and away from the gawking crowds.

"Excuse me?" a voice called behind them.

Mia let out a small sigh. She knew it was too good to be true. Even in a little town like this, first thing on Monday morning and Joel Coben still gets spotted.

They turned together to face the voice that had stopped them.

"I thought that was you, Mia Ryan."

Mia was startled to see an old school friend standing behind them. "Finlay, how are you?"

Finlay had been in Mia's year at school, right through primary school and into high school. In a place like Kinsale, you grew up with the same people. The town never changed.

"Grand, love, and yourself?"

"I'm doing great, long time no see!"

"Aye, it's been too long." He smiled warmly, the breeze from the ocean making his hair dance around the edges of his face.

"That it has, what are you doing with yourself now?"

"Ah, you know, same old. Still working for me dad. How's about yourself?"

Mia felt her lips twitching with a smile at Joel's puzzled expression. He was still having trouble with the accent. Finlay had lived in Kinsale all his life, his accent was rather strong.

"I've been working in Los Angeles, I've just signed a record deal."

Saying those words out loud to someone whose life hadn't changed much since high school made Mia realize just how far she had come.

"Bloody hell, Mia!" Finlay clapped her on the shoulder. "I thought you were still in Dublin! That's fantastic. I always knew ye would end up doing something like that."

Mia smiled gratefully. "Thanks."

"Who's this then?" Finlay changed topic, shoving his hands in his jacket pockets and nodding toward Joel.

"This is my boyfriend, Joel. Joel, this is my friend from school, Finlay."

Joel held out his hand to Finlay. "Pleased to meet you."

"And you," Finlay said with another warm smile. "You got yourself a Yank from Los Angeles?"

Mia laughed at Finlay's teasing. "Yeah, I have."

Finlay lived in his little bubble in Kinsale, but even Mia was surprised to see Finlay didn't know who Joel was. She then realized Finlay probably wouldn't know if she had just introduced him to the president.

"Anyway, I best be going. It was lovely seeing you again, Mia."

"And you," she replied.

"Nice to meet you, Joel," Finlay called over his shoulder as he strolled away down the street.

Mia chuckled to herself and shook her head.

"What?" Joel asked, smiling at her reaction.

"I wasn't expecting that."

"What were you expecting?"

She laughed. "Someone asking for your autograph."

"No, I think down here, it's your autograph they're more likely to be asking for."

Mia laughed again. "No, down here they're more likely to stop and ask what time the pub opens."

Joel took her hand in his as they continued on their way down the street, watching as the shopkeepers and café owners opened their businesses for the day.

Tables and chairs were being arranged outside cafes, menu boards were placed on the pavement, and shopkeepers hung out their wares to tempt in the passing tourists.

Joel's eyes scanned everything around them. Mia knew he saw everything, he wouldn't miss a thing. Someone like Joel who had such a way with words had to be an observer. A person couldn't write the words Joel wrote without seeing the world and having an understanding of mankind.

Mia found herself doing the same. People watching was one of her favorite pastimes. She could spend hours watching the world passing by, people going about their daily lives, and interacting with one another.

Their feet naturally found their way toward the beach. Neither of them said anything as they crossed the road together and descended the steps to the sand.

Overhead, the sound of dozens of seagulls cawed as they circled the bay, scouring the rolling waves for signs of life amongst the rolling water. One by one, they swooped and dived into the ocean, sometimes emerging with their catch proudly hanging from their beaks as they soared away into the jagged coastline to devour their breakfast.

The sand beneath their converse-clad feet was still wet from the recently retreated tide and made a soft patting sound as they walked across it. The ocean beside them gently rolled in and out from the sand, and the jagged coastline around them. Kinsale was nestled in its own little nook on the Irish coastline, its own spot seemingly carved out in the bay just for the town.

"It's so beautiful," Joel said to himself as he stared across the beach to the coastline.

Mia followed his gaze, appreciating the beauty he saw before him for the first time. The old adage sounded in her head as she stared. *Absence makes the heart grow fonder.* That saying really was true, Mia thought as she gazed at the pretty little town she called home. That same pretty little town she would have to say goodbye to all over again in a few hours' time. The bright lights of Los Angeles were once again calling her name, reminding her she had a job to do, a destiny to fulfil.

Staying in the privacy and solitude of Kinsale would only bring her just that—solitude. Mia reminded herself why she left the town in the first place, to chase her hopes and dreams, to make a name for herself, and for the world to hear her music.

She was beginning to find that dream, but the road she was taking wasn't as smooth as the sand beneath her feet. That, in itself, was a reminder of the journey she had taken. If she had stayed here in Kinsale, on the smooth, familiar ground, she would be safe. However, she had taken the long, very bumpy road to Los Angeles and to her dreams. Taking that road had caused her a few stumbles, falls, and crashes—of both kinds—but ultimately would take her to the place she wanted to be. Staying on the sandy beach would only leave her wondering what shores lay at the other side of the horizon.

e/ɔe/ɔ

The sun didn't last as long in Ireland as it did in Los Angeles, Mia thought as she watched the remaining light fading in the summer sky.

At eight o'clock in the evening in LA the sun would still be shining brightly in the sky, the evening still theirs for the taking. Here, on her final night in Kinsale, the sun was quickly descending into the ocean, reminding her how quickly her time here was drawing to a close.

If they were enjoying such an evening in Los Angeles, they would be sitting in Joel's garden, or their garden—Mia still wasn't sure which—and basking in the heat.

Now she was curled up in the garden furniture, watching Sharon pour the remnants of the bottle of wine into Mia's glass. Mike and Joel were deep in conversation about sports, and Max was resting his chin on Joel's knee. If only that dog knew how lucky he was, Mia thought.

Dogs didn't think like that. Max didn't know how many thousands of women would sell their souls to trade places with him right now. Max had no idea how famous Joel was or how rich he was. No, Max only cared about the hand petting his head and the scraps of food on the table above him.

Sharon placed the empty bottle down on the table with a clink and got up from her seat to turn on the lights above the patio around them. Mia smiled at her as she sat back down. The fairy lights wound around the trestles edging the patio, their soft little lights glowing in the early evening. The view was beautifully romantic in the fading summer night.

Mike looked up at the lights before rolling his eyes, shaking his head, turning back to Joel, and resuming his conversation.

"Men," Sharon said and shook her head.

Mia laughed, wondering if she and Joel would be the same in years to come. She pulled her cardigan off the back of her chair and around her shoulders. The breeze from the ocean was starting to give her goose bumps.

"You'll have to come out to Los Angeles," Mia said to Sharon.

Sharon nodded enthusiastically over the rim of her wine glass. 'I'd love to," she said once the glass was back on the table. "It sounds wonderful."

Mia picked up her own recently refilled glass. "Yeah, it is," she said, thinking of her earlier thoughts. "I really want you to meet Charlie too."

"Uh oh," Joel muttered beside her.

Mia playfully nudged him, making his beer swill in the bottle.

"Hey!" he said as he regained control over the bottle.

Mia felt the butterflies in her stomach return as he threw her a smile just for her—that knowing smile that only couples shared, a one that said you shared the joke together, you got the teasing, and understood each other's sense of humor.

"Charlie sounds lovely," Sharon said, chastising Joel.

"Colorful is a more appropriate term," Joel teased.

"Yeah, she's definitely that," Mia said, thinking of her beautiful friend's eclectic and varied tastes in fashion.

"Why the 'uh oh' then, Joel?" Sharon asked.

Joel laughed, throwing Mia another smile. "I'm just kidding. Charlie's great, she's my brother's girlfriend."

"Oooh," Sharon said, sitting up in her seat at the sound of gossip.

Mike rolled his eyes again and winked at Mia.

Joel laughed. "Yeah, she'll make an entertaining sister-in-law one day."

"*Sister-in-law?*" Sharon squealed.

Joel nodded, taking a sip of his beer. "They've liked each other for years. I know Josh is crazy about her. It's only a matter of time, I guess."

"I think they'll just turn up to work one day married," Mia joked. "They're so impulsive."

"I wouldn't be surprised," Joel agreed, "but could you imagine Charlie missing out on a wedding dress?"

"Hell, no." Mia shook her head. "Can you imagine the wedding?"

They shared a look together and burst out laughing.

"Speaking of weddings," Sharon piped up, interrupting Mia and Joel's laughter.

"*Sharon,*" Mike warned from across the table.

Mia felt the color drain from her face immediately. Surely, Sharon wasn't going to? Not in front of Joel?"

"What about them?" Joel asked politely.

"Does that impulsiveness run in the family?" Sharon asked.

It's the wine, Mia told herself. *She's had a few glasses, she's feeling brave.*

"*Sharon,*" Mike warned even louder.

Joel laughed, thankfully seeing the funny side. "Sometimes," he answered coyly.

"Because I don't want my Mia running off to Las Vegas and getting married. I want an invitation, you know," she told Joel. She was even pointing a finger at him across the table. She had a smile on her face and a devilish glint in her eye. Mia knew she was fishing.

Mia on the other hand, wanted the ground to swallow her whole. She pulled her cardigan tighter around her, tugging the sleeves over her hands, an excuse not to look up at the table for a moment.

"We won't be doing that, don't worry," he replied.

Mia felt her heart sink. As embarrassing as the conversation was, she was kind of eager to hear Joel's response.

"What do you mean?" Sharon said a couple of decibels too high.

Mike clapped a hand to his forehead and groaned.

Joel laughed, waving a hand at her to calm her down. "No, no, that's not what I meant," he said, between laughing. "I just meant a Vegas wedding isn't my idea of a wedding. The press would have a field day. And, besides, I think Mia deserves a lot more than that."

He smiled down at her, finding her hand in her lap amongst her sleeves, and entwining his fingers with hers.

Mia looked up into a pair of shining eyes, glowing down at her with meaning.

"Aww," Sharon gushed, her hand on her chest as she looked at Mia and Joel.

"That doesn't mean he's buying a ring anytime soon Sharon," Mike's deep Irish accent perforated through the moment.

Sharon reached across the table and swatted him on the side of the head, loudly.

Mia burst out laughing.

"I didn't say I wasn't either," Joel said, making Sharon's mouth fall open in shock.

"All right, all right." Mia waved her free hand. "Enough. Can we move on now?"

She felt mortified at having her adoptive parents discussing the idea of her marrying her world famous rock star boyfriend of only a few months.

Mia would be lying if she said she hadn't thought about it. She was dating the most beautiful man she had ever laid eyes on. Who wouldn't have dreamed of that? But thinking about it and saying it out loud were two different things altogether. She didn't want her rock star boyfriend running off into the hills behind the house.

Joel on the other hand, when Mia managed to look up at him after toying repeatedly with the sleeves of her cardigan, appeared unfazed. He was laughing with Mike and Sharon, smiling affectionately down at Mia, and still tightly holding her hand. Anyone would think he was keen on the idea.

Mia smiled back at him, quickly averting her gaze to the final hours of her hometown as the night dwindled away. The quaint little house overlooking the bay looked pictur-esque with the fairy lights twinkling around its trestles, the little bulbs glowing softly between the winding ivy. The candles on the table flickered and danced to the rhythm of the wind, and the ocean rolled lazily in toward the shore below them. The town was peaceful and quiet. The spatter-ing of lights across the coast was the only sign of life.

Mia stared up at the thousands of twinkling stars now staring back at her from the night sky above the ocean. How long would it be until she saw this view again? she won-dered.

Soon the crisp ocean air would be replaced by the smog of Los Angeles, and the twinkling lights above the bay would be replaced by thousands of streetlights and sky-scrapers. But Mia wouldn't change it for the world. She loved the stark contrast in her two worlds. It only made her appreciate them both even more.

She looked up at Joel, who was watching her taking in the view, a contented look on his face. He looked at peace with the world, happy to be away from the media, and even happier to be here with her. Mia smiled reassuringly up at him before nestling her head on his shoulder. She felt him rest his head on hers, both of them contentedly watching the sleepy town by the bay. Joel's hand was still interlocked with hers, his fingers stroking the back of her hand. It was only then that Mia realized that his thumb was stroking her ring finger.

Chapter 20

"Are you sure you've got everything?" Sharon asked for the fifth time.

Mia smiled to herself, remembering the last time Sharon had said those words to her outside the house. The last time she had asked that question, Mia had been loading her things into the back of a car and preparing to leave on a journey, as she was now. There was an odd sense of deja vu in the air, although this time, there was more certainty of where she was going. And her traveling companion was a lot easier on the eyes than staring at motorways for hours on end. "Yes," she answered as Joel slammed the boot of the car shut.

"Call me as soon as you get there, yes?" Sharon asked.

"I will do," Mia said, stepping into Sharon's outstretched arms.

Mia had been so busy recently, trying to keep in touch with everyone in a different time zone from her had been tricky. She reminded herself to make more of an effort. It was just so easy to get caught up in the Los Angeles bubble.

"Take good care of her," Sharon said to Joel, pointing a finger at him. Although she was teasing, both Mia and Joel knew there was a definite meaning.

"I will, you honestly don't need to worry," Joel reassured her.

Sharon reached up to Joel and gave him a great big hug, winking at Mia over his shoulder. Mia knew she was enjoying that far more than she should.

"Take care, Mia," Mike said, giving her a strong hug.

Mia nodded against his shoulder, safe in his fatherly embrace for a few precious moments.

"And you Joel," he said when he released Mia. Surprisingly, he gave Joel a brief hug. "It was great to finally meet ye."

"It was." Sharon nodded. "Especially after we've heard so much about you. Remember what I said. I want an invitation."

Sharon winked at him and Joel just laughed. Mike shook his head, looking to the skies for answers. Mia felt her cheeks flush immediately. Sharon was off again. You were never too old to be embarrassed by your parents, she thought.

After another hug from Sharon, Mia was seated in the passenger seat. This time, she was able to lean out of her window and wave to them both, instead of watching them fade in her rear view mirror.

"Bye!" she called as she leaned out of the window, waving at them both standing in the driveway and watching the car disappear into the distance.

Just before the car rounded the first bend in the road, Mia saw Mike reach down to Sharon and envelop her in a hug. Sharon sagged into his arms.

Mia smiled wryly to herself as she sat back in her seat, thinking what her coming and going must be doing to them both. "Thank you for all of this," she said to Joel.

Taking his eyes momentarily off the road to look at her, he smiled. "You're welcome. I think we both needed this."

Mia nodded. "We sure did."

"Sharon was right," Joel continued.

Mia felt her heart race a little faster, wondering what he was about to say.

"They really should come over to Los Angeles. Maybe when your album is finished. I think they'd love it."

Mia felt her heart sink a little. "Sure, sounds great. I think they would too."

"Are you okay?" Joel asked, his dark brows furrowing a little.

"Yeah, I'm fine, just a bit tired," she lied.

After all Joel had done for her, she could hardly bring up *that* subject again. Especially after last night. Mia still found herself wondering, though. She wondered if every woman did the same. Did she allow her imagination to run away with her all the time? Was it normal to picture marrying someone you'd only known for such a short time?

She stared out at the fading coastline of Kinsale, forcing every little thing she saw to commit to her memory so she wouldn't forget her picturesque little town.

"Are you ready to go home, *again*?" Joel cocked an eyebrow at himself, as if wondering whether Mia's home was here or in Los Angeles.

He was right, Mia decided. Again was the right term to use—both places felt like her home. "I sure am," she said, stretching her arms out in front of her.

She ran her thumbs over her fingertips. The skin there much less tender than usual. She hadn't played her guitar in days, and that was another absence that was making her heart yearn. She was itching to get back in the studio and pick up her guitar again, to continue with making the album she had so desperately waited and worked for.

Turning in her seat to take a final glance at the little town where all those big dreams began, Mia sat back down to watch the road ahead that would take her to the airport and back to Los Angeles, where those dreams were finally becoming a reality.

Chapter 21

W hat's this?" Mia looked up at Jackson, who had just dropped a few pieces of stapled paper on the table before her.

He nodded at the pages she was picking up. "Read it and see."

She scowled back at him. "No, really, what's this?" she asked again.

Thursday, February 9, 2017: Hollywood Bowl, Los Angeles, CA

Friday, February 10, 2017: Hollywood Bowl, Los Angeles, CA

Saturday, February 11, 2017: Verizon Wireless Amphitheatre, Los Angeles, CA

Sunday, February 12, 2017: Verizon Wireless Amphitheatre, Los Angeles, CA

Thursday, February 16, 2017: Staples Center Arena, Los Angeles, CA

Friday, February 17, 2017: Staples Center Arena, Los Angeles, CA

Saturday, February 18, 2017: Staples Center Arena, Los Angeles, CA

Mia's eyes scanned farther down the page and on to the next one. There were more and more dates and places, the list spanning from Los Angeles right across to the other side of the States a few months later.

Monday, May 8, 2017: Barclays Center, Brooklyn, NY
Tuesday, May 9, 2017: Barclays Center, Brooklyn, NY
Friday, May 12, 2017: Madison Square Garden, New York, NY
Saturday, May 13, 2017: Madison Square Garden, New York, NY
Sunday, May 14, 2017: Madison Square Garden, New York, NY

Mia read farther down the list. Flicking through onto the next page, she saw dates and places in South America, Europe, the Far East, and even Australia. The dates and places finally stopped at the end of next year in October.

She stared blankly up at Jackson.

"I thought you, of all people, would recognize a tour schedule when you saw one, Mia," he said, crossing his arms over his chest.

"Well, yeah, I kind of thought..." She trailed off. She *had* guessed it was a tour schedule, the dates and arenas gave that away, but nothing more. Why was Jackson showing her this?

"It's Joel's," Jackson said flatly.

"Oh," Mia said quietly.

She stared down at all the dates. Joel would be gone for most of next year, she realized. February to October, he would be travelling across America and the rest of the world. She would hardly get to see him.

Perhaps this was Jackson's way of telling her it was over, the label had finally decided they wouldn't let them get in the way of each other's music. Everyone knew artists were much more marketable if they were single. Mia *thought* she had landed herself too lucky when the label had just let her and Joel take off to Ireland for a few days. "Has he seen this?" she asked, not looking up at Jackson. She turned over the pages again, staring down at all the dates.

Joel was playing at the biggest arenas in the world. He had multiple nights at the Staples Centre, Madison Square Garden, London's O2 Arena, Sweden's Ericsson Globe, Norway's Telenor Arena, Hong Kong's AsiaWorld Arena, Sydney's Acer Arena and New Zealand's Vector Arena. These were some of the world's biggest music venues and Joel would be playing to them all. The thought was mind blowing.

So many thousands of people were going to watch him perform. But Mia knew, to Joel, this would be just another world tour, just another perk of being world famous. The thought wouldn't faze him in the slightest. Her stomach was churning with nerves for him just by looking at those arenas.

Jackson nodded. "Mmm hmm."

"What did he say?" she asked.

Mia didn't know why she asked. Joel would be going, regardless. Jackson had handed Joel one of these schedules a dozen times over.

"Nothing much," Jackson said.

Mia nodded, handing him the papers back.

Jackson didn't move. His arms were still across his chest.

"What?" Mia asked.

"That's it? You don't have anything else to say?"

"What can I say? He's going, anyway. I'm pleased for him. It's an incredible schedule."

"That's it? No drama? No tears?"

"No," she replied, raising an eyebrow at him.

"You sure?"

"No. Why would I?"

"Just curious."

Jackson pursed his lips, still not taking the papers from Mia.

"There's something else, isn't there?" Mia asked.

Jackson shook his head. "No."

Mia scowled. He wasn't telling her something. She looked up at his face. His expression was unreadable. She looked across at the door and saw that it was ajar. "Joel?" she called out, knowing he would be there.

She heard a small chuckle before Joel's head of messy dark hair appeared around the door.

Mia pursed her own lips in a smile at the sight of him. He ran a hand through his hair, making it fall around his face. As he walked toward her, she stared appreciatively at the sight of him in a fitted gray T-shirt and black jeans, both fitting all the muscular contours of his body the way they should.

"What's going on?" she asked him.

"Have you seen it?" he said, squatting down in front of her, taking her hands in his.

Mia nodded.

"And?"

"And what, Joel? I'm really happy for you. It's an amazing tour. You should be proud."

Joel frowned. "You haven't told her?"

He was staring up at Jackson who now had a more prominent smile on his face.

"Not yet." Jackson grinned. "I thought you were listening."

"I was talking to Josh. I only caught the end of the conversation," Joel replied.

"Will someone please tell me what is going on?" Mia exclaimed, looking between the two of them.

Jackson nodded at Joel with a smile. "Joel?"

Joel picked up the papers that were now abandoned on the table and placed them back in Mia's lap.

She sighed. "What's going on, Joel?"

"This is my tour schedule," Joel said.

"Yes, I—"

He held up a hand to stop her. "It's also *our* tour schedule."

"What do you mean?" she asked.

Surely, Joel wasn't asking her to abandon her album and join him on the road.

"You're coming with me, Mia." He squeezed her hands. "You're my opening act."

"*Me?*" she squeaked.

Joel nodded. "You're the opening act for my worldwide tour."

"*What?*" she said louder, shaking her head in disbelief.

Joel laughed. Standing up and leaning over her, he held her tightly. "Congratulations, baby."

Mia wrapped her arms around his strong shoulders for support. He pulled back and looked at her startled eyes. Still laughing, he kissed her lips.

"I—I…" Mia's sentence trailed away, words unable to form in her mouth.

Joel pulled her up from her seat and into his arms, embracing her properly. Mia clung to him for support, scared she was about to lose her balance or faint completely. She could still feel the murmurs of Joel's chest against hers as he laughed at her disbelief. TJ and Chad got up from their seats across the room and came over to congratulate Mia.

"Congrats, Mia." Chad clapped her on the back, his long brown hair falling in his face as he did.

"Looks like we've got an album to finish. *Quick*," TJ teased as he patted her arm.

"Thanks, guys," Mia said.

"Jackson, that was harsh, man," Chad said, shaking his head.

Jackson held up his hands, a smile still twitching at his features. "What?"

Mia laughed, finally finding her voice. "Yeah, please be a bit more direct next time."

"Okay, okay, I'm going before I'm put in the docks." He laughed. "Congratulations, Mia. Get to work." He pointed at the makings of her album on the computers behind them.

"Bastard," Chad said, laughing, going back to his seat.

Mia watched Jackson leave, winking at her before closing the studio door. She was happy he was finally showing a bit of his personality, but not at her expense.

TJ and Chad went back to their seats, snapping their large headphones over their ears and focussing on the task ahead.

"That was mean," Mia said to Joel who was still highly amused by the whole situation.

"Oh, come on, you have to admit that was pretty funny," he said, resting his forehead against hers so that his big dark eyes were level with her own.

"Not for me!" she said.

"Okay, but it wasn't my idea," he said, pulling her close to him. "I'm so happy you're coming on tour with me."

The eyes that filled her vision closed as he kissed her lips. Mia closed her own eyes, allowing herself to relax again.

"Are you really?" she asked when they parted. "Are you sure you're okay with this?"

This was a huge step to be making. They had only been together a few months and now they were guaranteed to be in each other's pockets for the next year.

Since returning from Ireland a month ago, the time had flown by. Mia had thrown herself headfirst into making her album, spending as many hours as she could in the studio with two very tired producers to ensure she gave it everything she could. She was determined to make the best music she had ever made.

"Of course," Joel said, giving her a small kiss again. "I couldn't think of anything better. I love you, Mia. I wouldn't want anyone else by my side for this tour. And I'm so pleased for you and your music to land such a big gig."

"Thanks," she said, finally allowing the reality of what was about to happen sink in.

She was going on a huge world tour with one of the music industry's biggest stars. Gigs like this were usually given to already established artists, ones who weren't quite as big as Joel but deserved the privilege of opening his tour. Things like this never happened to musicians like her.

"Are you sure you didn't have a hand in this?" she asked.

"No." Joel shook his head, and she knew immediately, from his expression, he was telling the truth. He was just as surprised as she was.

"I couldn't have any influence in this decision if I wanted to. It's completely down to the label to decide who supports my tour. They must really think something of you, Mia, to give you this opportunity."

"Wow," Mia said, shaking her head in disbelief. "*I'm* going to be supporting *your* world tour. I can't believe it."

"You'd better." Joel grinned. "It's going to be an incredible year, Mia, I can just feel it. Your album, the tour, us getting to travel the world together..."

"I can't wait," she said. Her smile felt as if it was going to split her cheeks, it was so big.

"Me neither." Joel smiled back at her before kissing her again, lifting her up in his embrace.

Chapter 22

"Look up at me, that's great. Now down at the floor again," the photographer instructed.

Mia was sat on the floor, her back against the wall, with her knees raised, her guitar between her feet, and her hand around the fretboard. Her hair was tousled in tendrils around her face and down her shoulders, and her eyes had stared back at her from the mirror earlier all smokey and gray.

Joel's eyes had almost popped out of his head when she emerged from the dressing room after an hour. The make-up assistant had insisted he wait outside to see the finished product, so Josh had taken him in search of the catering tables while Charlie bundled Mia into the room with the make-up assistant.

"You look amazing!" Charlie had shrieked and clapped her hands when Mia was finally ready.

"Are you sure?" Mia asked nervously, trying not to fidget with her hair.

"Yes! You definitely need to do your hair like that more often," Charlie pointed out.

"I think so too." Mia laughed, admiring the assistant's handiwork.

The young girl had made it look so easy, curling Mia's long brown hair around the styling wand, running her fingers through it afterward to make the waves look effortlessly chic.

"I'll teach you," Charlie offered.

"It's a deal," Mia had said to her after she had seen Joel's reaction.

"Back down at the floor again," the photographer called.

This modeling larky was hard work, Mia thought as she posed sultrily again. She used to casually flip through the pages of magazines, casting her eyes over the endless photos of over made-up models and celebrities. Now she would have a deeper understanding of their craft. This posing for pictures business was tough. And tiring.

Mia wondered what was on the catering tables that Joel and Josh had gone so eagerly in search of.

"No eating before the shoot," an assistant had snapped earlier when Mia asked. "You need to keep an empty stomach."

Mia had scowled back at her and then at Charlie who was stuffing her face with M&Ms.

"That's it, once more." The clicking of the camera sounded loudly across the room. Mia was nearly dazzled by the flashbulb. "And I think that's a wrap!" the photographer finally said.

Claps and cheers echoed from around the room at the signaling of the end of the shoot.

Mia went to stand from her seated position against the wall and found her back had stiffened.

"Here." Joel was immediately before her, taking the guitar and offering her his outstretched hand.

She sighed heavily, hauling herself off the floor. "Thanks."

"It's been a long day, huh?" he asked.

"Just a bit. I'm starving," she complained, scanning the room.

"I never like doing these," Joel continued as they walked across the studio to view the final shots.

"Really? I thought you would have loved them," Mia said sarcastically.

Joel threw her a look.

"But you're a natural," she added.

Joel pursed his lips. "That doesn't mean I enjoy it."

Mia laughed.

"But so are you. You looked fantastic out there today. Really, you did," he said, seeing the look on her face.

"Are you sure?" Mia had felt overly self-conscious all day, being prodded and poked with make-up brushes and told to stand this way and that—all with a camera in her face.

"Come and see for yourself." He jerked his head toward the computer where a group of people were now gathered.

"Ooh."

"Wow."

"Oh my God."

"Joel, you lucky bastard." Josh wiggled his eyebrows at Joel before being elbowed by Charlie.

Mia stood on her tiptoes to see through gaggle of assistants, make-up artists, and stylists, all eager to see the results of their day's work.

"Wow," Mia said when they parted to let her through.

"You look fabulous, honey," Kit, the photographer, said, smiling up from the computer.

"Thanks," Mia said, still shaking her head.

Staring back at Mia from the screen were dozens and dozens of shots of her from the day. She had been styled in several different ways for the album cover and the pages of the CD insert. Each outfit change had warranted several different poses to see which worked best with the concept.

Josh pointed at the screen. "That one's my favorite."

"Josh!" Mia exclaimed.

Charlie stood behind him, rolling her eyes.

The photo was of Mia lying across an amplifier, wearing

denim cut offs and black vest top. Mia hadn't felt comfortable in that picture. She could imagine Chad's girlfriend Tara looking right at home in it, though.

"I like this one best." Joel looped his arm around Mia's waist, speaking into her ear as he leaned in to point at the image as Kit scrolled through.

"That's mine too," Kit cooed.

Joel pursed his lips again, this time supressing laughter. Kit was so flamboyant and so eccentric, he would make Boy George and Perez Hilton's love child look tame.

The photograph Joel was pointing to was one of the final images of the day. It was one of the pictures of Mia sitting on the floor, the guitar between her feet, staring up at the camera through her eyelashes.

"You look really beautiful," Joel said quietly in her ear.

Mia could feel herself blushing.

"That's the one I think we're gonna go with for the album cover," Kit said, "I emailed all of them over to Sixth String. They love them. But this one—" He pointed to Joel's favorite. "—is the front runner."

"But we just finished?" Mia asked in disbelief. How had the label had time to look through all those images?

"We've been emailing all day, honey," Kit said. "They just got the last few."

"Oh," Mia said. "Who decided that one would be my cover?"

"Your manager," Kit said mater-of-factly, spinning in his chair back to the computer.

Mia stared open mouthed at the back of his head. He had gone back to clicking through the images, despite dropping the bombshell that he knew Mia had a manager.

She grabbed the back of the chair and span him around to face her. "*Who*?"

He winked at her, tipping his glasses as he did. "I said your manager, honey."

"I have a manager?" Mia asked.

The assistants and stylists around them had fallen silent

as they listened to the conversation. Mia could sense the baited breath held among them.

He winked at Joel this time. "That's what I said."

"How do you know this?" Mia asked. How did Kit know she had a manager and she didn't? When did she get one of those? And most importantly, who was it?

He spun dramatically in his chair again and crossed his legs once he was facing Mia. "In this business, it's not what you know, it's *who* you know, darling." He grinned devilishly at Joel.

Mia could have sworn she saw Joel squirm as he did. A few supressed giggles came from behind Mia. She ignored them. "Quit messing around. How do you know this? And, more importantly, who is my manager?"

"Me," said a small voice behind them.

The group fell silent. It was Mia's turn to spin dramatically and face those behind her. Not that she needed to. She would have recognized that voice anywhere. There was only one person in this world with such a cheery, musical Californian accent that Mia remembered hearing for the first time and feeling like she and that person were already lifelong friends. How right she had been. Within days of meeting, the two of them had begun lunching like best friends. Mia knew that she had immediately made a best friend for life in this person.

And Mia couldn't think of a better person to be her manager.

"Charlie?" Mia squeaked.

Charlie nodded before letting go of her giggles.

"What? When? How?" Mia stuttered over her words.

"They asked me a few days ago, I couldn't say anything until the papers were signed. I just got promoted!"

Mia untangled herself from Joel to hug her friend. "Congratulations!"

"So you're gonna be seeing a lot more of me over the next few months. I'm coming on tour with you," Charlie said, pulling back so she could see Mia.

"That's brilliant news." Mia shook her head. "I can't believe it. I'm so happy for you."

"Me too." Charlie grinned from ear to ear. "Things are finally starting to fall into place for us all."

Mia nodded, her lips pulling into a firm smile. Charlie was right, things were coming together at last.

"This is perfect." Mia closed her eyes briefly. "I couldn't ask for anyone better. You're the best person for the job."

Charlie laughed, tears of happiness brimming in her gold-glitter-laden eyes. "Thank you, Mia, that means the world to me."

Mia hugged Charlie tightly before either of them burst into tears.

"I'm so excited," Charlie gushed when they let go of each other. "I'm coming on tour with you guys."

"So am I," Josh chimed in, a mischievous smile plastered on his face.

"That's *not* so great news," Mia teased.

She already knew Josh would be coming. He was part of Joel's team. And there was no way he and Charlie would be parted for almost a year. It had taken them long enough to decide to get together. But Mia was elated that the four of them would be touring the world together. She already knew she had the best manager in the world in Charlie, and Josh was bound to keep them all entertained with his impish ways.

"Hey." Josh feigned being hurt, "I'll be on my best behavior, honest."

He winked at Mia, making her laugh. "Yeah, like that's gonna happen."

"Well." Josh shrugged. "Yeah, I guess you're right."

"I can't believe I have to put up with you every day for almost a year," Mia teased.

"You're going to love it." Josh winked, throwing his arms around Charlie. "A whole year on the road with my brother and beautiful sister-in-law."

Mia laughed, although she felt her cheeks blushing a little. She glanced at Joel who was smiling at the three of them, undeterred by his brother's words.

"One big happy family," Kit said, grinning from ear to ear and clapping his hands before him like a seal.

It was then that Mia could have sworn Joel's face turned a peculiar shade of gray.

Mia giggled and turned back to Charlie, still unable to believe her luck in landing Charlie as her manager. Working hard for years at the label had paid off for Charlie. They had promoted her straight up the ranks to the position of manager for one of their up and coming artists.

Mia felt her pride swell in her chest, knowing it was her career that was also launching the career of her friend. "I'm so happy for you," she told her again.

"I knew you were going to be big, Mia. I just didn't know you'd be taking me there with you," Charlie gushed.

Mia waved her off. "Don't be silly. You deserve this. You've worked so hard."

"And so have you. I'm so happy to be doing this with you." Charlie beamed, her gold rimmed eyes sparkling more than the eye shadow above them. "Team Mia!" she cheered, grabbing hold of Mia's hand and raising it into the air.

Joel, Josh, Kit, and the rest of the crew were all looking on with big smiles and pride at watching more than just the results of a hard day's work.

"Team Mia!" echoed the crew.

೧ഗ೧

"What do you mean you're declining?" Rebecca's voice snapped down the phone.

Since returning from Ireland, Mia had been conveniently forgetting to reply to her emails and had been too busy to take certain calls.

"Thank you again, but I want to stay where I am," Mia repeated.

"But you're turning down a huge opportunity," Rebecca continued. "Have you any idea how long you've kept us waiting for this decision?"

"I'm aware of that, but I've been incredibly busy lately. It was a very big decision to make."

"People don't take this long to decide on such offers, Mia," Rebecca snapped. "You should be thanking your lucky stars we gave you such an opportunity. We don't take making these kind of offers lightly."

"I know and I'm very grateful." Mia tried to keep her cool. "But I have to stay loyal to the company that gave me my break."

"Mia." Rebecca exhaled sharply. "I really need you to consider what you're saying. You're turning down the opportunity to work for Sky Records? You're turning down a six-figure contract?"

"I am."

"For Sixth String Studios?"

"That's correct. They're the right people to work with my music, they understand me and the direction I want to go with it."

"But we can offer you that *and more*!"

"I just think Sky Records are too pop-orientated," Mia explained. "I really do appreciate your offer. Thank you very much for the wonderful opportunity, but I want to stay where I am."

"That's your final decision?" Rebecca asked again.

"It is," Mia said firmly, beginning to feel like she was on a game show.

"Well, I wish you the best of luck, Mia," Rebecca said heavily. "You're a very talented girl. I'm just sorry we weren't able to have you working for us."

"Thank you," Mia said before hanging up the phone.

"Well, that's one down," Joel said, watching her toss the phone onto the table.

"Two to go," Mia replied.

"Two?" Joel asked, his big dark eyes looking all confused.

He was sat next to Mia on his sofa, one leg propped on his knee. He had been the one insisting she answered Rebecca's calls. He had said she needed to start tying up loose ends.

"Two more 'loose ends' to go," she said, quoting him.

"Yeah, about that," Joel said, sliding closer to her on the sofa.

"Go on," Mia said, trying to ignore the intoxicating scent of Joel and his cologne that was filling her nostrils, forcing her senses away from the conversation at hand.

Joel wrapped an arm around Mia's waist. "Lucy has been charged for the stories she sold to the press."

"Charged?" Mia asked. She immediately felt bad for Lucy. Although she hated what the woman had done—it wasn't easy seeing some girl's face plastered on every magazine cover claiming to have bedded her boyfriend—but now Lucy's name would be forever tarnished.

"Yeah." Joel nodded. "She's being sued, we won. I told you I wouldn't have someone talk about me like that anymore. I didn't care before. They could say whatever they wanted, which is why she thought she could get away with it. But I care about you, Mia, I don't want your name getting dragged into all of this. I want to prove to you that I love you."

"You don't need to sue someone for that," Mia teased.

Joel pulled a sad face. "That's not quite the answer I was expecting."

Mia laughed. "I'm sorry, you know I love you."

"I do." He kissed her briefly. "I don't want your name being tarnished because of mine, because some girl thinks she can make a few hundred dollars by claiming things happened that didn't. I don't want the world to think I'd do that when I'm with you," he said, looking up at her. His eyes looked so sad, so sincere, and full of meaning.

Mia felt her response catch in her throat. The sight took

her breath away completely. This man was too beautiful, too good, to be hers.

She nodded, it was all she could do to respond.

Slowly, his hand traced the edge of her cheek before his fingers ran nimbly into her hair, gently pushing her head down to meet his.

"I love you," he said again, whispering softly so that his breath danced against her lips.

He was so close, she could feel the edges of his lips against hers as he spoke, but he kept them apart for a moment longer.

Finding her voice again, she whispered back, "I love you too."

And on hearing those words, he closed what little distance was left between them and allowed the two of them to melt together completely.

Chapter 23

The room around her was silent as she strummed through the remainder of the song. Those few present were intently listening to what would soon be played out to thousands of fans across the globe on a worldwide tour. The pressure was immense.

Mia had been hard at work over the last few weeks, putting the finishing touches on her album and beginning work on her tour rehearsals. Sixth String Studios were fast forwarding the usual lengthy process, in order to have Mia as Joel's opening act.

Usually, Mia would have finished her album, done a media tour, and then begun tour rehearsals before jetting off around the globe on a sell-out arena tour, but all of the above was being done together at break-neck speed, in order to get Mia on tour with Joel in time.

She was trying hard to focus on the lyrics of the song she was performing, but really her brain was already stressing over the three interviews she had to do after the rehearsal.

Any day now, TJ and Chad were expected to finish the final touches on her album, and it would be prepared for worldwide release. The media had soon caught wind that Joel Coben's un-famous girlfriend was about to accompany him on tour and the world's press was waiting with baited breath for her album launch.

Everywhere Mia went these days, everything she did, she felt the pressure. She tossed and turned each night in the sheets of her bed, stressing over the things she had said in an interview. Was she funny enough? Did she talk too much about herself? Should she have said something different? Did she pose right in that photoshoot? How would the images turn out in the magazine? The pressure was incredible.

Joel, of course, offered an ever-empathetic ear. He had been there and done that hundreds of times before and could offer countless pieces of advice, all of which Mia took on board, but still she would fret to no end.

She looked up from the end of the microphone, her eyes scanning over the carpeted floor of the rehearsal room to where Joel was lounging against the wall opposite her. He smiled and gave her a thumbs up. Mia knew she already had her number one fan in him.

Standing beside him, wearing an impressive outfit of peg-leg trousers with zips at the hem, a gray chiffon blouse with a bow at the neck, and sky scraper stilettos was Charlie. Her long, manicured gold nails were clutched around a Blackberry, an iPad, a diary, and a folder bursting with papers. Charlie was taking well to her new role as Mia's manager, especially as the promotion had meant she and Mia had the excuse to spend a day trawling the luxurious shops in Beverly Hills, at Charlie's insistence, for a completely new work wardrobe.

"But my regular clothes just won't cut it," she said when Mia had finished pulling out dozens of more-than-suitable outfits for her new job.

"Why not? These look great," Mia said, holding up an armful of clothes she would have willingly given that arm to own.

"Yes, but not for the job of a soon-to-be world famous, multi-million-record selling artist's manager," Charlie said with raised eyebrows and her hands firmly on her hips.

Mia laughed. "Let's not get carried away now."

"Mia, you know as well as I do, that is true. The label wouldn't be going to all this trouble if they didn't think you were going to be a huge star. This kind of treatment only happens once in a long while. I've only seen a handful of new artists get this kind of treatment before. And one of them is your boyfriend," she explained. "And look where he is now."

Mia smiled. "Okay, okay, I see your point."

"So you can see exactly why I need a new work wardrobe? They don't just go handing out super-high end promotions to anyone you know? Your fast track to stardom is my fast-track to career success too! I *need* to look the part."

"Okay, okay!" Mia tossed the clothes on Charlie's bed and held up her hand in surrender. Let's go shopping. On one condition…"

"What's that?"

"That you help me pick out some new things too. I have to look the part as well."

Mia smiled across the room at Charlie who was watching her curiously.

In the end, Charlie helped Mia pick out almost as many new clothes as she had. Shopping with Charlie was a dangerous and expensive hobby. Mia had willingly surrendered her bank balance to the throes of the Hollywood boutiques, eager to look the part in her worldwide tour and not be ripped to pieces on the pages of fashion magazines. Though she hated those things, the thought of her career being tarnished so early on by fashionista journalists was stomach wrenching, those pages could be so cruel. Though Charlie had insisted Mia worked her rock-chick look with effortless style, Mia was sure a few new additions to her wardrobe wouldn't go amiss.

"Okay, guys, let's take a quick break," Charlie called to the room at the end of the song.

Joel's tour had been appointed a tour manager, who called in to check on Mia's progress from time to time, but his main focus was obviously Joel. Mia was Charlie's responsibility.

Mia lifted her guitar strap over her neck. "Thanks, guys, you sounded great."

Her backing band smiled and nodded, returning her compliments.

Mia still wasn't used to having a backing band. Sometimes when she'd performed at Glen's Tavern, the house band would join her for the odd cover song, but this was a whole new experience. Mia was used to playing acoustically with only her voice and her guitar. Now she had a whole band to work with.

"You sounded fantastic," Joel said encouragingly as he pulled her into an embrace before kissing her.

"Thanks," Mia replied after they parted. Her breath exhaled deeply. She was still feeling the stress.

"Stop worrying." His deep, thick voice sounded comforting in her ear as his hand caressed her lower back reassuringly.

"I can't help myself." Mia laughed. "There's just so much going on."

"I know, just a few more weeks and we will be on tour," Joel's eyes sparkled with anticipation.

It was December nineteenth, and all Mia could think about was getting Christmas over and done with so the tour could begin. Mia smiled up at him. "It sounds so easy when you say it like that."

He grinned, leaning down to her. "Because it's true."

The ends of his dark hair fell around his face. Mia reached up and brushed them back.

"You guys are too cute," Charlie cooed.

Mia reluctantly turned away from Joel's admiring gaze to realize her manager had been standing beside them the whole time.

"Where's Josh?" Mia asked, trying to take the spotlight off her for a minute.

Charlie shrugged. "Rehearsing, I suppose. Which is exactly where you should be," she said pointedly at Joel.

Joel turned his powerful stare to Charlie and laughed. "Don't worry about it. I got it covered."

"Hmm." Charlie scowled back at him. "We'll see."

"You worry about my girl right here." He kissed Mia's forehead. "And I'll worry about my show."

"All right, all right." Charlie shooed him away with her iPad. "I get it, not my responsibility. But I won't have your unrehearsed tour dragging down my client's name."

Mia and Joel laughed together as Charlie raised her eyebrows at Joel. A smile was threatening to burst behind her tightly pulled lips.

"I think you have more than me to worry about as far as the tour's concerned," Joel said to her.

Charlie's face fell.

"What do you mean?" Mia asked when she realized they both knew something she didn't.

Charlie looked up at Joel, scowling at him for giving Mia more to worry about than she already had, before explaining, "The support band has pulled out."

"They did what?" Mia asked.

Mia was Joel's opening act. She would take to the stage before Joel did, but prior to them both going onstage, a lesser-known band would warm up the crowd. A band which had now pulled out of the biggest tour of their careers.

Charlie rolled her eyes. "Yeah, they pulled out a few days ago. Said they didn't want to sell out."

The term "selling out" was used to describe bands or artists that had gone from playing small, indie venues to thousands of fans in arenas and stadiums. Some bands didn't want to "sell out." They wanted to keep out of the Hollywood limelight and the stigma attached to worldwide fame.

Mia thought they were crazy for passing up the biggest opportunity of their lives. How many bands got offered the chance to open for an artist as famous as Joel Coben? They would learn to regret that decision in the years to come, Mia thought.

"So Jackson is tearing his hair out, trying to find some-one to fill their slot so last minute," Charlie explained as she typed furiously on her Blackberry.

Joel shrugged. "It's not quite the final hour. He'll be fine."

Charlie shook her head. "You're so chilled out, it drives me insane."

Joel laughed. "There's no need to stress."

Charlie threw him a look of ridiculousness before walking away, her heels clicking softly on the carpeted floor.

Mia shrugged. "There's no point worrying about it. That's not our job."

"Exactly." Joel smiled. "We'll still be on the tour."

"You bet." Mia smiled too. Despite all her nerves and anxieties about interviews, her album, and the rehearsals, she was desperate to board the tour bus and get on the road.

After her initial shock of finding out she was Joel Coben's opening act, she had been bursting to get back on stage for so many months of the year. The thought that she would be finally getting paid to do what she loved, to spend her days traveling the world and performing to thousands of people each night, was incredible. Her dreams were final coming true.

"But first," Joel said, his dark eyes now looking all serious. "There's Christmas."

Mia laughed. "That's the last thing on my mind!"

"Well, it's coming, whether you like it or not," Joel teased, pulling her tightly to him again. "Are you not excited for our first Christmas together?"

Mia smiled, placing her hand on the side of his cheek and staring into his eyes. "Of course I am."

"Good, so am I," he replied, his eyes crinkling at the corners as he smiled.

Joel had turned into the biggest kid since Christmas had appeared on the horizon. By all of Josh's accounts, Joel was normally unfazed by Christmas, but somehow this year was different. Josh was insistent Mia had changed him, that she had turned his brother for the better into a softie. Josh told Mia how Joel usually passed the holidays alone at home, only making an appearance on Christmas day for dinner. The thought made Mia sad. Joel was so full of life these days, she couldn't imagine him spending the happiest time of year alone.

"Man, it's like you whacked him over the head with the Christmas stick," Josh explained a few days ago. "He's never been like this, not for as long as I can remember."

Mia had only laughed. A few months ago, she could have pictured the Joel Josh was talking about, but now she couldn't ever imagine it.

"You've changed him, Mia," Josh teased. "Not that I'm complaining. You're just going to have to put up with me this Christmas."

Mia had rolled her eyes dramatically, but she was only teasing. She was looking forward to spending Christmas with a house full of people. Now that she and Joel were officially living together, Joel had wanted a huge Christmas to celebrate. He finally managed to get Mia to change her address to his house, now that her visas were cleared and she was living in the States. Joel was planning a huge Christmas celebration to bring everyone together and have an unforgettable Christmas with their loved ones before they all left their lives behind and hit the road for the majority of the next year.

"Who's cooking, though?" Mia teased.

"Irish Christmas dinner or American?" Joel asked.

"There's a difference?"

He laughed. "I guess we'll soon find out."

Mia wasn't looking forward to the pressure of having to cook for so many people. She was secretly hoping Joel would hire caterers, although she doubted that would fit with his family-themed Christmas.

So far, they were expecting Josh and Charlie, Sharon and Mike were flying in from Dublin tomorrow for the holidays, and Luke and his partner Nittaya were even flying over from Koh Li Pe to spend the festive season with Mia and Joel. Mia was ecstatic about having her adoptive parents and her brother all under the same roof for Christmas. It would be the first time since they were separated into the system that either of them would be spending a holiday or birthday together. It would be the first Christmas Mia would be able to spend with her brother that she was old enough to remember.

She just needed to get through two more days of tour rehearsals and a few more interviews first.

Chapter 24

Mia giggled, trying desperately to maintain her one-handed grip on Joel's shoulder. "Hold on."

He had picked her up and was holding her high up in the air so that she could pin the Christmas decorations up on the walls. Surprisingly, Mia didn't think they'd bought enough garland, tinsel, and lights to decorate their Hollywood mansion.

Even after spending more money than Mia cared to think about online—it was easier than braving the shops together at this time of year, particularly with Joel in tow—on endless decorations, Mia could still see a few spaces in the house for a few more here and there. *The downsides to owning a fabulous Beverly Hills home*, she thought.

"You got it?" Joel asked. His face looked up at her from her stomach, his arms gripped around her thighs to hold her in place.

She laughed. "I'm sure standing on a chair would have been much easier."

Joel grinned, letting her slide down his body and catching her just before her feet touched the floor. "Yeah, but this is much more fun."

"I guess so," she said, looking up into huge, sparkling

eyes. She ran her hands up the back of his neck and into his thick hair, pulling his face close to hers.

"I can't wait to spend Christmas with you," he whispered.

Mia smiled in return and to herself, still amazed that this beautiful man was all hers.

Men like Joel Coben didn't exist. She told herself that over and over again. Each morning she would wake up and find herself entangled in his limbs and feeling his warm breath on her skin. Each night before she went to sleep, he would kiss her softly in the darkness and tell her he loved her.

Each morning and every night, Mia counted her blessings. She would stare out of the window in Joel's room at the clear starry skies above Los Angeles and say a silent prayer to the heavens. How they had found each other in this huge, crazy world, Mia had no idea. The heavens had clearly sent Jackson into Glen's Tavern that night for a reason. Of all the bars and pubs on Temple Bar, of all the places in a city as big as Dublin, they had walked into the bar where Mia worked. There were endless buskers, performers, and musicians to be found in Dublin, but out of all of them Jackson had chosen Mia.

She wondered if the universe had been scheming all along, if the fates had been plotting for more than her career when Jackson and Cole had wandered into Glen's earlier that year.

Men like Joel Coben didn't cross your path accidently. They didn't bump into you in your local Starbucks or climb onto the treadmill next to you at the gym. They didn't sit down for a drink at the kind of places you stumbled into on a Saturday night with your friends either. No, men like Joel Coben appeared out of nowhere and collided with your world head on. The universe had been plotting and scheming, unbeknownst to Mia, to bring someone as special as Joel into her life.

She really had gotten lucky.

Men this good were only to be fallen in love with amongst the pages of novels, daydreamed over through movie screens, or sung about in melancholy songs. Women spent their lives wishing and praying for someone like him to wander into their lives. Some never even found one. Mia, on the other hand, was already thanking her lucky stars that she had.

"Me too," she said. Squeezing him tightly to her—in case he would disappear at any moment, closing her eyes and then, just in case when she opened them he would be gone—she kissed him.

"What was that for?" he asked her afterward.

She smiled, gazing up into his eyes. "Just because."

His firm, muscular body was pressed against hers, rocking her gently from side to side, along with the music quietly playing out from the television in the corner of the room.

Mia closed her eyes again and rested her head against his chest, her cheek comfortably nestled between the contours of his muscles.

Joel kissed the top of her head and hugged her tightly. "Are you happy?" he asked quietly into her hair.

She smiled into his chest. "More than ever before."

She didn't need to see his face to know he too was smiling. He kissed her hair again and held her to him.

Mia could have stayed that way for a long time, comfortable and blissfully happy in the arms of a loving man who was more than a little easy on the eyes.

The universe, however, had other ideas.

Their romantic little moment was then rudely interrupted by the sound of the buzzer at the gates to the house.

"I'll get it." Joel squeezed her hand as he walked away to answer the flashing machine installed by the door.

Mia had a sneaking suspicion she knew who had arrived. She quickly followed Joel to the door, eager to see whose face would appear on the camera at the gates. They were expecting guests from two very different corners of the globe any day now and Mia couldn't wait to see either of them.

"Joel, hi!" Sharon's familiar Gaelic tones drifted through the intercom.

"Hey, I'll buzz you through," Joel replied, hitting the switch by the machine.

Mia heard the familiar buzz and then the sound of the gates in front of the house sliding open through the speakers, followed by the crunching of tyres on the gravel outside the front door.

"After you." Joel motioned to Mia, allowing her to head straight to the front door.

Mike was still putting the car into park by the time Sharon had already jumped out and was dashing across the drive to see Mia.

"Ah, I've missed ye so much," she gushed, grabbing Mia with open arms.

"I've missed you both too." Mia fell straight into her warm embrace, safe in the comforting arms of her adoptive mother.

Despite being on the other side of the world, Mia felt like she had come home again as soon as Sharon was with her.

"You're looking gorgeous, Mia, Los Angeles looks good on you," Sharon gushed. She held Mia away from her and looked her up and down before giving the seal of approval.

"Thanks. I really love it out here," Mia said truthfully.

"How are ye doing, love?" Mike came over and hugged Mia in his big, strong hold.

"Grand," Mia replied, already hearing her accent returning stronger now that she was back in the presence of her family.

"Nice to see you again, Joel," Mike said, clapping Joel on the back.

"Yes, of course." Sharon hugged Joel with a pleased smile on her face. "You're both looking well. I'm glad to see you both looking so happy."

Joel smiled down at Mia. "We are."

Sharon gave Mia "the eye."

"Are we the first ones here?" Mike asked Joel, ignoring his wife's not-so-subtle behavior.

"You are," Joel answered.

"Oh, that's good. It'll give us chance to catch up before anyone else arrives," Sharon said with a nervous smile.

Mia knew Sharon was apprehensive about Luke's arrival. While Mia couldn't wait to see her brother again, Sharon was somewhat nervous about meeting the person who had been absent, presumed dead, for most of Mia's life.

Sharon and Mike had been the ones to see Mia's years of heartache, the teenager who locked herself in her room with her guitar and wrote books full of songs, the young woman who exhausted herself physically and emotionally trying to track down a missing person long forgotten about. Mike and Sharon had been there through all of that. They had seen just how much Luke's disappearance had affected Mia, and now he was suddenly back in her life.

They were, of course, eager to meet Mia's brother. They'd had a long time to adjust to this new addition to Mia's life before actually getting to meet him. But it would be a surreal, strange mix of emotions when they did finally meet.

Mia was nervous, excited and apprehensive all at the same time. Joel, naturally, was as cool as a cucumber. He insisted she was over analysing, and everyone would get along just fine. Mia sincerely hoped he was right.

As they filed up the front steps together and into the house to admire Mia and Joel's decorative handy work, Mia knew it was only a matter of time before they would discover which one of them was right.

∽∾∾

"Has everyone had enough?" Mia asked, glancing up and down the table.

"There's more potatoes if anyone wants any?" Sharon tried to pass the dish along the table but everyone around them mumbled they were stuffed.

Despite Mia's insistence, Sharon had more or less taken charge of the cooking.

Mia had wanted to cook for all their guests and family, but Sharon's maternal instincts had overruled and overpowered Mia's complaints. She had been instantly demoted to sous chef as soon as Sharon had stepped through the front door. Mia should have known.

"No, thank you," Luke politely declined. "Though that really was the most delicious meal ever."

Sharon blushed. "Why thank you, Luke."

"Yes, it was," Nittaya agreed. "You'll have to show us how to make this when you come to visit."

"Ooh, I'd love to," Sharon began, immediately off on a tangent about what foods she could show Nittaya how to make when she visited them in Koh Li Pe.

Any excuse for a holiday to Thailand, Mia thought.

She looked up from her abandoned plate to see Joel smiling at her.

*Smug ba*stard, Mia thought. She smiled back at him. She couldn't help it. He was just too darn nice. There wasn't a thing she would change about him, even if she could.

Ever the oracle, Joel had been right about Luke meeting Mia's adoptive parents.

Luke and Nittaya had arrived from Koh Li Pe the day after Mike and Sharon's flight had arrived from Dublin. Their plane had been delayed slightly, meaning Mia had been gifted with a night with her adoptive parents before having to play happy families with an eighteen year absence to deal with.

She had fretted for nothing. As soon as Luke and Nittaya had arrived at Joel's house, they had gotten on swimmingly with Mike and Sharon. There had been an initial moment of awkwardness when Mia introduced them, but as soon as Sharon had begun to cry, the barriers were down.

After grabbing a box of tissues and brewing an extra-large cafetiere of Christmas blend coffee, they had sat down in Joel's living room to fill in the blanks on the last eighteen years. Mia had relayed as much information as she could to Mike and Sharon since meeting Luke and, likewise, she had told Luke as much as she was able to about her adoptive family, but some things just needed to be said in person.

Stories always sounded better first-hand, even if they were repeated ones. Luke willingly answered all of their questions and explained his story over again to Mia's family. Mia smiled gratefully at him throughout. His willingness to have the acceptance of her adoptive parents was truly warming.

Once they were on comfortable, familiar ground, Mia could have sworn Luke had known her adoptive parents for years. Some things were meant to be, she thought.

Charlie patted her non-existent food baby. "Sharon, Mia, this was the best Christmas dinner I think I've ever had."

Honestly, that girl could eat for America and not gain a pound. Mia wondered if she fretted it all off with the stresses of work. Or perhaps walking in stilettos twenty-four hours a day burned thousands of calories. Mia thought about taking a leaf out of Charlie's book if it meant her waist would be as tiny as hers.

"Oh, man," Josh groaned. "That was grand."

He had been perfecting his Irish accent all holiday season. Now that he had Mike's deep, broad accent to imitate.

Mike smiled. "Almost there, kiddo."

"Damn it." Josh punched the air. "So close."

"It's getting better," Mike teased.

"Please don't encourage him." Charlie rolled her eyes. "You don't have to live with him."

Mia and the rest of the table laughed at Josh's dismayed face.

"I thought you liked my Irish accent?" he asked.

"Not when I have to hear you repeat the same words a hundred times a day," Charlie quipped.

Mia could see her lips twitching in the corners, she loved winding Josh up.

"Yeah, yeah." Josh waved her off and changed the subject, offering her the Christmas cracker that was before him on the table. "Pull a cracker?"

Charlie winked. "I think you already have."

"Don't I know it, baby." He smiled adoringly at her and kissed her cheek before the cracker popped with a loud bang.

Mini-fireworks sounded around the table as everyone crossed their arms and pulled crackers with those either side of them.

For the next several minutes, horrendously bad jokes were read out from little paper slips, novelty toys and gimmicks were thrown around the table, a plastic frog even landed in the left-over potatos, and people wrestled with their neighbor over not wanting to wear flimsy paper hats.

"Don't even think about it," Mia warned Joel as he came toward her with a bright purple paper crown.

"Every queen needs a crown," he leaned in and whispered into her ear.

"Queen?" Mia asked.

"Queen of my heart," he said with a dopey smile and planted a large kiss on her cheek.

Despite the little butterflies in her stomach doing a celebratory Mexican wave, Mia playfully punched him in the arm. "You're such a douche," she teased, allowing him to drape the paper crown over her head and kiss her in front of everyone at the table.

Not that anyone minded. They were all too full of food, drink, and Christmas spirit to care.

"But you love me," he said, his eyes level with hers.

Mia draped her arms around his neck, wishing for a moment they really were alone so she could savor this sweet, private moment. "I do." She kissed him again. "But I think you've had way too much to drink."

"Probably." Joel hiccupped, his eyes losing a little focus.

He really was a cute drunk, Mia thought. She wished she could keep him like this, all to herself. Maybe she should get him drunk more often.

"Anyone for coffee?" Mia asked her rowdy table of joke tellers, frog throwers, and over-stuffed turkeys.

Several murmurs of agreement replied and, after several minutes spent fingernail tapping impatiently waiting for the coffee machine and several attempts to sit down an overly affectionate Joel later, Mia could finally sit down on the sofa, surrounded by her loved ones.

She curled up into Joel's lap, not that his sofas weren't big enough for everyone, and relaxed comfortably in his warm, safe hold.

Surrounded by everyone she loved dearly, full of delicious food and more than enough alcohol, and riding on a contented wave of the best Christmas she had in...well, ever, Mia recounted her blessings once again.

Luke shuffled around the table, topping up everyone's mugs with the remaining coffee, and tried not to get in the way of their view of *Elf*, the Christmas movie that was playing on the television.

He sat back down beside Nittaya and draped his arm around her shoulders. Mia smiled at them both, happy to see her brother enjoying the love of a woman as sweet and as beautiful as Nittaya. He deserved to be happy, after everything life had thrown at him.

Mike and Sharon were sat on the sofa beside Luke and Nittaya, comfortably sitting hand in hand as they watched the movie.

Josh and Charlie were beside Mia and Joel. They too were curled up together in the other corner of the sofa. Charlie was dozing against Josh's chest, and he was stroking her blonde streaked hair. For once, Charlie's sky scraper heels were lying abandoned on the floor of Joel's living room, and her bare feet were tucked up in Josh's lap. Mia wondered if Charlie would notice if they went missing.

"Merry Christmas, baby," Joel whispered so that only she could hear.

She looked up into his eyes, their blackness almost merging with the darkened room. The faint glow of the television reflected in his eyes, and Mia could see the glow within them was emanating from more than just the screen.

"Merry Christmas," she said.

His hand caressed her cheek, his fingers stroking her cheekbone before trailing down her neck and lightly fingering the diamond pendant she now wore around her neck.

"For the next chapter in your life," Joel had said to her when he removed her silver guitar pendant that morning and replaced it with his gift.

His eyes were level with hers, his breath soft and slow against her lips. He was just tantalisingly out of reach.

His hand snaked back up her collarbone and along her neck, making her shiver. She closed her eyes briefly and wished he would close their distance and kiss her.

"I love you," he said quietly, "more than anything in this world."

She opened her eyes to respond, but she knew that Joel had already seen her response in her face. He didn't need to hear the words back.

He already knew.

Gently, his hand trailed up the back of her neck and into her hair, bringing her head those final few millimetres closer.

That moment was so passionate, so intense, Mia had never felt anything like it before. She thought her heart would burst in her chest it was pounding so loudly.

His full, soft lips finally kissed hers, and she melted into him completely. No, Mia reminded herself, men like Joel Coben didn't appear out of nowhere. They collided with your entire universe head on, its course forever altered.

Men like Joel Coben were sent into your life for a reason. They turned your world on its axis, never to be the same again. Their two worlds had now collided and were forging a pathway all of their own, full of heart-stopping moments just like this one.

At that moment in time, she really couldn't have asked the universe for anything more.

Chapter 25

Throwing her head back as the band riffed through the bridge of her song, Mia felt as though she hadn't a care in the world. She was lost in her song, her music was coming alive in the small rehearsal space, and she was dying to get out on stage with the band and truly bring it to life.

It was only a matter of weeks.

The album had been released and as anticipated, was flying off the shelves. Mia had jumped up and down with glee when Jackson told her how many copies had been bought and downloaded after the first week.

"They're some fantastic results, Mia. It's going down a storm," he said when congratulating her.

"Thank you!" she squealed with delight.

"The media are loving it too. You've got some fantastic reviews." Jackson tossed a couple of folded magazines at her. The interviews had been booked in advance. The press had been anticipating Mia's album release in the new year and had been waiting to print their interviews with her on its release, along with their dreaded reviews.

Five Stars: You have to hear this girl!

Four Stars: Unmissable
FIVE STARS: Mia Ryan ~ one to watch!
FIVE STARS: Hot on the heels of Joel Coben
Four Stars: Sixth String's female answer to Joel Coben

Mia stared in disbelief at the magazines in her hand. From tiny, inch-wide columns in the music sections to two-page features, the reviews on her album and her interviews were incredible. She couldn't have anticipated a better response.

A delight to work with, Mia Ryan will go far in this industry...
Filling the room with her infectiously sweet personality...
Polite and sincere, Mia shows exactly why she deserves this opportunity...
Spend only two minutes in her company and you'll soon see why this sweet Irish girl won over Joel Coben...

The last one made Mia smile more than the others.

She needn't have worried. The press had been more than kind in their reviews and interviews with her. Mia had fretted for weeks over the release, wondering what the critics would say and if the media would devour her whole, but the response was phenomenal. She was on the fast track to something good. She could just feel it. The introduction to world of show business seemed to be putting itself to rights after a rocky start.

"Congratulations," Joel had murmured in her ear, draping his arms around her shoulders and squeezing her tightly.

Mia relaxed back into his hold, allowing herself to absorb how truly happy she was at that moment. Things were looking good, she couldn't deny that.

Joel brandished a bottle of very expensive champagne before her eyes.

"I think we need to celebrate your success," he had said

with an allure in his voice that suggested more than champagne.

Now, her pick hit the strings of her guitar and the final note sounded through the amplifiers and into the room. The room vibrated with the sound and Mia let the feeling wash over her.

It was only a matter of weeks until she would hear that sound a thousand times louder, and the aftermath would be thousands of cheering fans, rather than an empty room with a spattering of applause from a handful of roadies.

The humming wall beside Mia told her that Joel was hard at work rehearsing in the next room, putting in the last few weeks of hard work before he headlined his biggest world tour to date. She didn't know how he did it. He was so laid back, so relaxed about the thought of thousands of people turning up to see his show all over the world.

Mia's back up guitarist nodded at her as he unplugged his amp. "I think we got it."

She returned his enthusiastic smile. "I think so too."

The amount of people needed to put on a tour like this had never occurred to Mia before. Not only the artists but their backing bands, their managers, the amount of roadies needed to assemble the stages and rigging each night, the crews that supported the tour—there was so much planning involved.

There was an awful lot more to it than walking out on stage each night.

Mia wouldn't get to see the stage until a couple of days before their first show at the Hollywood Bowl in a few weeks' time. The crew was hard at work designing and setting it up, but she and Joel couldn't do their final rehearsals on the big stage until then. Thinking about the tour made Mia remember Jackson was still stressing over finding a support act.

"How's it going, Jackson?" she asked when she unplugged from the amplifiers and made her way across the room.

"Not great." He sighed, shoving his phone back into his pocket. "The original band pulled out before Christmas and are insistent they won't do it. We're struggling to find someone just as good. We don't want to drop the standard on a tour this big."

Mia offered him a smile. "No pressure."

He looked tired, really tired. She wondered when he last took a holiday.

"That's exactly it," he said. "We don't want to take on just anyone. They need to be good, I mean really good."

"There's no one signed to the label?" she asked.

"No one that's ready." Jackson tugged at his tie, loosening it from his neck. "We thought we had a band we could use, but the lead singer quit."

"Oh," she said.

He shook his head in disbelief. "This support band seems cursed. It's the one thing that just won't fall into place."

"Can't you find anyone to take the lead singer's place in this other band?"

Jackson sighed. "Ready-made singers who can play guitar well *and* fit in with the rest of the band *and* who are good enough to come on this tour don't just fall out of the sky."

Mia hesitated, considering, for a moment.

Jackson thrust his hands into his pockets and stared skyward for inspiration, as if searching for the artist he described to literally fall out of the sky.

"Actually, they might," Mia said.

"They what?" Jackson asked.

"They might just fall out of the sky. Well, so to speak."

 ❧❧❧

"Bloody hell, Mia!"

The familiar, deep Irish tones of Dylan's voice called across the foyer of Sixth String Studios. Striding through the glass doors of the building, he already looked every inch the ready-made rock star Jackson so desperately needed.

Dressed in a fitted black T-shirt, distressed blue jeans, and Converse trainers, Dylan's rock star image was completed by his tattooed arms, messy dark hair, and brooding dark eyes which lit up when he saw Mia.

He's almost a mini Joel Coben, Mia thought. "Dylan," she called, rushing to greet her friend. "How are you?"

"Bloody fantastic," he said as he grabbed Mia and hugged her tightly.

She squeezed him back, glad to be back in the tattooed arms and familiar embrace of her friend. She smiled when she looked him in the eyes again. "I can imagine."

Seeing Jackson so stressed about the support band made Mia eager to help. She wanted to do anything she could to support those who had given her this shot at stardom but also to help anyone else she could too. Dylan fell into the latter category.

Jackson needed a singer, a singer who was good enough to come on a global tour with a Grammy-award-winning artist and front his opening support band. That singer ideally needed to be a ready-made rock star, one who wasn't fazed by the thousands of screaming fans, one who could sing well, play the guitar, and fit in with a band of age-twenty-something musicians, as if he had always been their frontman.

Jackson said singers like that didn't just fall out of the sky. Mia disagreed.

They did indeed fall out of the sky. Only after boarding a rather large airplane out of Dublin airport and flying for several hours before 'falling' out of the sky into LAX airport.

Mia suggested Dylan to Jackson. He was everything Jackson needed in an artist and could be in Los Angeles in a matter of days. Mia knew Dylan would relish the opportunity. He would throw himself headfirst into the challenge of coming on tour with a new band.

It had taken a grovelling phone call to Glen to apologise for stealing yet another member of his staff for the bright lights of Los Angeles.

"There must be something in the water in this feckin' place," Glen had muttered over the phone. "I'm losing another one of ye musicians, flying off to LA."

"I'm so sorry, Glen," Mia apologised again. "I really think Dylan would be great for this."

"I know, I know, Mia," Glen teased. "You're costing me my second star attraction."

"Second?"

He laughed. "Yes, second after you, ye daft beggar!"

And, with that, Mia had the green light to let Dylan board the plane to Los Angeles. Not that Dylan wouldn't have come anyway. Her conscience simply insisted she speak to Glen first.

Mia had shown Jackson all the YouTube videos she could find of Dylan performing at Glen's and other gigs across Ireland.

It only took two videos for Jackson to make the phone call to his assistant, asking her to book Dylan's flight.

"He's not in the same league as you," Jackson pointed out, "but he definitely has something special. He can work the crowd too, which is what we need. The girls love him."

Mia smiled. "They certainly do."

Mia knew all too well how Dylan affected women. She had seen it for years at Glen's and knew just how easily the female fans would quickly begin falling at his feet on this tour.

Niamh wasn't accompanying Dylan out to Los Angeles. The label was only paying for Dylan to fly out on such short notice. But now that the two of them had realized how they felt about each other, they would be rock solid.

No amount of female fans or groupies would come between Dylan and Niamh. And Mia would be there throughout the entire tour to keep an eye on Dylan, just in case.

"Mia, I really can't thank you enough," Dylan whispered as he released her slightly.

"Don't even mention it," she said with a shrug.

"No, I'm serious. How many people get offered something like this? I'm here because of you."

"I honestly couldn't think of anyone better. As soon as I heard, I told them all about you."

"I'm honored." Dylan flashed her one of his rare smiles, hitting her hard with the full force of his Irish charm.

Oh dear, Mia thought, *those fans have no idea what they're about to see.* "How's Niamh?" she asked, changing the subject.

"She's grand, as always." Dylan's dark features warmed as he spoke of Niamh. "She's gutted she can't come out here with me, but she's going to come out and join the tour when she can."

"That'll be great. I can't wait to see her again."

Dylan smiled, running a hand through his dark hair. "Me, too, I miss her already."

Mia smiled back, warmed at seeing her friend so openly declaring his love for her best friend. She really hoped they would survive the pressures of fame and the band, as they were so good together.

"So, are you ready to meet your new band?" Mia asked, untangling herself from his embrace.

"I sure am." He nodded enthusiastically, clapping a hand on Mia's back as he followed her across the foyer to the studio where the rest of his band were waiting.

Jackson introduced himself as soon as Dylan walked through the door. "Dylan, it's great to finally meet you."

He hadn't been expecting Dylan just yet, but Dylan had texted Mia to say he was almost at the studios and she was eager to meet her friend before the rest of the studio could pounce on him. She knew the minute Jackson and the band got hold of Dylan, he would be thrown into a hectic schedule of non-stop rehearsing until the tour began. She had wanted to be the familiar face to greet Dylan when he arrived at the studio before Los Angeles and his new band swallowed him whole.

"And you, Jackson. Thank you so much for this opportunity," Dylan replied, shaking Jackson's hand.

"You have Mia to thank for that, which I'm sure you already have," Jackson replied.

Dylan smiled over at Mia. "I have. She's the best."

"Let's introduce you to the band, shall we?" Jackson asked, gesturing behind him to where a group of twenty-something rockers were eagerly awaiting Dylan's arrival.

Well, as eager as age-twenty-something males can ever appear, Mia thought.

Lounging in the comfort of the studio's leather sofas were three young Americans. Mia already knew of the band's history through Jackson—Rivera 64 was a band from Seattle, Washington, and up until recently was a four-piece pop-rock band that played their own instruments and wrote their own songs. Their lead singer and guitarist had been offered a scholarship, so he had quit in the midst of signing a deal with Sixth String Studios and opening Joel Coben's headline arena tour, much to the rest of the band's dismay.

"Fecking idiot," Dylan had said when Mia explained the scenario to him over the phone.

Jack, Ryan, and Tom were a drummer, bassist, and guitarist without a frontman who were eagerly awaiting a small-time musician from Dublin to fill the gaping void in their band.

"Right, guys, allow me to introduce you to Dylan," Jackson said as he led Dylan over to the band.

The first guy peeled himself off the sofa and stood up to greet Dylan. "I'm Tom, bassist, pleased to meet you," the dark haired bassist said, smiling politely as he introduced himself. The band all wore similar attire of grungy tees and skinny jeans. Tom seemed quiet and reserved.

The second band member, who had spiky blond hair and wore heavy boots. His blue eyes twinkled and he flashed

Mia a smile over Dylan's shoulder, one that suggested he had a mischievous side. "Ryan, fellow guitarist."

Uh oh, Mia thought. She had seen that look before on Josh. It was bad enough with one of those to contend with, let alone two.

"I'm Jack, the drummer," said the final member of the band as he introduced himself to Dylan. Jack wore a vest that showed how muscular drumming had made his arms.

Mia had to admit they were pretty impressive.

"You guys have a lot of hard work to cram into these next few weeks," Jackson said, interrupting the friendly banter between the boys, to remind them all what they were there for. "I need to see you rehearsing hard, practise like you've never played an instrument before in your life. Dylan, I need you to work harder than anyone else. You've got a set list to remember, songs to familiarise yourself with, and lyrics to learn. I need you guys to look like you've always been together."

"Apart from the accents," Ryan joked.

Everyone laughed, even Jackson. There was only so much rehearsing they could do. Nothing was going to disguise the fact that Dylan didn't share the rest of the band's history.

"All right, apart from that," Jackson agreed. "You guys could have met anywhere. I've heard stranger stories, trust me. You guys just have to get it together by February seventh, you hear me?"

"We hear you," Tom affirmed.

"Now get out of here and let us get to work," Ryan said to Jackson with the same mischievous smile Mia saw earlier.

"All right, I'm going." Jackson dismissed the room with a wave, happily leaving the band members to get to work and teach Dylan their music.

"You joining the band too, sweetheart?" Ryan asked Mia.

"You wish," she teased.

The rest of the boys fell apart laughing as Ryan blushed, momentarily lost for words.

"See you later, Dylan," Mia said as she left the room.

He grinned widely across the room at her. "Thanks again, Mia."

Mia closed the door behind her, still able to hear the band laughing as she walked down the corridor. Her heart felt light in her chest. She had the swelling feeling that she had just done a wonderfully good deed. Dylan was happy. He had a promising start in a band that was about to tour the world. Not many guys his age were handed that opportunity. And to be able to hand it out to a friend like Dylan was certainly a good feeling.

Mia couldn't wait to see him shine on stage as Rivera 64's frontman. She had a gut feeling Dylan had found his place in Los Angeles, just as she had a only few months ago.

Chapter 26

Joel held his beer aloft to the crowd gathered in the living room. "This is it, our final night of freedom. Cheers, guys."

Our living room, Mia reminded herself. She still thought of the place as Joel's, despite his many insistences that it was as much hers as it was his.

"Cheers," the crowd echoed back to Joel.

"This is it," he repeated in Mia's ear once he took a swig from his bottle. He looped his arm around her waist, gently holding her body to his.

She nestled into the crook of his arm, contentedly comfortable in the embrace of her very own rock star. "Mmm," she mumbled back.

"Our last night before we hit the road," Joel continued, "our last night at home."

"I know, scary isn't it?"

"Scary, exciting, nerve wracking—"

Mia laughed. "Nerve wracking? Joel Coben you of all people do not get nervous."

"Okay, that one was mainly for you," he teased.

Mia leaned farther into him. She could faintly smell the beer on his breath as he kissed her cheek. She didn't care, even Joel could make that appealing. She wrapped her arm around his lean frame, nestled against his sculpted chest, and watched the gathering of people before them.

Joel had decided to throw a going-away party at his house—something else Josh insisted he never did—before the tour officially began tomorrow. The rehearsals were finally wrapped; the stage was built, assembled, and dissembled into the back of a truck; the guitars were tuned; and the tour buses were ready and waiting. There was no going back. Mia would be opening the first night of Joel Coben's worldwide arena tour at the Hollywood Bowl in twenty-four hours.

She took another sip of her beer.

Ryan, the guitarist from Rivera 64, beamed his cheeky smile at them both. "Thanks for the party, man."

"No worries." Joel shrugged. "There will be loads more of this once we get on the road."

"Swee-eet." Ryan elongated the word, his voice filled with admiration.

Mia wasn't sure if Ryan was more enthusiastic about the tour or the after parties.

The rest of his band were mingled among the crowd in Joel's—their—living room. Mia could see Dylan's tall, dark-haired frame across the room, talking to Tom, the bassist. Jack, the drummer, was farther across the room, talking to TJ.

Intermixed with the rest of the crowd were Charlie and Josh, Jackson, Ruben, Lyle, Chad, and his girlfriend Tara, numerous roadies, and crew members who would all be assisting the Joel Coben World Tour. Mia only wished the rest of her friends and family from Ireland were there to complete the night entirely.

"Are you okay?" Joel asked her quietly, watching her observe the room.

"Never better." She beamed up at him. "I just wish a few other people could be here with us tonight," she told him honestly, the joy in her heart now bittersweet.

"They soon will be." Joel hugged her tightly. "Just imagine the after party when we play Dublin, everyone will be there then."

Mia smiled, already picturing all of her friends and Mike and Sharon waiting for her backstage in a few months. "I can't wait."

"They'll be watching and reading everything online. They'll practically know the set list by heart by the time we get to Dublin," Joel teased.

"That's true," Mia said. She knew Mike and Sharon would be Googling her every day and scouring YouTube for videos uploaded by the fans in the crowd.

"And I'm one hundred percent sure Niamh will be watching the show first hand long before then," Joel added.

Mia looked up at him watching Dylan across the room. "Me too, at least I hope so."

She was really missing her friends back home. As many new friends as she was making in Los Angeles, they would never replace the ones from Dublin. She just couldn't wait to have them all together in the same room.

Of course, there was another presence missing from the party that night. Luke. Her brother had flown back to Koh Li Pe after Christmas and Mia was already missing him. Emailing and Skyping just weren't the same as having her brother in her daily life. She marveled at how far they had come in their relationship since the accident. They were already building bridges and forming a close brother-and-sister friendship. Mia couldn't wait to tell him about the party he was missing tonight. She was sure he would love to be right here with her and all their friends.

She wondered if Luke could get across to the mainland when the tour reached Thailand and Malaysia next year. It was just a pity he couldn't be with everyone when the tour reached Ireland.

"That's going to be a great few days," Joel said, "when we get to Dublin."

"It sure is," she replied.

"The highlight of the tour I reckon," Joel winked at her.

Out of all the places in the world they would soon be visiting, they both knew having everyone together in Dublin would be the best part of the tour. And nothing compared to the hospitality and eagerness of an Irish crowd, something Mia reminded Joel of.

"Is that so?" He laughed. "You have yet to play to the rest of the USA, Miss Ryan."

"Home crowd." Mia shrugged. "Dylan and I will blow the roof off that place."

"And I won't?" Joel asked, his face alight with amusement.

"Nope, sorry we got that one down."

"Not that it's *my* tour or anything," Joel teased.

Mia giggled. "No, they're only coming to see us."

Joel grabbed her waist and pulled her close to him, his arms tightening around her body. His eyes were sparkling and full of life as he came toward her. At that moment in time, Mia didn't think she'd ever seen him happier.

The whole room was alive with anticipation, eagerness, and appreciation for the journey they were all about to take together.

Mia could already sense the makings of their own little family assembled in the room.

She had a good feeling about this tour. There wasn't one person in the room she wasn't looking forward to sharing the majority of the rest of the year on the road with.

There was music playing through the surround-sound system, people were dancing or talking, and the drinks were flowing. Mia couldn't have asked for a better send off for their tour.

Across the room, someone dimmed the light switch and turned up the volume on the sound system.

Joel laughed, leaning in and kissing her deeply. "That's what I'm talking about."

Mia looped her arms around his neck and together their bodies swayed along to the steady beat of the music. Their foreheads rested against one another, and Joel was softly singing the words of the song to Mia. She smiled as he did, relishing in one of her own private Joel Coben performances. Soon she would have to share this man with thousands of screaming fans every single night before she would get him to herself again.

Thankfully, the hours whittled slowly by in a blur of dancing and mingling with their guests. There was a great sense of anticipation in the air. Everyone in the room, whether they were coming on the tour or not, knew that this was the eve of something great. Mia almost found the feeling akin to the same one felt on Christmas or New Year's Eve, that exciting, eagerly anticipating feeling as you ticked by the hours for the day that was to come.

"We're gonna head off," Charlie shouted in Mia's ear above the noise of the music several hours later.

Mia nodded. "Okay, we'll come see you out."

She motioned to Joel to follow her out of the room to say goodbye to some of their last remaining guests.

The alarm system by the front door glowed brightly as they walked past. Mia noticed the time was one-thirty a.m. They would soon be getting up again to hit the road.

As soon as they were outside, Charlie grabbed Mia's hand. "Don't worry about this, okay?" she said to Mia, pulling her to one side away from the brothers.

Mia smiled. "I'm okay, honestly."

"You sure? I know how much you've been stressing?"

"I think I'm finally okay." Mia laughed. "It's taken me long enough, but tonight let me see what a great team we've got with us and how well everyone gets along. I think this tour's going to be the best."

"You got that right." Charlie winked. "You deserve all of this, Mia," She gestured around to Joel, the house, and the party behind them.

Mia knew she was including the tour and everything else in that statement too. "I hope so," she said.

"You do, trust me. You'll see." Charlie embraced her into as big of a hug as her little frame could manage. She beamed at Mia before stepping aside to hug Joel. "Thank you for a great party."

Josh immediately took Charlie's place and grabbed Mia into one of his giant bear hugs before setting her back down on the steps. "See you in the morning, kid."

Joel laughed, shaking his head as he watched Josh return Mia to his side Joel clapped his brother on the back. "See you in the morning, bro."

"Bye, guys," Charlie called over her shoulder.

"Tomorrow it begins," Josh shouted and punched the air. "This is it!"

Mia laughed, shaking her head in unison with Joel, as they watched the couple climb into a car before being driven out of their gates.

"I've no idea where they get that much energy from," Joel said in disbelief, still watching the car's taillights.

Mia laughed. "Me neither, but I know I need some of it."

"I'm sure you could find some from somewhere," Joel whispered into her ear as he pulled her close to him, his voice full of promise.

"Eww, can you guys at least wait 'til we've all left?"

Mia knew without looking that voice belonged to Ryan. She had a feeling the Rivera 64 boys would be often interrupting moments like this soon.

"Hurry up then," she teased.

"We're leaving now anyway." He winked. "So you don't have to wait much longer."

Mia laughed, reluctantly untangling herself from Joel's embrace to bid goodbye to the last of their guests.

Once the final car had pulled out of their driveway, and the gates were firmly closed behind them, Mia and Joel shut the front door of the house.

"Our last few hours of privacy." Joel's voice was filled with promise again as soon as they were alone.

"Mmm," Mia said, giving him a teasing smile, "plenty of time to sleep."

Joel laughed. "That's not quite what I had in mind."

"Come on." She entwined her fingers with his, reaching behind her to turn out the light switch in the living room before pulling Joel up the stairs behind her.

Their bedroom was dark. The only light that filtered into the room was through the curtains from the moon's pale glow outside. There was an beautiful glow about the room, as if it too knew what lay ahead. "Give me two minutes," Joel whispered behind her, kissing her hair before pulling away from her.

"What?" Mia asked, surprised.

"I really, *really* need a shower after that party," he said over his shoulder as he disappeared into the bathroom.

Mia shook her head. He was worse than some women. Talk about killing the moment.

While she waited, refraining from counting all of 120 seconds, she undressed and perched on the edge of the bed, hoping the pale light from the moon outside their window was casting her in the same beautiful glow it gave to the room.

Sure enough, Joel materialised shortly afterward. He turned off the bathroom light before stopping when he saw her waiting for him on the bed.

"Wow," he breathed heavily, "you look beautiful."

Mia managed a smile in return. She could no longer think about what she looked like right then. For the sight of Joel wrapped in a small cotton towel, his sculpted body still covered in droplets of water from his shower completely took her breath away.

Moisture trickled over the contours of his chest and stomach before falling into the plush cotton of the white towel that was wrapped around his waist. Mia stared hard. His hair was still wet. Water drops fell from the edges across his cheek, and he ran a hand through it, as if trying to keep it away from his face.

Mia felt as if she were watching an advertisement. Life, at that moment, seemed to play out in slow motion. She could almost hear the slow, pulsing beat of music as he walked across the room toward her.

One bare foot in front of the other came toward her across the carpet. She let her eyes drift upward to the towel stopping above his knees and tied loosely about his waist. Only a gentle pull would cause it to fall to the floor. As he drew closer, she found her eyes drawn to the trickling beads of water that cascaded over his sculpted chest, ran down the tattooed inkings on his body, and over the hard lines that defined his stomach. She swallowed, hard. No matter how many times she saw that body, she never tired of looking at it.

"You okay?" he asked, shaking a hand through his wet hair again.

"Mmm hmm," she replied, staring as he trailed a hand over his chest and down his stomach, flicking away stray drops of water.

"I envy that hand," she muttered, immediately feeling her cheeks flame red as she realised she had said the words aloud.

A low chuckle came from Joel's chest. Mia watched it rise and fall as he did, her eyes drawn to the curves of muscle that lay there.

He sat down beside her on the bed. Taking her hand in his, he placed her palm on his chest, retracing the route his had made only seconds before. He stopped just millimetres away from the edge of the towel. "Better?" he asked.

She could still feel the dampness in her hand from the water on his skin. The dampness on her bra was now beginning to soak through to her skin as she leaned into his body. "Not quite," she whispered, her fingers snaking back up his stomach, tracing the lines of his tattoos and muscles alike.

Joel chuckled again. This time, the noise was against her lips. The feeling resonated into her own chest as he pressed his against hers, her own body now feeling the dampness still on his. "Better?" he asked again as he pulled his lips away from hers.

"Almost," she said breathily, her eyes sparkling as she gave the towel a gentle pull and watched it fall onto the bed around his hips.

Chapter 27

Although Joel's house was only a short drive from the Hollywood Bowl, the tour officially began today and the management team was insisting that everyone board their tour buses, in preparation for the coming months.

Some had moaned and groaned about carting all their stuff onto the bus when their homes were so close by, but others—Mia included—had jumped at the chance to get straight onto the buses and bag their bunks in their "homes-away-from-home" for the next few months.

"You won't be saying that in a few weeks' time," Joel had said with a laugh, when Mia insisted they sleep on the bus that night.

"Why?" she asked, although he wasn't disagreeing with her. Joel had his own bedroom at the end of a particularly large tour bus, so he didn't suffer the same 'roughing it,' as the rest of the boys on the tour did.

Mia, of course, would be sharing Joel's rather large room with him. Dylan and the rest of Rivera 64 and the other crew members on the tour would be crammed into bunk bed style cubbies that lined the length of the buses. Each person had their own single bed, a shelf inside their cubby to store things and just enough head room to sit up in bed. *The perks of a rock and roll life*, Mia thought.

The band members seemed unfazed. They couldn't wait to throw themselves into tour life and were already planning tour bus parties and working out what games they could play in the space they had to keep themselves entertained for hours on the road.

Mia knew it wouldn't be long before the narrow, carpet-lined corridor would be littered with beer bottles, guitar picks, and dirty laundry. She was glad she and Joel were sharing a tour bus with Lyle, Charlie, and Josh. The rest of the boys had their own bus.

The inside of the bus looked just as rock and roll as Mia had imagined it would.

When their car pulled up in the parking lot behind the Hollywood Bowl, the tour buses were ready and waiting for their arrivals.

Side by side sat several long, shiny black buses in the car park. Each one's paintwork reflected their faces back at them as they approached. The chrome glinted blindingly in the morning sunlight. They were beautiful. Mia stared with admiration up at them as she climbed out of the car and walked across the tarmac to the bus doors.

Lyle pointed out to the third bus in the line-up. "This one's ours."

Joel grinned at him. "Of course."

Mia could see why. Of course, Joel had the biggest tour bus. He was the star of the tour. This was his tour, and he deserved the biggest bus.

"After you." He held out his hand to Mia and briefly curled his fingers around hers as she climbed aboard the tour bus first.

"Wow," she said breathily once she had ascended the steps into the bus.

"Cool, huh?" he said into her ear, placing his hand on her waist.

Mia smiled. "It's more than cool."

The interior of the bus wouldn't have looked out of place on an episode of *Cribs*. Everything looked ultra-modern and ultra-expensive. The front of the bus was lined with cream leather seats. Some sat opposite one another booth-style with little tables, and others lined the sides of the bus like sofas. A large, flat screen television hung off one wall with an assortment of games consoles and DVDs in the cubby underneath mid-way between the sofas. Farther along the bus there was a kitchen where Joel opened the fridge door to reveal shelves stocked full of food and bottles of beer. Next, there was a small bathroom followed by four of the bunk-bed style beds that stereotypically lined the tour buses. Of course, these were larger and comfier looking than the standard issue beds Mia knew the band would be living in on the bus next door.

"And this," Joel put his hand over Mia's eyes as he pushed open the door at the end of the tour bus, "is our room."

"Our room?" Mia squeaked when he took his hand away.

"Uh huh," Joel confirmed.

"Wow," Mia said again. She had said that word more times that she remembered in the last few minutes.

At the end of the tour bus was a bedroom. But it wasn't like any other beds on the other tour buses. With Joel being the star of the tour, he naturally had the biggest and most impressive bedroom. Mia wondered if it was possible that this bedroom was cooler than his bedroom in his mansion.

"This cannot be on a tour bus," she said in disbelief.

Joel chuckled, sliding past her and throwing himself down on the cream bedding. "Well, you're standing in one."

The bed took up a huge portion of the room. The circular bed was larger than king-size and had enough pillows to accommodate everyone else on the tour. There was yet another flat screen TV on the wall and wood panelled wardrobes and cupboards lined one side of the bus wall.

"You coming to join me?" he asked, patting the bed beside him.

Mia smiled and perched on the edge of the bed next to Joel's legs, still staring in disbelief that this would be her home for the next few months.

She often dreamed of touring the world on a tour bus, gigging her way up and down various countries, and living in the confinement of a cramped bus, but she hadn't imagined anything like the one she was now sitting in.

She had gone straight to the top, that was for sure.

She felt Joel shift his weight behind her before placing his hands on her waist and pulling her down on the bed next to him.

Mia shrieked in surprise before laughing as she lay back on the bed beside him.

"Happy?" he asked, placing a kiss on her cheek.

Mia smiled up at him. "Very."

He had propped himself up on one arm so that he stared down into her eyes. His hand brushed a stray hair away from her face, his fingers leaving a gentle trail on her skin as he did.

Mia gazed up into his eyes. What she saw reflected in them was not the haunted, troubled image she had seen when she first arrived in LA. Now she saw her own reflection staring back at her from their dark surfaces. But the surface was where the darkness ended, for Mia knew her image was what was giving those eyes their newfound light. Joel's soul was no longer troubled. He was happy and content, the light was finally back in those darkened windows.

"I love you," she told him.

"I love you too," he whispered back before drawing the curtains on the windows and closing his eyes to kiss her.

∽∘∾

From the comfort of the green room backstage, Mia could already hear the chatter and hum of the crowd gathering in the arena. She sat on the sofa next to Joel, both of them having just finished an interview with a local television station before commencing the painful wait until they took to the stage.

Nearby, Dylan and the other members of Rivera 64 were anxiously pacing up and down the room, waiting to be called to the stage to open the show for the night.

"You all right Mia?" Dylan asked from across the room.

Mia nodded. Her throat was too tight with nerves to manage words. She had no idea how she was going to sing soon.

Dylan laughed. "I've never seen you this nervous before," he said, coming to sit beside her.

"Neither have I," Joel said from her other side.

"I'm starting to freak out," she admitted. "I've never played to a crowd this size before. What if they don't like me? What if your fans hate me for being with you?"

Joel shook his head. Mia could tell he was trying not to laugh. "Don't be stupid," he said. "As soon as you start to play, they'll fall in love with your music."

Mia wrung her hands together in her lap. "I don't know."

She had been worrying for days about going on stage before Joel. Some of his fans were crazily obsessed with him. They had camped out for days at the arena just to get to the front of the crowd this evening and be within yards of their idol. Mia had seen them rip people to pieces on Twitter for saying the wrong thing about Joel. These girls were more than overly protective. She was throwing herself to a wild pack of lionesses in the form of teenage girls.

"Don't sweat it, Mia." Dylan patted her arm. "You'll be great."

"That's easy for you to say, mini Joel," Mia teased.

"Huh?" Dylan and Joel echoed in unison.

"You're practically a mini Joel," Mia explained. "They're going to love you, regardless of what the band sounds like. And you're young, gorgeous, and a musician. Girls will automatically love you."

Dylan shrugged. "Suppose you're right."

Mia rolled her eyes. She knew she was right. Teenagers and girls in their early twenties often went weak at the knees for musicians. Mia could have sworn they saw the guitar first and the man second. She, on the other hand, was the most envied person in the entire arena that night. She would be sharing a bed with their idol after the show, something those girls could only dream about. That was bound to have repercussions.

A roadie stuck his head around the door and summoned Rivera 64. "Guys, it's show time."

The band whooped and cheered as they filed out of the room.

"You coming to see us go on, Mia?" Dylan asked.

"Sure we are," Joel answered for her, hauling her out of her seat by her hand and tugging her after the band.

They followed the band through the winding maze of corridors and empty equipment containers to the backstage area.

Mia could hear the crowd already, their constant hum of chatter and singing along to the background music that was being played into the arena to keep them entertained until the band went on.

Joel clapped each member of the band on the arm in turn. "Knock 'em dead, guys."

"Thank you so much, Joel," Tom said.

Jack hugged Joel. "Yeah, thanks for bringing us along for the ride, man!"

"We can't thank you enough," Ryan said to Joel.

"We'll celebrate after," Joel promised them.

"I can't thank *you* enough, Mia," Dylan said as she made her way down the line of musicians after Joel and finally reached him.

"Don't even mention it." She grinned. "I know you'll be amazing at this."

Dylan laughed before pulling her into a hug. "We'll soon find out."

"Let's do this!" Ryan cheered as the band formed a huddle and gave each other their final words of encouragement.

"Good luck, guys," Mia called out as the band parted and filed their way up the steps to the back of the stage.

The lights in the arena went out and spotlights began to swirl around the stage. The crowd immediately began to scream and cheer. The change in the atmosphere was instantaneous. Mia could feel their excited anticipation, their eagerness for the show to begin as the dancing spotlights taunted them further.

The crowd screamed louder and whooped as the band began to file on stage. Dylan was the last to go on. He looked back over his shoulder and gave Mia a final thumbs up before heading out onstage to thousands of screaming girls welcoming him to the front of the stage.

"Come on." Joel grinned at her, tugging her along to the side of the stage, where they could watch from the wings without being spotted by Joel's eager fans.

The band had kicked off their set and already the crowd was jumping up and down, singing along to the songs, and calling out to the members.

As Mia had imagined, Dylan worked the crowd effortlessly. The female members of the crowd called out to him; screamed when he walked by; and snapped away on their phones, grabbing as many pictures of him as they could.

Mia felt her chest swell with pride as she watched him. She knew she made the right decision in bringing him to Los Angeles. He belonged on stage, as did she, not pulling pints behind a bar. She was just grateful she had been able to give him the opportunity. Jackson would never have known what a star Dylan was if Rivera 64's original member hadn't quit. Mia hoped that guy's scholarship was worth it.

Joel stood behind Mia, pressing his body against hers and wrapping his arms around her waist. Mia leant back into his chest and contentedly stood in his protective embrace, watching the band play through their set.

All too quickly it was over, and Dylan was waving

goodbye to the crowd, asking them to check out the band on iTunes and follow them on Twitter. Mia could already see dozens of phones light up under their owner's noses as they logged on to find the band's Twitter page.

"That was incredible!" Dylan shouted as they stepped down from the stage.

"Man, what a crowd!" Ryan agreed as he leapt over the railings.

Mia smiled to herself and then up at Joel as they watched Rivera 64 revel in the post-show adrenaline.

All of the guys were covered in sweat, their T-shirts clung to their bodies, and their hair fell about their faces in dripping tendrils. They shook it off, swigging heavily from cold bottles of Evian that were in constant supply backstage.

"That was an awesome set, guys," a faded Irish accent said from across the room.

Mia turned from their group to see Luke striding across the backstage area toward them.

"Luke!" she called, running to greet her brother.

"How you doing, kid?" he asked as he grabbed her, pulling her into an enormous hug.

Mia laughed. "Even better now.

"I can't wait to see you go on," he said, stepping back so he could see her.

"Yeah, I'm a little nervous about that," Mia admitted. Although seeing the band receive such a reaction from the crowd and seeing how elated they were afterward had reignited her desire to go on.

"What are you doing here?" she asked suddenly.

Luke laughed. "It's nice to see you, too."

Mia shook her head. "No, I just mean I wasn't expecting it, that's all."

She had spoken to Luke most days, keeping him informed on how the tour preparations were going. She hadn't expected him to be here on the opening night. He never said anything about coming over to the States again. Mia couldn't imagine Luke had the spare cash for return tickets to Los Angeles, and for two people at that. Luke's partner Nittaya was standing patiently behind him while he greeted his sister.

"Hey, it's so good to see you again," Mia said when she realized who was standing behind him.

Nittaya looked as stunningly beautiful as ever. Her long dark hair cascaded over her bare shoulders and her big, dark eyes were made up with brown eyeshadow.

"Joel arranged this for us," Luke explained once Mia and Nittaya had greeted each other again.

"Joel?" Mia asked, turning to look at her boyfriend.

Joel held up his hands. "Guilty, as charged."

Mia looked from her brother to Joel, wondering how long they had been planning this for.

"I thought you might like to have your brother here to see you play on the opening night," Joel explained. "He's never seen you perform yet either."

Mia stepped toward him. Putting her arms around his neck, she reached up and kissed him. "Thank you."

Joel's face broke out into a huge smile and his eyes brightened to the same level Mia had seen hours earlier when they were alone on the tour bus. "Anything for you," he said before kissing her again.

A roadie wearing a headset came up and interrupted them. "Mia, it's your turn."

Mia took a deep breath in, holding on to Joel's embrace a moment longer before letting go.

Luke gave her another hug. "Good luck."

"You'll be great, Mia," Nittaya said.

"Seriously, it's fantastic out there!" Dylan encouraged her.

When Mia had spoken to each of them, she followed the roadie, who was carrying her guitar, to the steps behind the stage.

She turned and looked at her friends, who were now filing toward the front of the stage so they could watch her perform. Joel, of course, was right behind her.

"Show them what you're made of," he whispered so that only she could hear. "Show them exactly why you deserve this. Show them why I love you."

With those words, he kissed her deeply. His hands cupped her cheeks, and Mia felt every ounce of sincerity behind his words before he let her go.

"I will," she whispered as they parted, taking one final look into his familiar eyes. Within them, she saw everything she needed. She saw every reason she needed to give this show everything she had. She saw everything Joel wanted her to see. She saw how much he loved her.

The roadie grinned at her as he handed her the guitar. "Showtime."

"It sure is." Mia grinned back, placing the strap over her head and walking out onto the stage.

She took a deep breath, looking out at the crowd in front of her. The stage was dark again, the spotlights were doing their swirling dance around the arena as they waited for the artist to step out onto the stage. Mia saw all the thousands of faces waiting for her to make an appearance. She saw the glow of thousands of phones waiting to capture her every move. The atmosphere was electric. The air itself was alive with crackling energy of the adrenaline yet to come.

Suddenly, Mia had difficulty placing one foot in front of the other. She paused for a second as she prepared to step out onto the stage.

This was it. This was the moment she had waited her entire life for.

Her moment, her shot.

Her moment in the spotlight was finally here.

And it was in the Hollywood Bowl.

That part of the scenario Mia had difficulty wrapping her head around. She was about to perform at a sold-out show in the Los Angeles Hollywood Bowl. This was exactly the kind of moment she had spent hours, days, and months dreaming of. She, Mia Ryan from little Kinsale, was about to open Joel Coben's sold-out tour.

She walked out across the stage. The expanse of space to the microphone at center stage was seemingly endless. The lights began to swirl out over the crowd before dancing across the stage as Mia approached the microphone. She could hear the deafening noise of the crowd welcoming her to the stage through her earpieces. That was the part she was most nervous about—how the crowd would react to her being on Joel's tour.

Joel and Mia had been official for some time now, and Mia had long feared how Joel's ruthlessly loyal fans would react to her. Joel had told Mia to just let her music speak for itself and the fans would be won over by her talent.

Here goes nothing then, she thought as she adjusted her guitar and took her place behind the microphone.

Mia gave a small smile of relief as the blinding spotlight shut out most of her vision of the thousands of people before her. She knew, eventually, the lights would spin out to the crowd and the harsh lighting would lift and change throughout her set, but, for now, the familiar blinding of the light was comforting.

The backing band kicked off the first song and the crowd fell silent as Mia began to sing. Only the few stray whoops and cheers could be heard throughout the room as she launched into her first verse. The familiar silence descended upon the room, and Mia was once again comforted by the feeling, knowing she was the touching thousands of hearts with her words as they quietly listened to every heartfelt one she sang.

She reached the crescendo of her first song. The bridge after the final verse between the last chorus was always Mia's favorite part of music. The song was in full swing and she could really lose herself in it at that point.

The lights lifted with the music and Mia was finally able to see the thousands of people watching her, riveted. Her eyes drifted across the front row of people hanging over the security barriers, and she was surprised to see many of the faces staring back at her singing along with her word for word. She scanned along the front row and beyond them into the crowd as she sang, her eyes finally resting on the wings of the crowd.

There, that was where she saw him. Eerily, he was standing exactly where Mia always pictured *them* standing. Every time she performed, she always looked out into the crowd and pictured her parents standing there, singing along to her music, their eyes brimming with pride as they watched their daughter take to the stage.

And that was where Luke was now standing. He wore exactly the same expression Mia had pictured her parents wearing. All the hundreds of shows she had performed before this, all the endless songs she had written about him, and now he was standing there watching her sing them.

The sight was surreal. Mia wondered if Luke realized all these songs were about him. Years of scanning the crowd looking for him, endless songs she sang through closing her eyes and picturing him, and now he was finally here.

She thought she might faint with the overwhelming reality. Everything was coming together on one night.

Then there was Joel. He was standing discretely in the wings of the stage, tucked out of sight of his waiting fans but still with the best ticket in the house to Mia's first show.

The sight of them both so proudly watching her made her heart flutter in her chest.

This is it, she thought. *I'm finally doing it.*

The last notes of her first song faded into the crowd, and the audience immediately burst into applause, whooping and cheering their support for her.

Mia shook her head in disbelief as the lighting lifted and she could see the thousands of people rooting for her.

"Thank you very much," she heard her own voice echo through the sound system, and they cheered again in response.

Mia adjusted her fingers on the fretboard again before beginning her second song. She quickly glanced to the side where Joel's face was brimming with pride as he watched her. She smiled at him before turning back to the crowd and kicking off her next song.

Before she knew it, she was working her way through the set, chatting to the crowd between her songs and laughing at the signs the eager fans had prepared for Joel.

"He's going to love that one," she said with a laugh, as she pointed out a fairly rude one.

Those close enough to see turned to look at the sign and laughed with her. Mia loved the engaging response she got from the crowd. They already loved her, and she felt as though she was performing to her own fans. *Hopefully someday these guys will be coming to my own tour.*

The crowd sang eagerly along when Mia played her original version of the song, *Hear Me*, which had been a huge hit for the band Glasshearts. It had been Jackson's idea for Mia to add the song to her set list. He'd said artists often performed a cover track at live shows and this would go down a storm with the crowd as the song was now so popular. It was an added bonus that Mia had originally written the song and the crowd would get to hear the original version of it.

All too soon the last bars of her final song had echoed out into the thousands of listeners in the crowd, and it felt as though every person in the arena was cheering for Mia. In the space of a few songs, she'd had them singing along with her, chanting, and clapping, and she'd even seen more than a few teary eyes in the arena when she'd played her most emotional song. Reducing the Hollywood Bowl to tears was definitely going down in Mia's journal. That kind of thing didn't happen every day.

"Thank you so much, Hollywood Bowl, you guys have been incredible!" Mia shouted to the crowd as she took her final bow.

As she walked off the stage, she turned and waved once more and what she saw took her breath away. Thousands of hands were in the air, clapping and cheering, all for her. Thousands of phones were glowing in the masses as they captured her one last time and, most of all, thousands of voices chanted in unison as she walked away.

"Mia! Mia! Mia! Mia! Mia!"

She felt her heart race in her chest as she heard them calling for her. She had pictured them chanting at her but not in this way. She'd imagined them booing her for being with Joel. But this audience loved her. They were shouting their love for her.

Mia unhooked her guitar from around her neck, thrust it into the waiting arms of a roadie, and threw herself into the waiting arms of her biggest fan waiting in the wings.

Chapter 28

Touring was singlehandedly the most taxing, tiring, and exhilarating experience Mia had ever endured. Nothing compared to the adrenaline surge that coursed through her body each and every single night she took to the stage. Each time the crowd seemed bigger, louder, and more supportive than the last.

"Your fan base is growing," Joel told her one morning as he scrolled through the entertainment news on his phone.

Mia shook her head. "We've only been on tour a couple of weeks."

"Word travels fast." Joel smiled as he inched closer to her on the tour bus sofa. "The world of social media is going crazy for you."

Mia glanced down at the phone in his hand and blinked a couple of times.

"Look." Joel laughed again at her disbelief, picked up her hand, and placed his phone into it.

Mia scrolled down the touch screen at all the comments and replies—Twitter, Facebook, Instagram—they were all full of responses from fans, showering Mia with praise and adoration. The gossip websites and entertainment news pages were full of positive reviews about Mia's slot on Joel's tour.

Joel nudged her in the ribs. "I think you're getting better reviews than me."

"I never expected anything like this." Mia stared up at his big dark eyes, "I thought they were going to hate me."

"Because of me?" he asked, his eyes clouding over.

Mia nodded.

"You were so wrong," he whispered into her ear. "They only see exactly why I love you."

Mia titled her head to look back into those big dark eyes and felt her own smile mirror the one that was plastered on his handsome face.

ↄ◦ↄ◦ↄ

Before she knew it, their stint in California was over and their tour buses were packed up and heading east across America.

Joel's tour was headlining arenas and venues across the States before they would fly out to Brazil and tour South America, then they would fly on to the UK and tour Europe before heading across the Far East and on to Australia.

Mia could only take the tour one day at a time. She didn't dare allow herself to think so far ahead to the dates that were planned for the rest of the year. It already baffled her to be playing to sold-out crowds in California, where she had spent the last few months of her life, let alone performing to sold-out arenas across the globe. The tour moved so fast, she barely had time to realize what State they were in, let alone which town.

They soon headlined shows in San Francisco and, after that, were driving out of California and into Nevada, where a run of shows on the famous Las Vegas strip awaited them.

"We're here." Joel's hand was nudged Mia awake as she had peacefully dozed off in his arms in the back of the tour bus late one afternoon.

"Huh?" she asked sleepily as she peeled open her tired eyes.

Joel grinned, squeezing his hand around her waist and opening the curtain wider so Mia could see what he was looking at. "Las Vegas, baby."

In the fading dusky light of the early evening, the Las Vegas strip was already coming to life. Mia could see, in the distance, the bright glow of the numerous lights on the strip as the buses approached the city in the middle of the Nevada desert. She frowned as she stared out of the window. She had never visited Las Vegas, until now, and she marveled at how strange it looked just plonked in the middle of the desert. A place so vibrant and full of life should have been closer to civilization, somewhere with endless suburbs and highways connecting it to various other towns nearby. But then, Mia realized, Las Vegas was probably a law unto itself. It was the kind of place that needed to be in its own little bubble out here in the middle of the desert.

She smiled as she recognized some of the landmarks they passed—the Paris Hotel with its replica Eifel Tower, the palatial fountain of Caesar's Palace Hotel, the numerous hotels and drive-through wedding chapels that littered the boulevards of one of the most famous cities in the world. Mia stared in disbelief as they drove past the sites of numerous TV shows and movies that she had watched over the years as they passed one after the other.

"There's nowhere else on earth quite like it," Joel said quietly beside her.

Mia knew, he too, was admiring this unique city from behind the privacy of their tinted tour bus windows. Soon the bright lights and citizens of Las Vegas would be admiring them, and it would be Mia and Joel's turn to headline here.

❧❦❧

"Thank you so much, Las Vegas! Goodnight!" Joel's deep, sultry voice echoed through his microphone and into the arena where thousands of screaming fans were begging him to stay onstage, cheering him one final time, and waving goodbye as he left the stage.

"Wow." He beamed from ear to ear as he left the stage and immediately swooped Mia into his arms. "That was some crowd."

Mia laughed as he set her down in the wings of the stage. "I know, they were crazy."

She never tired of watching him perform. Just as she never tired of playing the same songs of her own each night, she never tired of watching Joel sing his over and over again.

When Joel took to the stage, he came alive in the way that was usually only reserved for her. He gave away a little piece of himself each time he performed. He put his heart and soul into every performance, and every crowd got just as good a show as the one before them. Mia saw every ounce of passion and determination in Joel's performances, she saw exactly why he had worked as hard as he had and just how much his fame meant to him when he took to the stage.

He chatted to the crowds between his songs, as if he was sitting and having a one-on-one conversation with each of them. He laughed at the signs they made. He pointed and waved to the overly enthusiastic fans, and he aimed the microphone into the crowd for them to sing his songs back to him.

It always made Mia's heart swell with pride and admiration to hear the crowd loudly singing along with Joel's music word for word, to hear them appreciate and understand his painfully personal music was heart wrenching. It was as if every person in that room shared the same pain, the same emotions, and the same heartache.

And that, Mia realized, was what brought his fans together.

That was exactly why Joel's fans identified with his music. They had all felt exactly the same way before at some point in their lives. Joel just had a beautifully poetic way of describing the things that so many people encountered in their daily lives, and that was what made him so successful. People believed he was singing about them, or to them.

Mia wrapped her arms around his sweat-drenched back and pulled him in to her. "I'm so proud of you," she gushed.

"Really?" Joel asked, pulling back to look at her. He ran a hand through his damp hair and let it slick back onto his head.

Mia nodded. "Every show seems as good as the last one. They love you so much," she said, gesturing to the crowd who were now slowly filing out of the arena.

Joel stared in the same direction and nodded. "They do. I couldn't ask for better fans. That's why I'm so glad they've taken to you as well as they have. One day, they'll support you as much as they do me. You'll be playing to your own sell-out world tour, hearing them sing back your songs word for word, and adhering to a deafening request for an encore."

Mia laughed. Each night when Joel's set finished, he left the stage and, as was typical in live music, he waited for the crowd to begin to chant. Still riding high from the energy of the show, they would begin to call for an encore, their applause and stomping feet getting louder and louder until the lights would go back up, and Joel would take to the stage for two more songs.

Tonight, the encore chant had been particularly loud.

"We've still got two more nights of this," Mia reminded him.

"I know." Joel shook his head. "Imagine what they're going to be like."

"It's Vegas, anything could happen."

കൈ

"Guys, look!" Charlie called over her shoulder and

pointed at the The Venetian Hotel where gondolas were sailing around the man-made rivers of the Venice-inspired hotel.

"We should totally go on one," Josh said, pushing Charlie in the direction of the hotel.

The first evening they arrived in Las Vegas hadn't left much time for sight-seeing by the time the buses had arrived at the arena. The first full day had been spent unloading the equipment, running sound checks, and rehearsing.

Day two had mainly been filled with press duties—giving interviews to local magazines, newspapers, and radio stations—and a few photo shoots. Their third day in Las Vegas was thankfully a day off before the show that night and Mia and Joel finally had some free time to act like tourists before their buses packed up again and moved on to the next town.

Joel, of course, had been to Vegas numerous times on tour but was happy to go along with Mia and Charlie's requests to visit every tourist attraction imaginable in the time they had. Joel and Josh dutifully followed them around, enjoying their few hours of freedom in the heat of the Nevada desert. Both of them were wearing sunglasses to attempt to disguise themselves from the hordes of fans and tourists that were congregated in Las Vegas, but they were still approached dozens of times by fans as they wandered their way across the city.

"Wait until we actually get to Venice, you can go on a real one," Joel pointed out.

"Oh, yeah." Charlie paused. "I hadn't thought of that."

"And in Paris, we can go up the real Eifel Tower too," Josh said, pointing at Vega's own version of the landmark.

"Don't be getting any romantic ideas now," Ryan teased, elbowing Josh.

Mia rolled her eyes, Of course the Rivera 64 boys had insisted on joining their sightseeing outing. Truthfully, she was enjoying their company. They were a constant source of entertainment and often livened up the atmosphere on tour. Even if it meant having the equivalent of four irritating little brothers constantly at their side for the next nine months.

"We're in Vegas, where else would be better?" Josh replied.

Charlie scowled up at him and Mia laughed. She couldn't imagine Charlie getting hitched at the Little White Wedding Chapel. How would she cope without the big dress, the ceremony, the reception, the flowers, the centre-pieces, and seating arrangements? For someone as organised and controlling as Charlie could be, the idea of missing out on the most organised day of her life was torture. Charlie folded her arms. "I don't think so, mister."

"Going to the chapel, and we're—" Ryan began singing.

"Gonna get maaaaaaaarried," Josh chimed in.

Mia and Joel fell about laughing with Josh and the Rivera 64 boys, much to Charlie's displeasure.

"Men." Charlie rolled her eyes, shaking her head she carried on walking, while a chorus of "Gee, I really love you and we're gonna get married. Going to the chapel of love," followed her down the street.

"Do you think they actually would?" Joel asked Mia once Charlie was out of earshot.

"Are you kidding?" Mia asked. "There's no way Charlie would miss out on her big day."

"I guess it's not her style," Joel mused.

"Not quite." Mia laughed. Seizing an opportunity, she probed, "Do you think Josh would?"

"Would what? Get married?"

"Well, yeah…"

"Sure," Joel said without hesitation. "He's crazy about her and he's more than spontaneous enough to go for it."

"He hasn't even asked her," Mia probed further.

"It wouldn't surprise me if he did." Joel glanced up at the two of them farther ahead. "He has mentioned it more than a few times."

"Really?" Mia asked a little too loudly.

Joel laughed. "Yeah."

"Do you two talk about that kind of thing much?" she bravely asked, trying not to sound too obvious.

Joel laughed again, a wicked glint filled his eyes, which Mia didn't need him to remove his sunglasses to be able to see. His lip curled into a teasing smile and he simply tapped the side of his nose in response.

Chapter 29

Charlie blinked. "Really? He actually said that?"

Mia thought that was the first time she'd ever seen Charlie's elegant quiff of hair almost move on her head. Her surprise at hearing Mia recall her conversation with Joel earlier that day had caused her to whip her head around in shock.

Mia nodded before taking a sip of her drink. "Uh huh."

They were sitting outside a coffee shop just off the Las Vegas strip, drinking wonderfully cold iced beverages to cool off from the heat of the sun while the boys larked around, taking photographs for their Instagram pages.

Mia was surprised how readily Joel had agreed to get involved. He usually shied away from the media at every opportunity.

"It's you," Josh had reminded her again.

"No, I think he really likes those guys." Mia nodded at the Rivera 64 boys. "They're like his prodigies."

"Maybe so, but you've definitely changed him for the better." Josh took every opportunity he could to remind Mia how she had brought Joel out of his media-cocooned shell.

"What else did he say?" Charlie plonked her drink down on the little table and grabbed Mia's arm, jerking her attention away from the boys. Dylan was currently being held aloft by Josh as he made a huge V sign with his arms in the air.

"V for Vegas baby!" Ryan shouted, just in case anyone needed confirmation.

"Mia?" Charlie demanded.

"Sorry." Mia stopped laughing, pulled her eyes away from the group, and returned her attention to Charlie. 'Not much else, just that he's mentioned it more than a few times."

"That's not exactly 'not much else,'" Charlie squeaked.

Mia shrugged. "Joel said he wouldn't be surprised."

Charlie stared open mouthed at her across the table. Her sunglasses were lying forgotten on the glinting silver table top which shone almost as brightly in the Nevada sun as the many studs in Charlie's ears.

Charlie shrugged with a glint in her eye. "Well I guess that makes two of them."

"Wha—" Mia spluttered, almost covering Charlie in her drink.

"Just saying." Charlie shrugged again, picking up her drink as if nothing had happened.

"Are you being serious?" Mia asked.

Charlie knew all about the rest of her conversation with Joel, how he had secretively tapped his nose and not said anything when Mia had asked more.

Mia scowled, scanning Charlie's face for tell-tale signs of humor. There weren't any. "You're messing with me."

"I guess we'll both find out, won't we?" Charlie said indifferently.

"But—" Mia began, desperate for more information, but at that moment, Josh bounded back over to their table.

"Hey, baby," he said, greeting Charlie, wrapping his arms around her and enthusiastically kissing her cheek. He sighed, picked up her drink, and took a long sip. "Man, it's hot."

"Please, help yourself," Charlie mocked.

"What's mine is yours." He winked at her before kissing her again and dashing back over to the other guys.

Mia and Charlie stared at each other in disbelief.

∽∾∽

"Do you think this is it?" Charlie whispered to Mia as they filed through security with the rest of their group.

"With these idiots in tow?" Mia pointed at the Rivera 64 boys. "I hardly think so."

Charlie's face fell slightly. "I guess you're right."

They were currently shuffling through the security checks at a Las Vegas helipad for their own private flight over the Grand Canyon. The company had gotten in touch with the tour and offered all the artists private tours over the Grand Canyon while the tour was in Las Vegas, all in exchange for a little publicity. Managers Charlie and Lyle, of course, thought it was a great idea.

"It's a free private flight. All you have to do it give a little Twitter shout out or an Instagram picture," Charlie pointed out.

"You mean *you* have to," Mia reminded her.

Charlie ran Mia's official music Twitter page. Mia was still hesitant about putting herself so readily out there to the masses.

"These guys will do plenty, I'm sure," Charlie said, gesturing at the band who were already on the helipad, snapping away with their cell phones.

"Guys, can we take a couple of pictures before we board? Is that okay?" a member of the helipad flight staff asked.

"Sure, what do you need?" Charlie asked, instantly taking charge.

For the next couple of minutes, Mia, Joel, and Rivera 64 took turns posing in front of the helicopters before finally doing a group shot together.

"Okay, I think we've got everything," the staff member announced. "Let's get you guys in the air."

"Yeah, baby!" Ryan shouted as they made their way across to the chopper.

"Let's do this!" Dylan whooped as they piled inside the helicopter, one after the other.

Mia smiled to herself. Dylan was already feeling right at home with his new band members. It was as if he'd always been a part of the group.

"I guess we're taking this one." Charlie gestured to the remaining helicopter, following Mia, Joel and Josh into the back seats.

Inside was surprisingly spacious. Three seats took up the back wall, while two more comfy-looking leather seats were backed against the pilot's, facing the other three.

Charlie, Josh, and Lyle took up the three seats together, and Mia and Joel sat together on the backward seats.

"Are you guys okay going backward?" the pilot asked as he switched the helicopter to life. "No motion sickness?"

"No," Joel said, checking with Mia. "We're good."

"Awesome. Ready to go see this baby?" the pilot called over his shoulder as the helicopter began to lift from the ground.

They all placed headsets over their heads so they could communicate with each other over the deafening roar of the helicopter's blades.

They were soon airborne, once Rivera 64's helicopter was off the ground and leading the way. Mia and Joel laughed as the boys passed. They were all huddled together around Tom's iPhone, taking a selfie of the band together in the helicopter.

Joel laughed. "That'll be on Twitter as soon as we land."

They quickly flew over the dazzling sights of Las Vegas from the sky, marveling at all the famous landmarks and hotels along the strip and out across the desert to the Arizona border where the Grand Canyon awaited.

"Oh my god," Mia exclaimed.

As soon as it came into view, it took her breath away. The flat, rolling expanse of desert gave way to the impressive natural beauty of the Grand Canyon. The desert simply seemed to fall away beneath itself, the dusty orange ground stepped down into the phenomenal landscape of the canyon. Mia could find no words to describe what she saw. Eerily their whole cabin fell silent as they flew over the canyon, every single one of them breathless at the beauty they saw.

For several minutes the helicopter seemed to glide silently over the canyon, the pilot effortlessly navigating his way over the landscape to give his passengers the best view there was.

"We're gonna take a stop now. Let you folks get some pictures," he announced.

"Sounds great," Joel called over his shoulder, despite wearing the headset.

Mia peered over Joel's lap to watch as the helicopter circled for a moment, waiting for Rivera 64's helicopter to touch down on the ground before it could follow suit.

"He makes parallel parking look like rocket science," Mia marveled as the pilot smoothly navigated the helicopter down onto the ground beside the other with only the briefest bumps as it touched the desert floor.

"Holy cow, that was awesome!" Ryan shouted as soon as he climbed through the open door.

"Mia, did you guys see that?" Dylan called, bounding over.

She laughed as he hugged her. "I couldn't exactly miss it, Dyl."

"I didn't expect anything like this when I came here," he said so only she and Joel could hear.

"Enjoy it." Joel winked at him. "Look how happy you've made him," he said into Mia's ear, wrapping his arms around her waist and kissing her neck.

"Me?" she asked, toying between watching how happy Dylan was to marveling at the Grand Canyon before them.

They were standing on the edge of the canyon. A steep

drop into the descent below was only inches away from their feet, but before their eyes was one of the most beautiful sights in the world. The danger of being so close to the edge melted away with the sight they were witnessing. It was easy to see why it was one of the seven wonders of the natural world.

"Yes, you. You gave him this opportunity. If you hadn't suggested it, Jackson would have picked some pretentious Californian kid who would have everything handed to him on a plate. Or, even worse, he would have dropped these guys and picked another band altogether. You've made this happen for all four of them," Joel said from behind her.

His arms were wrapped protectively around her, keeping her tightly in his arms as they stood close to the edge. Mia happily nestled back into his embrace.

"I guess so." She sighed contentedly, her eyes leaving the boys and scanning the canyon before them.

One of Joel's arms left her body and Mia felt him pull his phone out of his pocket. His iPhone was quickly pointed before them, snapping away at the beauty of the Grand Canyon.

"Have you been here before?" Mia asked as she watched him take pictures

Joel shook his head. "No. I guess I never really had anyone to enjoy coming out here with."

Mia thought for a moment as she let those words sink in. "Not even with Josh? Or the other bands on tour?"

"No," Joel replied, focussing on his shot. "They weren't into this kind of thing. We'd sleep all day, go on stage, and drink afterward. Sometimes I'd stay up writing music or recording on the road, but we never did anything like this."

"Huh," Mia said, "I guess this is a different kind of tour for you then?"

"In all the right ways," he answered, kissing her on the cheek.

"You guys want me to take a photo for you?" the pilot asked.

Mia and Joel paused, turning to look at him. Mia then realised how their embrace looked, clinched together with Joel pointing his phone outwards it looked like they were trying to take their own photo.

"Sure, that'd be great thank you." Joel readily gave his phone over to the pilot.

"Three, two, one. There you go, that looks great." The pilot smiled as he handed the camera back.

"Oh man, can you take a group shot?" Dylan asked.

Dylan and the rest of the band had been taking as many pictures as they could think of from their view of the Canyon.

The pilot shrugged. "Sure."

Mia glanced down at the photo on Joel's phone as almost everyone present handed their phones or cameras to the pilot.

"Pete, can you come give me a hand?" the pilot called to the other one who was having a cigarette nearby.

"No problem." Pete stubbed out his cigarette and came over to take his fair share of the cameras and phones.

Mia smiled at the one on Joel's phone. "I love that picture." She could feel his own smile against her cheek.

"Great isn't it?"

They looked so blissfully happy together. They had their arms wrapped around each other, both of them with huge smiles on their faces and the stunning backdrop of the Grand Canyon behind them.

"I'll send it to you." Joel tapped away, inserting the image into a text to Mia. Mia then smiled to herself, watching as Joel set the image of them to his wallpaper on his phone.

He replaced his existing one of them together, one they had taken themselves with the much better one taken today.

"That's gorgeous." Charlie smiled over Joel's shoulder at the picture. "You guys look so great together."

"Thanks," Mia replied.

"Right, you all ready?" the pilot called, interrupting their moment and gathering their group together.

"Yeah," came a chorused a reply.

Mia quickly handed her phone along with Joel's to the pilots as they prepared to take their group picture.

Huddled in together on the edge of the Grand Canyon, Rivera 64, Charlie and Josh, Lyle, Mia and Joel all happily posed together for one big tour photograph.

The pilot grinned as he handed back the phones and cameras. "There you go, that looks awesome, guys."

"We should totally make this our thing," Tom suggested as he looked down at the photo on his phone.

"What do you mean?" Josh asked.

"You know some bands take pictures along the way on their tour? Like shots of them with the crowd each night, or tour bus pictures? We should take pictures like this of us all at big landmarks we visit on this tour," Tom explained.

"We already have that one from Santa Monica pier," Jack said.

"And the San Francisco bridge," Ryan added.

"I think that's a great idea," Joel agreed. "We can put them on our tour blogs, websites, and Instagram pages."

"The fans will love it," Lyle chipped in.

"And it gives us a good excuse to go see all these places," Mia thought aloud.

"Yeah, dude," Ryan said, "Think where we're gonna be going to. We can take one at the top of the Empire State building, in front of Christ in Rio, the Eifel tower, the Great Wall of China, and the Sydney Harbour Bridge."

Tom shook his head. "Man, we are some lucky bastards."

Everyone marveled at the list of only a few of the places they would soon be visiting over the next few months.

"I think that's a great idea guys," Charlie agreed.

"Come on, you lot, time's almost up," the pilot announced. "It'll soon be time to get you back to Vegas."

Everyone hurriedly began taking their last few photos of the canyon before they had to leave. Mia posed for a few more pictures with Rivera 64, one with Joel, Charlie and

Josh, and one with just her and Charlie.

"Charlie, would you mind?" Dylan held out his phone to her, gesturing that he wanted a picture with Mia.

She grinned. "Of course,"

"You guys should send this to Niamh," Charlie suggested.

"She'd love that," Mia agreed, handing her phone over too.

Mia stood with her arm around Dylan, smiling in the bright desert sunshine for their photo together.

"Come on, you need to get in too," Mia grabbed Charlie and pulled her in for one final picture with her and Dylan.

Once their photo session was finished, everyone reluctantly filed back into their helicopters to be whisked back to Las Vegas.

"You guys have got a show to put on," the pilot called over his shoulder as the helicopter whirred to life again.

"Are you coming down to see it?" Joel asked.

"Man, I'd love to," the pilot replied, "but I couldn't get tickets to save my life. You guys sold out so fast."

Joel glanced at Mia and they both smiled to one another.

"Do you have a card with your number? I'd be able to get you some tickets," Joel offered.

"Really? You could do that?" the pilot's voice asked through their headsets.

"Sure, it's the least I could do after today," Joel said.

The pilot shrugged. "Just doing my job."

"We've had a great time," Joel said, squeezing Mia's hand in his. "Let us return the favor."

"Okay, man, if you insist." The pilot grinned from ear to ear, handing a business card through the gap in the seats to Joel.

"Leave it with me, I'll give you a call this afternoon," Joel told him.

"Thank you so much, I'm a huge fan," the pilot admitted.

Mia could have sworn she saw him blushing.

"No problem," Joel replied.

Mia smiled to herself. The day seemed full of good deeds and reminders of past ones. This tour was turning out to be more than she could ever have hoped for. She was constantly reminded of how blessed she was in life, despite the rocky start she had endured.

She looked out of the window, as the Grand Canyon began to vanish beneath them, disappearing into the desert as dreamily as it had appeared. and marveled at the beauty of it. These blissfully happy times made her reminisce about how truly grateful she was. At that moment, she had wonderful friends, her family, her brother back in her life, her career was off to a flying start, and she had Joel in her life. She couldn't have asked the universe for anything more if she tried.

Chapter 30

Well, perhaps there was one more thing, Mia thought.

As she watched the green room door burst open later that evening and Niamh came rushing into Dylan's arms, Mia realized the only thing better than having such wonderful friends in her life, was having them there with her.

"What are you doing here?" Mia asked with a laugh.

Niamh had eventually untangled herself from an affectionate reunion with Dylan and had come over to greet her.

"I missed you guys so much! And I just had to come and see you both headlining in Vegas. How could I miss that?" Niamh squealed.

"Well, we're not technically headlining, Joel is," Mia corrected.

"Same thing." Niamh waved her off. "You're both on the tour."

"If you say so."

"You guys were all so incredible. Glen's going to be so jealous when I show him these pictures and videos from tonight," Niamh said. She was practically dancing up and down on the balls of her feet with excitement as she waved her phone in her hand.

"We did good then?" Dylan asked her with a proud grin on his face.

Niamh threw her arms around his neck and kissed him. "You did more than good, you were unbelievable."

Turning away from them both to leave them in their moment, Mia headed away from the green room down the long corridors that wound around behind the stage to head in search of Joel, who had been doing a meet and greet with his fans somewhere backstage.

"Mia." Lyle stopped her in her tracks halfway there. "Have you seen Charlie anywhere?"

"Not since before the show, why?" she asked.

"I can't find her anywhere." He frowned. "It's not like her."

"I'm sure she's fine," Mia reassured him. "She'll be with Josh. Have you checked the bus?"

"Yes." Lyle pulled a face. "They're not on there either."

"She'll be around somewhere. Don't worry." Mia patted his arm and Lyle strode off down the corridor back in the direction she had just come from.

"Hey, gorgeous." Ryan appeared at her side, draping his arm around her shoulders. "You coming to the party to-night?"

"What party?" Mia asked, ignoring the fact that his arm was around her. Ryan was overly friendly with everyone.

"Me and the other guys are going into Vegas tonight, to that club we were telling you about," Ryan explained, "Dylan and Niamh are coming too. You up for it?"

"Sure, I'll ask Joel," Mia said as they reached Joel's dressing room door.

"All right, we're meeting in the green room in about an hour," Ryan added, glancing at his watch.

"Okay, see you soon," she called after him as he headed down the corridor.

Mia knocked on Joel's dressing room door and, after

hearing him call out to come in, she entered. Thankfully, Joel was alone in his dressing room, crashed out on the sofa.

"Hi." She smiled, closing the door behind her. "You okay?"

"Just tired," he replied, sitting up. "Lock the door, will you? I could use a few minutes' peace."

"Do you want me to come back later?" Mia teased.

"No, silly, I meant a few minutes alone with you." He reached out, grabbed the waistband of her jeans, and pulled her onto his lap.

Mia landed softly on his legs and curled her own up beside her. Wrapping her arms around Joel's body, she then snuggled into his chest.

Joel held her tightly to him. Resting his head on hers, he let out a deep sigh.

"You sure you're okay?" Mia asked again, this time to his chest.

"Mmm," Joel murmured beneath her. "I'm just tired. The last few weeks have flown by."

"They sure have," she agreed.

"Did Ryan ask you about the party?" Joel asked.

"Yeah."

"Do you want to go?"

"I don't care," she answered truthfully.

"Good," Joel whispered, "because I have a better idea."

And with that he turned on his side, pulling her with him so that they were both lying side by side on the sofa in his dressing room. Mia giggled, as he did, before settling back down into his arms.

"I've missed this," he whispered to her after a moment.

"What's that?" she asked.

"Just spending time together like this, just me and you. There's always someone else on the tour bus or someone else in the room."

"I know. But we knew it would be like that when we came on tour."

"I know," he agreed, stroking her hair. "I've never been

on tour with someone like this before. I guess we both need to figure this out, how to make time for ourselves."

"Yeah, it's so easy to get caught up in everything that's going on," Mia agreed, thinking how much time they had spent in the company of everyone else recently. They just needed a balance, that was all. They needed to remember they were a couple, that they were together as well as with their friends on this tour.

"It's only early days," Joel said into her ear before kissing her cheek.

"Early days?" Mia asked, pulling away slightly.

Joel laughed deeply and held her tightly to him so she couldn't escape farther. "I meant on the tour."

Mia laughed, feeling herself blush. "Oh."

"So where were we?" Joel reminded her, resuming the trail of kisses he was placing on her cheek.

"You were saying how we needed to find a balance?" Mia teased.

"Balance sounds good right now," Joel said with a tantalising smile.

With those words, he kissed her deeply, wrapping his arms tightly around her, and closing the curtains on his nearly black eyes. Despite being backstage at a sold-out tour in the middle of the Las Vegas strip, for the next few hours they were in their own private world.

❧❦❧

"Mia? Joel? Guys, open up!"

Mia stirred in Joel's arms at the knocking on the dressing room door. Realizing she wasn't wearing a watch, she pressed a button on Joel's cell phone on the table to see the time.

"Crap," she muttered, regretfully untangling herself from the comfortable embrace they had spent the last few hours in.

"What?" Joel mumbled sleepily beside her.

She gently shook his arm. "Wake up, Joel."

Mia glanced back down at the table and Joel's phone, which was still illuminated, and saw several missed calls. Knowing Joel wouldn't mind, she swiped her finger across the screen and tapped the call button.

"Joel," she said, turning behind her and putting the phone under his nose. "Look."

He squinted through tired eyes at the screen, trying to focus on what Mia was showing him. "Huh?"

There were several missed calls displayed there, from Charlie, Josh, Lyle, Ryan, and Dylan.

Mia wondered what on earth could have happened. They'd only been gone a few hours.

So much for finding a balance, she thought.

"We're coming," Joel called out to the pounding on the door.

Running a hand through his messy hair, he forced his eyes open. Mia smiled to herself. He looked so adorable.

He hauled himself to his feet and offered Mia his hand, lifting her up from their now abandoned love nest on the sofa.

Joel scowled at the door before unlocking it and tugging it open. "Can't we even have—" he began.

Outside their dressing room door was a cluster of people, and right at the front were Josh and Charlie.

Everyone around them was smiling, albeit with baited breath.

Mia's mouth immediately fell open. *No,* she thought, *surely not.* She knew straight away what they had done. She knew immediately where Josh and Charlie had been these last few hours.

Charlie was dancing up and down while Josh beamed from ear to ear.

"We got married!" they announced.

"You did what?" Joel asked, his face pulled back in a confused expression.

"We. Got. Married," Josh repeated slowly for him.

"Can you believe it?" Charlie screamed, pushing past Joel to get to Mia. "Look!" she squealed, grabbing Mia's arm and thrusting her hand in front of Mia's face.

"Wow," Mia replied. She took hold of Charlie's hand and looked down at the diamond solitaire engagement ring and wedding band now sitting on Charlie's finger.

"What? When? You guys weren't even engaged?" Mia asked, confused.

"How long were we asleep?" Joel asked Josh, shaking his head.

"Josh asked me this afternoon and then we went straight out after the show. We decided to keep it a surprise," Charlie explained.

"But didn't you want a wedding?" Mia asked, her head spinning with this sudden overload of information.

Charlie shrugged. "We wanted to get married, and that's all that mattered. I didn't care about the big day or anything, just as long as we were married."

Mia still held Charlie's hand in hers and stared to and from the rings now glistening on her finger to her friend's deliriously happy face. Seeing the look Charlie was now wearing was all Mia needed to see. She knew straight away this was the right thing for them to do. Charlie was on cloud nine and so was Josh. *These two were meant to be together*, Mia thought.

"I can't believe it." Joel was still shaking his head. "Congratulations, guys. I'm so happy for you, bro."

Joel then seemed to snap out of his sleepy haze, stepped forward, and hugged his brother tightly.

"Thanks, man," Josh said over his shoulder. "I was worried you would be mad we didn't tell you, or that you weren't there."

Joel pulled a face. "Well, I am kinda pissed I didn't get to see my little brother tie the knot."

"But I'll get to see you tie the knot one day." Josh winked at Mia. "We can make up for it then."

Charlie was listening to their conversation too and squeezed Mia's arms when Josh hinted at another wedding.

"It's just so sudden," Joel said, bypassing the subject. "I think I'm still in shock." He glanced down at the wedding band on Josh's left hand that matched Charlie's thinner one.

Josh laughed. "Me too."

"So you actually had a Vegas wedding?" Joel asked, "at the Little White Wedding Chapel?"

"Uh huh." Josh nodded. "It was just quick, easy, stress free—everything we wanted. We talked a lot about it and we decided neither of us wanted a big day. All we cared about was just being married to each other. All we wanted was to say our vows and to have the marriage certificate. It was between me and Charlie only, and that's just how we wanted it."

"I guess I can see your point," Joel said. "It's only about the two of you. Why would you need anything else?"

Josh grinned. "Exactly."

Mia hugged Charlie again, seeing how elated they both were. "I'm so happy for you. Congratulations."

Charlie smiled, her eyes brimming with tears of joy. "Thank you."

It was then that Mia noticed Charlie was dressed in white. She wasn't wearing a typical wedding dress, but she had on a short, white-lace dress that was both elegant and quirky at the same time. It was Charlie down to a tee. Her hair was styled up in its usual blonde-streaked quiff, and the only jewellery she wore was her wedding and engagement rings and a pair of diamond stud earrings.

"You look beautiful," Mia said to her.

"Doesn't she just?" Josh agreed, looking proudly at his wife.

Mia smiled. "And I love those shoes."

Charlie's wedding shoes were white satin peep toes with a five inch heel and a little bejewelled skull at the peep toe. Her outfit was so elegant and beautiful, but with little hints of Charlie's eccentric, fashionable style along the way. The tiny skulls on the front of her shoes summed her up perfectly. Mia always knew Charlie would look perfect on her wedding day, even if it was in Vegas.

Charlie winked at her. "You can borrow them one day."

"I think this calls for a celebration," Joel announced to the crowd gathered in the corridor. "It's not every day my little brother gets married—and especially to such an incredible woman."

Josh came over to Charlie's side and kissed her proudly on the cheek, making her blush.

"Lyle, can you organize some champagne?" Joel asked his manager.

"Sure." Lyle nodded, already pulling out his cell phone and hurrying away down the corridor.

Joel grinned down at Mia. "Let's go celebrate with the new Mr. and Mrs. Coben!"

Chapter 31

Ugh," Mia groaned, turning over in bed and hitting the wall.

She tried to move the other way but found herself squashed against something softer than the wall. She painfully opened her eyes and realized she was sandwiched in between Joel and the wall of a very small tour bus cubby.

"What the hell?" she mumbled.

"Morning," Joel grunted beside her, turning over to face her.

Mia squinted at him. "Glad I'm not the only one who looks rough."

Of course Joel still looked impeccably handsome, even when he was hungover. Mia narrowed her eyes at him. She was more than sure she didn't look anywhere near as good as he did right now.

He laughed. "Thanks." His voice came out dry and choked, like he hadn't spoken for weeks.

"Just why are we squashed into this stupid bed?" Mia asked, trying to sit up in bed without banging her elbows and knees on the wall.

"Because we gave ours to the bride and groom," Joel explained.

"We did *what*?" Mia asked loudly.

Joel squinted, holding his hand up to his forehead in pain. "Ssshhh."

"Sorry," Mia whispered. "Why did we do that?"

Joel raised an eyebrow at her over his hand.

"Okay, okay. I get it." She waved him off. "I need some water."

She clambered over Joel and almost fell out of the cubby into the corridor lined with more beds like theirs.

"Good morning, gorgeous," came a voice from opposite.

Mia snapped her head around to see Ryan's face poking out from behind a cubby curtain.

"I wish you appeared by my bed every morning," he quipped.

"Careful," Joel warned, leaning out of their bed.

"Oh, hey, man." Ryan nodded. "Good night last night, huh?"

"Sure was," came another voice.

Mia turned again to see Jack clambering down from one of the beds above them.

"I don't think I've ever drunk so much champagne in all my life." Jack massaged his forehead before stumbling past them all toward the kitchen.

"Thanks for that, Joel," Dylan's Irish tones drifted down the corridor from behind one of the other curtained beds. "That was a good call."

"Yeah, thanks, Joel," Niamh called out from the same direction. "Morning, Mia," she added.

Mia turned back to face Joel. "Remind me why are we on their tour bus."

"Yeah, Joel, why are we on their tour bus?" Lyle asked, rolling himself off the sofa at the end of the corridor of bunk beds.

"Because." Joel sighed, sitting up in the tiny bed and almost cracking his head on the one above it. "We gave ours to Josh and Charlie for the night, to give them some privacy."

Tom laughed from one of the beds above. "Dude, say it like it is."

Mia shook her head at him. "Well, you're washing the bed sheets."

The tour bus erupted into laughter.

Even Joel laughed before pulling a face. "Okay, maybe I didn't think that idea through too well," he said, "but we couldn't stay in a hotel. We had to keep moving. The tour had to leave Vegas last night to stay on schedule."

Ryan nudged Mia, once he clambered out of his bunk. "What a shame you had to stay on our tour bus instead."

Mia rolled her eyes and playfully shoved him out of the way to head in the direction of the kitchen to look for much needed water.

She fumbled with the refrigerator door before being able to pull it open. She narrowed her eyes at the bright light that immediately shone from within. It was far too early and too painful too be looking at a light that bright.

Inside the refrigerator was what Mia would only expect to find inside a college frat house—an assortment of beer bottles, coca cola cans, squirty cheese, and leftover takeout food.

She rummaged around, wincing at the clanking's of beer bottles as they fell over, before finding some bottled water at the back of the fridge.

Before she went back to their squashed little cubby bed, she stopped at the one of the tour bus's many tinted windows and looked outside. Beyond the window the world was whizzing past as the driver took them along Highway 93 toward their next show in Phoenix, Arizona.

Outside the window Mia could see barren desert and rocky hills in the distance. The landscape was flat until it reached the outcrop of mountains in the distance. The beige-colored desert was littered with stones and little greens shrubs that were scattered among the dust. It looked like something straight out of a movie.

"Beautiful, isn't it?" Tom said, appearing at her side.

"It is," Mia agreed, watching him crack open a can of coke.

"Think of all the places we'll soon be driving through," he added, taking a long sip from his can. "It blows your mind, really."

Mia smiled. "Yeah, it does."

The landscape she was now seeing was nothing compared to the landscape she was used to back home in Ireland, where rolling green hills and fields dominated the scene before meeting beautiful little picturesque towns that spattered the coastline. She truly was a million miles away from Ireland, but she couldn't have been happier. Despite waking up in what could only be described as a touring, musical frat house, she was blissfully happy to be on the road on America's highways, touring the States with her friends.

"Wait until we get to Texas. Now, that's beautiful," Jack quipped, reaching into the fridge.

"Yeah?" Mia asked.

"Uh huh," he mumbled over a mouthful of water. "Nowhere else quite like it. But it's so darn hot."

"Canada is amazing too," Tom said. "You'll love it there."

Mia smiled again. "Sounds great."

"What about Ireland?" Jack asked. "We're going there, aren't we?"

"Man, we're going to so many places, I can't even remember," Tom replied.

Mia laughed. "Yes, we get to Ireland in a couple of months."

"What's it like? Green?"

"Yes," Mia agreed, rolling her eyes at Tom, "very."

"But Dublin's grand." Jack imitated an Irish accent. "Full of great people and music."

Mia fell about, laughing at his accent. "That's true, it is."

Tom grinned. "You can show us around, Mia."

"I can, I'll take you to the bar where I worked and performed."

"That's where Dylan did too, right?" Jack asked.

"Yeah, that's how I know him." Mia smiled, fondly remembering their time at Glen's. Her heart panged with the memories. She dearly missed the place, the familiarity, and the feeling of being so at home there. She couldn't wait to visit there on tour and take the Rivera 64 boys to Glen's. She was sure they would love it as much as she and Dylan did.

"Before you know it, Mia, we'll be flying down to Brazil, then Europe, the Far East, and then Australia. These next nine months will fly by," Tom said.

"I hope not." Mia pressed her hand against the glass. "I want to remember every second."

ノンくノン

Eventually, Tom was right.

Before Mia knew what had happened, their next few weeks touring across the States flew by faster than she could have imagined. It was all she could do to sit tight on the tour bus and hold on for the ride.

They soon zigzagged their way up and down the States, traveling from the west coast to the east. They alternated between heading north and south, depending on which venues had been booked first. One day Mia would wake up and peer out of the curtains to see a hot, dusty Louisiana dirt road. The next, there were snowflakes falling outside their frosted window on a cold Minnesota morning.

They drove through huge, sprawling towns and cities, only to pass them by and watch seemingly endless highways and lonely, empty roads roll by their window for hours upon end.

Mia found herself mesmerised by the ever-changing landscape outside their tour bus window. The inspiration she found there had her writing more music than ever before. Joel simply watched her with a thoughtful smile on his face as she did so. Their relationship went from strong to stronger. Mia knew she and Joel were perfect for each other. They were at ease with one another, as if they had known one another their whole lives and sometimes longer. Joel was Mia's best friend. They could talk to one another about anything in the world. She had no fears, no jealousy, no worries with him, and that was more than she could ever ask for.

The fans seemed to get stranger, louder, and crazier as the tour went on. Mia went from being a virtually unknown singer to an overnight sensation. Her debut single skyrocketed to third place in the singles chart. There were already high expectations for her second single after her album release saw it heading straight up the charts too. Mia was blown away by the praise she was receiving from the fans. She had initially been nervous about accompanying someone as well-known as Joel on tour. And being his girlfriend, too, had left her dreading the response from the crowd.

Joel, of course, told her he had predicted just as much all along. Each night, the crowd would chant and cheer loudly, the singing was also getting louder as the weeks went on. As they progressed across the States, the word was spreading about Mia's music, and the sound of the crowd singing along to her songs word for word was getting louder by the day.

As the tour bus pulled up to the backstage of another arena, a huge crowd was already assembled by the gates, awaiting their arrival.

"Look," Joel called from the window. "They have banners for you too."

Sure enough, he was right. Mia peered over his shoulder to see dozens of banners for Joel among the screaming gaggle of female fans, but dotted among them were several banners for Mia and Rivera 64 too.

The fans were everywhere. They managed to get themselves into the strangest of places in their desperate bids to get themselves closer to their idols. Security found them lurking in the backstage toilets, behind the tour busses, underneath the stage and even inside equipment cases on the back of the lorry. Mia wondered how on earth they had managed to get themselves inside the last one and how long they'd been in there too. They really would do whatever it took to get closer to their idols. Mia admired their sheer determination. They were creative with their methods too.

She smiled through the tinted glass of the tour bus window at the crowd gathered below early one Friday morning as the bus pulled through the gates behind Madison Square Garden. The breathtaking sights of New York City's skyscrapers stood all around them, but all Mia could focus on was the enormous arena that loomed before them.

Madison Square Garden.

Their tour in the United States of America was almost over. Three very fast months had passed by in a blur of stage lights, screaming crowds, late nights, and endless highways. And it all came to a head in three night's time. *Three nights. That's all, just another three shows*, Mia told herself.

Just three sold-out shows at Madison Square Gardens, no big deal.

"You okay?" Joel asked, his big dark eyes looking up at her full of excitement.

Mia nodded. "Sure."

He looped his arm around her waist and pulled her close to him. Mia ran her hand through his messy, bedhead hair that still always managed to look impeccable, despite him living out of a suitcase.

"You'll love New York," he said casually. "The crowd is always great."

She nodded, resting her head on top of that impeccable head of hair of his.

Madison Square Gardens was no big deal to Joel, just another night and another arena.

Just three more shows in his home country before they all boarded a plane out of JFK airport to touchdown in Brazil where the tour kicked off again in a few days' time.

"And we have a couple of days off before it starts again," he said, as if reading her mind.

"Yeah that should be nice," she said absentmindedly.

"We could hit the beach in Rio?" he suggested.

"That'd be great," she replied more enthusiastically, mainly due to picturing Joel in shorts on a blistering hot day at the beach. And they would be accompanied by more twenty something musicians hitting the beach in shorts too. It was a hard life.

"Look." Joel laughed. "You see that?"

He was pointing to one of the signs in the crowd gathered behind the now closed gates. It read *NYC 'hearts' Mia* in the style of the typical *I 'heart' NYC* tourist T-shirts.

"That's so sweet," Mia said. "We should get a picture of that."

"Want to go and say hi?" Joel asked as the tour bus pulled to a stop.

"Sure." Mia looked over her shoulder again. "Looks like someone's already beating us to it."

The crowd's screams intensified. They called out and shouted as the Rivera 64 boys bounded off their tour bus to greet the assembled fans.

"Let's go join them." Joel took her hands in his, pulling her toward him. "But first." He stopped her and held her close. "I just need to do one thing."

Mia giggled. "What's that?"

"This," he said, cupping her face in his palm and bringing her lips up to his. He kissed her softly, then deeply. His hand caressed her waist before he pulled her tightly into his arms, and she melted against him. "I love you," he said. His lips brushed against hers as they were still so close. His forehead rested against Mia's and he held her to him, as if holding on for dear life. 'Forever," he added.

"I love you too," she managed to whisper back, her heart

thudding loudly in her chest at his last word. She could feel her hands shaking against his chest as she held him, terrified she had imagined the last word he'd said.

She closed her eyes and kissed him again. "Forever," she whispered.

Though her eyes were still closed, she didn't need to see Joel's face. His touch and his kiss told her everything she needed to know. She hadn't imagined it. He'd said the word just as clearly as she had. They were each other's forever. She knew deep in her heart as he kissed her more passionately than he'd ever kissed her before that they belonged together. And that, together, they would take on the world, right after Madison Square Garden.

Chapter 32

T his is it," came a deep, dulcet voice from behind Mia.

It was her favorite sound in the world. His voice seemed to melt into her ears, whether he was singing or simply talking. She'd never tire of hearing that sound.

"This is it," she repeated with a smile on her face that was bigger than the arena they were standing in.

She remembered him saying those words three months ago. How quickly time had flown by since then.

Joel came up behind her and wrapped his arms tightly around her waist. Mia was still sitting on a stool in the middle of the stage, an empty Madison Square Garden staring back at her, its empty seats just waiting to be filled one last time.

They were two shows down, and their last one was that evening. Mia had just finished her sound check early in the morning and had the rest of the day free before they would headline the arena one final time.

Their three day stint in New York had already allowed them time to sample some of the city's famous tourist sightseeing and nightlife, but Mia wondered what else they could cram into their last day.

"What do you want to do today?" she asked as he rested his head on her shoulder and stared out at the empty arena with her.

It was a strange feeling, staring out at thousands of empty seats just waiting to be filled. Knowing that in several hours' time those seats would be filled with thousands of screaming, shouting, and singing fans all desperate to hear Mia's favorite sound in the world.

"Actually." Joel hesitated. "I have a couple of interviews to do this afternoon."

"What?" Mia tried to turn and look at him but failed. he had hold of her too tightly.

"I'm so sorry." He kissed her neck several times. "They were really last minute. I can't help it."

"You're a changed man, Joel Coben," Mia teased. "You would never have agreed to all this promo before."

"Women do that to you, you know?" he teased right back. "They change you without you even realizing."

She laughed wriggling out of his hold to stand up from her chair. "You know exactly what you're doing, mister."

Joel laughed and pulled her back into his arms again. "I'm sorry, I'll make it up to you."

"It's fine, honestly," she said, kissing him.

"Are you sure?" he asked.

She shrugged. "Yeah, I'll see if the guys want to go and do something."

Rivera 64 were always up to mischief. She was sure she could tag along to whatever they were entertaining themselves with that afternoon.

"Oh, you're ditching me for a younger model now?" Joel teased.

Mia threw her head back and laughed. The wicked glint in his eye told her he was joking. She giggled. "Yeah, something like that. The old ones can't keep up, you know?"

"I'll show you I can keep up," he said with a delicious tone in his voice before kissing her again.

They broke apart moments later, their breathing heavy and ragged.

"Are you sure you have to do the interviews?" Mia asked, clinging to him.

"I wish I didn't." He grinned, his lip curling into a smile that made Mia want to forget they were in the middle of Madison Square Garden.

⌘

"Wait, wait, one more," Tom said through fits of laughter.

Mia giggled as she watched Ryan and Jack pose for yet another silly picture.

The boys had been at it all day. Mia had accompanied them across what felt like all of New York, taking crazy pictures for their blog pages, along the way.

They had hit the Top of the Rock, the Statue of Liberty, trailed through Central Park, and along numerous shops along Fifth Avenue. It was a lot to cram in to one day, particularly when following a rock band of twenty something boys across the city.

They clambered out of the back seat of yet more taxis and almost fell onto the tarmac outside the rear entrance to the arena.

Mia heard several screams and shouts from some of the fans who were still gathered at the gates and the boys went rushing over to greet them and pose for more pictures.

"They just love the attention," she said to Charlie who had come out to meet her.

"They sure do," Charlie agreed, watching Dylan, Tom, Jack, and Ryan take pictures of themselves with the fan's cell phones.

"Have you guys had fun?" Charlie asked as they headed back inside the arena.

"Yeah, we've had such a laugh," Mia said, shaking her head. "I'm exhausted."

"Only a few hours to go," Charlie reminded her, glancing at her watch.

Mia looked at her own. Four hours until the doors opened to the waiting fans. "As if I could forget," she said. "How's Joel getting on with his interviews?"

"O—oh," Charlie stammered. "Yeah, great. He's been looking for you, actually."

"What's wrong?" Mia asked as they headed for the green room.

"Nothing," Charlie said, avoiding Mia's eyes. "Wait here, I'll go find him. He's been waiting for you."

"Okay," Mia said as the door closed behind Charlie. *That was odd.*

Something was definitely wrong. Charlie had seemed out of sorts, preoccupied even. Come to think of it, the Rivera 64 boys had dashed away to the fans really quickly.

And backstage was eerily quiet, Mia noticed. She was sitting in an empty green room, the rider of water, coca cola, and beer looked untouched. Their walk from the tour buses through the corridors to the green room had also been strangely deserted. It was only a few hours until show time, the place was usually crawling with people.

Where was everyone? Something was definitely wrong.

Suddenly the door opened again and Charlie materialised.

"What on earth is going—" Mia began but was immediately silenced.

Charlie held up a finger to her lips. "Come here," she ordered.

Mia felt her stomach begin to swirl and dance with butterflies.

It was then that Charlie held up a blindfold. "I need you to put this on."

"What?" Mia asked.

"Just do it," Charlie said, her lips twitching with a smile.

Mia knew then that, while something was indeed going on, it was not of the worrying kind. Charlie knew something Mia didn't. They were all up to something. Even Joel's surprise party for her on her birthday two months ago hadn't involved this kind of heist.

Mia held up her hands. "Okay." and

Charlie walked around her, placing the blindfold over her head, and tying it tightly in place. "Give me your hand," she instructed.

Mia did as she was told and was led blindly down the corridor, hanging on to Charlie's arm and following the sound of her clacking heels beside her in the empty corridor.

Mia realized that Charlie's hand was shaking slightly, and she could feel her palms beginning to sweat. What in the world was happening? Mia knew from memory, the few times she had taken this journey over the last couple of days that they were heading in the direction of the stage. She knew from the now-echoing sounds of Charlie's footsteps that they were behind the stage, and everything was deadly silent.

The sensation was eerily strange. The hairs on Mia's arms stood on end, and she felt her own hands beginning to tremble in Charlie's.

Charlie rounded a corner and the clacking of her heels grew louder, echoing into the vast empty space they were now inside.

Mia felt her breath catch in her throat. They were walking into the middle of the empty arena. Charlie then pulled Mia tightly to her side as they made their way across the large expanse of floor. Their footsteps echoed loudly into the arena, an eerie reminder of how quiet the place was. The walk seemed to last forever. Mia held on tightly to Charlie's hand in the silence.

Suddenly they came to a stop. Charlie put her hands on Mia's shoulders and squeezed them, signaling for Mia to stay in place.

Then Charlie began to walk away in the direction they had just come from, her footsteps echoing loudly into the vast expanse of empty space.

Mia suddenly began to feel extremely foolish, standing on her own, blindfolded in the middle of an empty arena.

It was then that she felt his hands take hold of hers. She knew, just by his touch alone, that Joel was there with her, standing in front of her in the arena. As if on cue, music started up from the direction of the stage, and Mia immediately recognised the song.

She could feel her smile breaking on her lips, which had been tightly clamped shut with nerves until now. Out of all the songs he could have picked, the dozens of his own songs, Joel had chosen Mia's favorite song in the world.

A beautiful, acoustic version of *Iris* by the Goo Goo Dolls was playing across Madison Square Garden.

Upon hearing Dylan's voice begin to sing the first words of the opening chorus, one of Joel's hands left Mia's and reached up to remove her blindfold.

She squinted her eyes at the sudden release of the darkness before being able to adjust her senses again. She blinked rapidly. *No,* she thought, *surely not?*

Indeed, she was standing in the middle of Madison Square Garden. Rivera 64 were standing on the stage in the distance, playing an acoustic version of Mia's favorite song just for an audience of two.

The arena itself was completely empty, aside from the band, her, and Joel and several thousand flickering candles in the darkness.

Mia and Joel were standing together in a cleared circle among the thousands of candles. Behind them was a narrow pathway which Charlie had just led her through. All around them, tiny little lights flickered together in the darkness. They weren't just covering the arena floor. They made their way up the dozens of staircases, across the aisles and amongst the thousands of empty seats around them.

The image was so haunting, so painfully beautiful, it took Mia's breath away completely.

And it was all for her.

She had never seen anything so wonderful in all her life. Except for the man who was standing before her now, the man who had made all of this happen just for her.

"Mia," Joel began, taking both her hands in his again.

She took hold of his fingers, squeezing them tightly, and nodded, unable to speak at the overwhelming sight of it all.

"I want to start by saying I love you, that all of this is for you. Each and every candle is for you. They've been lit to represent many of the ways in which you've lit up my life. I was living in the dark for so long, afraid to show the world who I was. Sometimes, I don't think I even knew myself. I think I was afraid to find myself. I'd gotten so used to being that way, I couldn't see a way out and everyone around me accepted that. They admired me and looked up to me. And then you came along, this shining, fiery beacon of Irish light. I'd never seen anything like you before."

He paused, as if trying to catch his breath.

He was so nervous, Mia noticed. She squeezed his hands again.

"You came along and you changed my world completely. You tore down all those walls I'd spent years building, trying to hide myself away from the world behind them. You reminded me that I was only a human being, that money and fame made me no different from anyone else. You reminded me of myself when I first started out, I knew then that you and I were one of the same. That we were two halves of the same whole. I knew there was something so completely different about you from anyone else. I knew you were my soul mate."

Hearing him say that, Mia felt a tear trickle down her cheek.

"The more time I spent with you, the quicker I began to fall in love with you. I'd watch you for hours on end. I saw the passion and devotion you poured into your work. You gave your music your heart and soul, and I wanted to steal that for myself. I wanted you. I wanted all of you to myself."

Mia fondly remembered how Joel used to materialise at her studio door. How, at first, she was so irritated by him and then how quickly her opinion of him changed when he immediately connected with the words of her songs. He'd heard them how no one else in the world heard them, how, only she knew, they were meant to be heard.

From that moment on, she knew there was something special about Joel Coben.

He was hers.

He smiled, as if reading her thoughts. "And then you finally let me in."

Mia smiled in return, tightly holding on to his hands as the song continued and the candles glowed around them in their thousands. She had finally pieced together her broken jigsaw. Piece by piece, she had put together the whole picture that made up Joel Coben. She saw the image that the rest of the world did not. He was hers and she was his.

He knew her better than she knew herself. He knew her every thought, her every move, and she knew his. He seemed to know exactly what she would say or do before she even did herself. He knew every single little part of her and Mia realised in that moment that she knew his. They understood each other better than anyone else. They were two halves to the same whole. They weren't one without the other.

"You turned my world from being upside down to right again, Mia," he continued, "I owe everything to you. I couldn't ask you for anything more. You've given me your heart and your love, and that's more than I could ever dream of. To know that I have the love of a woman so incredibly talented, so smart, and more beautiful than anyone else in this world to me. That's more than I could have ever dreamed of. Fame, money, success, none of this would ever matter because they could never bring me you. That would all mean nothing without you in my life. I love you, Mia, more than any words or any song could ever describe to you. I know that you and I belong together, that, no matter, what we'll stand by one another and love each other for the rest of our lives."

Mia swallowed. Her tears were falling thick and fast now.

"There's only one little thing that's missing," Joel said. Letting go of one of her hands, he reached into his pocket and produced a small box. "I have something to ask you. I want to know if you'll do me the honor of making me the happiest man who ever lived. Say that you and I will be together forever, that we'll love each other long after this world stops turning. I know you and I were made for one another, Mia, I know you're my soul mate."

And, with that, he sank to one knee. "Will you marry me?"

In that moment, her world stopped turning on its axis. The universe was stood still with baited breath. Everything she had ever wanted in life she now had. Joel Coben was offering her his hand in marriage. She knew every word he'd said was true. They were soul mates. They belonged together.

Without thinking, her mind already knowing the answer, the word fell effortlessly from her lips. "Yes."

Joel let out a relieved exhale. Taking the ring from the box with shaking fingers, he slid the diamond up onto her finger before standing up again.

He clasped her hands in his. Bringing her ring finger to his lips, he kissed it tenderly before placing her hands on his shoulders.

Mia slid her arms around his neck and pulled him to her body. Joel's eyes were brimming with emotion, tears of happiness and relief were welling in his dark eyes.

"Forever," she whispered. Holding his head, she brought her lips up to his.

"Forever," he said against hers, before closing his eyes

and kissing her with every ounce of love and passion he'd ever felt.

> "And I don't want the world to see me
> 'Cause I don't think that they'd understand.
> When everything's made to be broken.
> I just want you to know who I am."

The words of the song came hauntingly through the speakers, and Mia understood why Joel had chosen that song for the band to sing.

The words mirrored their story completely. Joel had been hidden away from the world, hiding his true self away from everyone under years' worth of hardened exterior until Mia had arrived. She had been the one to break down his walls and peel away those layers. She had revealed the real Joel Coben underneath all of that. In finding each other, she had helped Joel find himself again.

"I just want you to know who I am." Dylan's voice sang out the final lines of the song and Mia understood everything. She and Joel belonged together, they understood one another in a way that no one else on this earth ever would.

As the music echoed around them into the empty arena, only the thousands of glowing candles and her soul mate for company, Mia closed her eyes and let go completely.

Lost in the arms of a man she knew would love her long after his heart stopped beating—that, no matter what the world would throw at them, they would always have each other.

She felt the cool metal of the large diamond ring now weighing on her finger, a token of the everlasting love that Joel felt for her, and she tried with all her might, to show him in her kiss that she felt exactly the same.

The final bars of the song played out. The acoustic guitar resonated hauntingly through the speakers and into the empty Madison Square Garden arena. Joel opened his eyes, and his achingly beautiful, almost black eyes stared deep into Mia's.

She stared back into them. No longer did she see a black abyss, a haunting image, or an endless void. No longer did she see pain and hurt in those dark irises. All of those things had been replaced by light. Joel was finally, truly happy, as was she.

"Forever," he whispered again, his eyes level with hers.

Now, in those irises she saw her own.

The End

About the Author

Melissa Speight lives close to the historic city of York, in the United Kingdom, with her family. After studying for an honors degree in Journalism, she has since written three romance novels. Besides writing, Speight's main passions are travelling, adventure, running, yoga, and live music.

She is also an active supporter of cancer charities in the UK and, after conquering Mt. Kilimanjaro in Tanzania, she is planning her next fundraising challenges for charity.

Speight dedicates her literary career to the memory of her mum.